I'LL TAKE EVERYTHING YOU HAVE

Also by James Klise

The Art of Secrets

Love Drugged

I'LL TAKE EVERYTHING YOU HAVE

James Klise

Algonquin 2023

Published by
Algonquin Young Readers
an imprint of Workman Publishing Co., Inc.
a subsidiary of Hachette Book Group, Inc.
1290 Avenue of the Americas
New York, New York 10104

LIBRARY OF CONGRESS
CATALOGING-IN-PUBLICATION DATA

Names: Klise, James, 1967- author.
Title: I'll take everything you have / James Klise.
Other titles: I will take everything you have
Description: First edition. | New York, New York : Algonquin, 2023. |
Audience: Ages 12 and up. | Audience: Grades 7-9. |
Summary: While running a con in 1934 Chicago,
sixteen-year-old Joe splits his time between Eddie, a handsome
flirt, and Raymond, a carefree rich kid who shows Joe
the queer life of the big city, but as danger closes in,
Joe must decide who he wants to be before disappearing.
Identifiers: LCCN 2022035891 | ISBN 9781616208585 (hardcover) |
ISBN 9781643753652 (ebook)
Subjects: CYAC: Swindlers and swindling—Fiction. | LGBTQ+
people—Fiction. | Interpersonal relations—Fiction. |
Chicago (Ill.)—History—20th century—Fiction.
Classification: LCC PZ7.K6837 Il 2023 | DDC [Fic]—dc23
LC record available at https://lccn.loc.gov/2022035891

10 9 8 7 6 5 4 3 2 1
First Edition

For Mike,
otherwise known as Walter.
Also answers to "Wally," "Wallace,"
"Uncle Walt," and "Uncle Mike,"
among numerous aliases.
Known around town
as my husband.

I'LL TAKE EVERYTHING YOU HAVE

ONE

AT L<small>A</small>S<small>ALLE</small> S<small>TREET</small> S<small>TATION</small> <small>IN</small> C<small>HICAGO</small>, the first thing I did when I stepped off the train was count the tracks, nearly a dozen total, all pointing the same direction: back toward home. Loudspeakers blared platform numbers and destination cities, the fuzzy stream of words passing like clouds overhead. A mob jammed the waiting room.

Before I felt licked, my cousin's cap shot up, waving above the sea of black fedoras and brown trilbies.

"Bernie!"

"Hurry up, kid. Let's bust out of this circus and find some fresh air."

Everything around us looked swell, marble walls and brass ticket counters, nothing like the dumpy brick station we got stuck with downstate. Bernie led me toward the exit, and we passed vendors selling magazines, Lucky Strikes, PayDays. One stand displayed the most colorful flowers I'd ever seen, except on postcards. The long waiting-room benches reminded me of the pews at St. Mark's, and the idea struck me that the station was like a church, people saying their prayers at each arrival and departure. Even though I was flat broke, the train station made me feel hopeful—first I'd felt that way in a long time.

I guess I was still running my mouth about it later, after we dropped off my suitcase where Bernie was staying. He snapped, "Enough about the station already! You sound like a goddamned hick when you squawk about it."

More gently, he added, "LaSalle Street isn't even one of the fancy ones, Joe. You gotta see Union Station, or Grand Central over there on Harrison. I'll take you sometime, if you're so bananas about locomotive travel all of a sudden."

We snaked our way on foot down Clark Street in Towertown. The afternoon sun blazed hot. At this hour, there was no shady side of the street. The entire city seemed to be made of brick and concrete, the apartment blocks and office buildings rising higher and higher toward the cluster of skyscrapers called the Loop.

"Golly," I exclaimed.

"You'll get used to it," Bernie said, but I hoped I wouldn't.

My father never lived to see such sights. He died in 1918, when a team of horses ran off, dragging a hayrack and my father behind them. He missed seeing everything—not just skyscrapers, but modern automobiles and traffic lights, living room radios and air travel and penicillin. He'd missed Cole Porter and Charlie Chaplin and bubble gum. He'd almost missed seeing me. When they put him in the ground, I was only eight months old.

"Shake a leg, champ!" Bernie hollered. "You want to be late for your very first shift?"

It was the end of June, with 1934 predicted to be the hottest year in American history. After too much sun and no rain, crops had shriveled across the state. That was before swarms of chinch bugs flattened what was left. We all wanted to work, but Mother Nature wouldn't meet us halfway. The previous winter, we'd heated

2

the house with corn rather than coal. This year we wouldn't even have corn. My mother had sold my father's gold watch and his cuff links; she'd hocked half the furniture. By the time I boarded the train to Chicago, she couldn't afford tears in her eyes.

Bernie had set me up with a job in the hotel kitchen where he worked. He was nineteen, three years older than me. He'd only been in Chicago a year, but already he seemed to belong. He boasted, "I go anywhere I want. Don't even glance at street names anymore."

The area where he stayed was dingy as hell. Trash filled the gutters; every block had broken windows. Grown men in rags lingered everywhere, hands stuffed deep in their pockets, like they'd been waiting years for luck to change. When a breadline jammed the sidewalk, we crossed traffic to the other side.

At Walton Street, we came to a park, a square block of uncut grass and weeds enclosed by a picket fence. The park was surrounded by two churches, a stately old library, a picture house, and an assortment of mansions. The houses had gone to seed, with torn awnings and peeling iron fence posts. In dirty windows, cardboard signs offered rooms for rent.

"Take my advice," Bernie muttered, "and steer clear of this park."

"What for?"

"It's no good, Joe. Not for us. Filled with radicals. Not to mention the place is crawling with pansies."

My ears perked up. "Repeat that?"

"I mean, this neighborhood. It may be the best we can afford for now, but it's a pansy paradise or something. Near that fountain over there, you can't look at a fellow without getting a smile you don't need."

The sign on the picket fence read WASHINGTON SQUARE PARK. My shirt collar felt wet against my neck, the same as whenever Mary Toomey invited me over for Sunday dinners with her family. At least I would be spared those crooked afternoons for a while.

I fanned my face with my hat and changed the subject. "Listen, Bern, who should I speak with about getting an advance on my first paycheck?"

"Advance? Come on, you'll get paid same as everyone else when they start. End of the second week. No way you're getting any *advance*." He said it like the word disgusted him.

"I can't wait that long."

"Where's the fire?"

"We've got so many bills staring down at us, they'll cut the power if we don't make a payment by the end of the month."

Bernie looked offended. "I've been sending cash back home, haven't I? Not just to my folks, either—"

"And we've appreciated every nickel."

"We're family, pal, but I haven't got extra dough sitting around gathering dust. Isn't that what I got you this hotel gig for?"

"Sure, but the job's only at night. My days are free. Maybe I could paint houses or something. Lookit, every storefront we pass needs paint. You know anybody who could get me extra work? I could cut grass—"

"You didn't come here to cut nobody's grass."

"No, listen, I'll do anything. Cut grass. Wash windows. I'll go door to door, if I have to—"

"Shut your trap for half a second."

We walked in silence. I knew my cousin would help me if he could.

Sure enough, he snapped his fingers in my face. "Okay, listen," he said. "I got a little plan."

Bernie always had a little plan. He walked with a limp, due to childhood polio, and he came up with plans all the time to show the bum leg hadn't made him sensitive or weak. He could get down a city sidewalk quick as anyone.

"There's this jerk in the kitchen called Hannigan," he explained. "He's been at the hotel longer than any of us, and he acts like a hotshot, even though he don't know squat about the world outside that kitchen. He needs to come down a peg. Remember That Old Black Magic?"

A parlor trick we played to fool the kids on neighboring farms. "Sure."

"We get this crumb to believe you got a special ability. Like you can read minds, right? Maybe if he thinks you can see inside his head, he'll make both of our lives easier. You'll get a few bucks to send home tomorrow, at least."

"Sounds great. But I mean, this is your job. Mine, too, until August. I don't want to mess with steady work."

"Nah, I'm talking about a simple put-on. We'll chisel a few bucks out of him. At the end of the month, I'll come clean. We'll have a good laugh. The dope's got too much pride to get bent over being had."

There was no one I trusted more than Bernie. My cousin had always been too smart to make serious trouble.

We zigzagged along the sidewalks. The second we turned onto Michigan Avenue, everything changed for the better. I struggled to take it all in: brand-new automobiles clogging the wide street, gleaming office buildings and art galleries, bustling restaurants, newsstands lined with papers from New York, Washington, DC, and London, England. I'd never seen prosperity like this, not even before the stock market crashed. "Doesn't seem fair, somehow," I said to Bernie. "Not when things are so lousy back home."

"Someone said life was fair? Say, wait until you see all the picture houses downtown. A fellow can see a different picture every day of the week."

A fellow with money could. There was nothing I loved more than pictures, but my goal was to save every penny I earned.

On Michigan Avenue, people looked like they had never gotten word about any hard times. I could not fathom where so many folks in glad rags needed to be going so quickly on a Thursday. Every man walked purposefully in a fine suit, and all the ladies wore their summer hats on a slant like Greta Garbo, along with elegant gloves. Back home in Kickapoo, my mother could wear her apron anywhere in town, except church.

It pained me to think of her spending the summer alone. Gray-haired in a gray dress in the gray farmhouse. I added "all the color" to her life, she liked to say. But I'd write and keep sending cash, and we both knew what a difference it would make.

✳✳✳

The Lago Vista was a handsome pile of bricks with nearly two hundred guest rooms. While the hotel was past its glory days, it still booked weddings and retirement parties, especially in June and July.

Bernie had arranged everything with Mr. Mertz, the banquet manager, who said he could use me in the kitchen, helping with food prep and washing dishes. I could get more hours if I looked presentable and could help serve in the ballrooms. Up to nine dollars a week, he said, if I worked hard.

The basement kitchens were hot. Over the buzz of electric fans, I could hear a baseball game from a radio. More than anything, the kitchen smelled like a holiday. Onions and celery frying in oil, meat cooking and chocolate cakes browning in the oven. I sniffed, my nose working to identify the different aromas, and my stomach growled.

"You'll eat this summer," Bernie promised. "Maybe even put on a few pounds. The chow here is outstanding."

Bernie introduced me to Jackson, the pastry chef and one of the kitchen managers. His dark forearms were dusted impressively with flour.

"Don't be fooled by the funny hat," Bernie told me. "Jackson here knows the score. How long you been working here, Jackson?"

Jackson shot Bernie a glance that said he wasn't in the mood to recite his résumé. "Four years, just about."

"You hear that, Joe? Four long years. Listen to Jackson, and you'll be aces."

Handing me a pecler and a soiled apron, Jackson pointed me toward the largest steel pot I'd ever seen, filled with a mountain of potatoes. "Once you finish those up, I'll introduce you to some carrots."

The men on the line worked in their undershirts, so I did the same. I hung my white waiter's shirt on a hook. I sat on a metal milk crate, grabbed a spud, and got started. I could peel spuds in my sleep.

Every now and then, I snuck a look back at Jackson. The fellow was handsome, with a stylish mustache. He looked Bernie's age, or not much older. He handled the two industrial mixers at once like they were toys.

Bern stood at the stove, stirring thick brown gravy in a big pot. Waitresses came through in pairs, barking orders for clean settings and linens for the ballroom setup. These women carried the heavy glass racks themselves and laughed at the same jokes as the men. I'd never heard ladies cuss before. Rules of behavior were different in the big city, that was clear.

A greasy-faced man came into the kitchen carrying two enormous cans of mayonnaise, the size of tom-toms. This was Mertz, the banquet manager. Dressed in a suit and fine shoes, Mertz didn't look like he'd peeled spuds in a long while. His necktie was so loose, I wondered why he even bothered. He set the mayonnaise cans on the counter. Seeing me, he scratched at his red, speckled nose. "Who the hell are you?"

I jumped to my feet. "Joe Garbe, sir. My cousin Bernie set it up with you. I'm much obliged for the opportunity." My fingers were slick with potato juice, so we couldn't shake mitts.

"Go make yourself useful in the alley. Liquor delivery just pulled up."

I nodded quickly, eager to demonstrate my willingness. Plus, I was curious: Prohibition had ended in December, and it was still a kick to see booze trading hands in broad daylight.

In the alley, the muggy air smelled rotten. An orange-and-brown truck was parked to the side, rear gate lifted. Inside the cargo area, between the stacks of wooden liquor crates, stood two men, one older, one younger. Both looked plenty rugged, with broad shoulders and leg muscles that strained against their ratty trousers. The older man held a bottle of Old Forester whiskey and an invoice. Without a word, he hopped off the truck and went inside.

Like me, the younger fellow was only wearing his undershirt. When he turned around, I saw he was my age, give or take, with large brown eyes and a prominent nose. His thick dark hair, without any oil in it, put me in mind of a top-quality scrub brush. When he jumped off the truck, I saw he was taller than me by several inches. Strong arms, too.

"Golly," I heard myself mutter.

The fellow held my gaze longer than was typical—almost the way Mary Toomey did back home. Something told me he wasn't saying his prayers. His face seemed to soften.

"Never seen you before, have I?" His voice was warm and low, and I felt all the blood in my body rush to my—

"You shy or something?"

—face. Around most people, I was shy, but in the presence of a beefy looker like him, I clammed up entirely.

. . .

"You work here long?" he prodded.

"Just started today." To avoid staring, I looked at the crates stacked inside the truck, and then at the brick pavement between our feet, and then, when enough time had passed, back at him.

"Eddie," he answered, as if I'd asked.

"Joe."

"Nice to meet you, Joe. Mind giving me a hand? I got nearly thirty crates to move, and Pop never lifts a finger."

"My supervisor sent me out to help."

He smiled like I'd said something clever. "He did, did he? How about that?" His tone was teasing now. It wasn't a fair fight, because

I'd been raised to speak sincerely to strangers. "I'd say your supervisor did me a favor, Joe. I'll thank him sometime."

I didn't wait for instructions. Just reached for the nearest crate and got moving.

The delivery was mostly spirits, along with club soda and seltzer. While Eddie stacked crates onto a metal dolly, I carried them one by one. They were heavy as hell, but I acted like the weight didn't give me any trouble. We worked separately, without speaking, going back and forth from the truck to the kitchen. Each time we passed, his eyes sought mine, and the corners of his lips lifted in a brief, discreet, unmistakable grin.

I let myself look, every single time, until my cousin's voice broke the spell.

TWO

"HOLD UP, JOE," Bern said. "I want to introduce you to someone."

I set down the last liquor crate with the others. We'd built a mountain in the center of the kitchen.

Hannigan, our mark, turned out to be the hotel's butcher, a giant with curly red hair and thick forearms. His freckled hands were huge and cruel-looking. The second I laid eyes on him, I wanted to forget the whole thing.

"Hann, meet my cousin Joe," Bern told him. "Kid's with us for the month."

Hannigan barely looked up from the bloodstained cutting board. "Pleased to meet ya," he said gruffly. *Chop!* He didn't look up again.

"Listen to this, Hann. My cousin's got this fascinating mental ability."

"Yeah, how's that?" *Chop! Chop, chop, chop!*

"Fact is, he's a mind reader."

"Sure he is," Hannigan said, raising his cleaver high into the air. "And I'm the maharaja of Kashmir."

General laughter sputtered from the fellows on the line.

"I'm being straight with you," Bern said. "If the kid concentrates hard enough, he can see right into a person's brain."

A man called O'Malley, washing lettuce at the sink, spoke up: "He don't wanna see what my brain is thinking right now!" O'Malley raised his head and hooted at the ceiling, even before the others joined in laughing.

"You both can go climb a tree, in my opinion," Hannigan suggested.

"Let's drop it," I muttered.

Bernie nodded. "Okay, I get it. It's not something you see every day. In your shoes, I wouldn't believe me either. How about a demonstration?"

By now the men had stopped working. Someone lowered the volume on the ballgame. Eddie, the liquor kid, propped up his dolly to watch.

Faced with an audience, I lost my nerve. "Lookit, Bern, I'm moving these crates, and I'm still buried in spuds over there."

"Come on, Joey, it'll only take a minute. I want the crew to see how special you are."

"It's malarkey anyhow," Hannigan sneered. "He can't do it."

"Can so!" Bernie said. "He's had this ability his whole damn life. In fact, I'll wager you some real jack saying the kid can do it."

Hannigan's fists pressed the meat counter. "How much?"

"One dollar," Bern said.

"Now you're really cuckoo."

"Think so?" Bern shrugged. "Prove it then. Prove I'm making it up. For one dollar. Because that's what it'll cost to have him prove his ability to you. Fifty cents for me, fifty for the kid."

"And if he can't do it?"

12

Bernie reached into his pocket. He pulled out a dollar and placed it on top of the liquor crates. "Here, I'll make the payment for my cousin and me. It's easy money for you, if you honestly think the kid can't do it."

Hannigan pulled a bill out of his wallet and laid it on the crate next to Bernie's. "You're on."

"Anyone else think I'm blowing smoke?" Bernie opened his wallet, too. "Looks like I've got another three bucks to pay out, if anyone's interested. Easy money, if you think I'm wrong."

That's all it took. Jackson, the pastry chef, put down a dollar, followed by a skinny line cook called Arroyo. Their bills joined the two Hannigan and Bernie had already laid on the crate. With a sheepish grin, Eddie contributed one more. "How can I refuse?" he asked.

My throat only tightened, as I stood watching.

Bernie held up three more bills and added them to the pile. There were now eight one-dollar bills on the crate. Nearly my weekly pay. Eight dollars was more than the cost of my train ticket. This thought buoyed my confidence a little. Sure, I'd only get a piece of it, but even two bills would be worth the nerves. Every buck I earned that summer would make a difference.

Hannigan crossed the room to me. He bent forward, his face so close to mine I could smell the stink of lunch between his teeth. He pointed to his temple. "Okay, pally, what number am I thinking of?"

"Nah, Hann," Bern said, "you can't bully the kid like that. You'll only change the number if he guesses it right. It's got to be fair and square." He scratched his head, as if he was thinking it over, and then looked at me. "Say, Joe, go take a breather in the alley, while we set it up in here."

Eddie pushed aside the dolly so I could pass by on my way outside.

My heart was racing like a jackrabbit's, but only in part due to Bernie and the piece-of-cake trick. Eddie's keen attention had rattled me good. Had my own staring been so obvious? I wouldn't have known what to do with a fellow even if I got my hands on one.

Twenty seconds later, Bernie called my name, and I went back inside.

My cousin grinned as I stood next to him. "So then, Joe, I asked Mr. Hannigan here to identify one object in this kitchen. Any item he fancied. And we instructed him, without speaking, to point to the object, so we would all know what it is. None of us have said the name of the item out loud. Gentlemen, is that correct?"

The men nodded. A few of the ladies had stopped to watch. They leaned against the counter, trays tucked under their arms.

"Now concentrate, if you will, Joe, and use your spectacular powers to summon this object to your mind."

The only thing I could see for certain was that if Mertz walked in and saw the whole group of us standing idle, we'd all be cooked. This needed to happen quickly.

"I'm ready."

"All right. Now then, I will point to several items in the room, and you tell us if it's the item Mr. Hannigan has selected. Got it?"

I nodded. It had been years since we'd played That Old Black Magic, but it wasn't complicated. The name alone gave the whole thing up, but only if you knew it.

Bernie pointed first to a mirror, square and smudged, that

hung above the utility sink. "Consider the mirror over there, Joe. Is that the item Mr. Hannigan chose?"

"No."

He indicated the sky-blue electric clock on the wall. "How about the clock?"

"No, that's not it either."

Next, he pointed to the biggest skillet I'd ever seen, big enough to scramble seventy eggs, crusted with ancient-looking black grease. "How about this skillet?"

"No," I said quickly. I needed to get back to those spuds.

Finally, he pointed to a whisk on Jackson's pastry table. "How about that whisk over there?"

"Yes, the whisk. That's what it was."

I didn't need anyone else to confirm it.

Hannigan pounded his fist on the cutting board. "It's a damn trick!" he hollered. "You let him know somehow."

"How?" Bernie asked. "We're all here together, aren't we?"

"You got a system?" Jackson asked me, smiling.

"They got a signal," one of the gals suggested. She looked peeved, even though she hadn't lost a nickel herself. "Like, it's the *way* Bernie asks the kid. The specific words."

"We can do it again, folks," Bernie said. "Write down my exact words. We can do it as many times as you like, as long as you pay up each time the kid gets it right."

"You both can go take a hike." Grumbling under his breath, Hannigan turned to wash his hands at the meat sink.

Bernie retrieved the crumpled bills from the crate, as the crew stood glaring, like they'd been conned by him one too many times.

My cousin gave me two dollars. "Be sure to scrub your hands, too, kid. Nothing's filthier than cash."

Drying my hands, I noticed the dolly standing in the corner where Eddie had pushed it. I looked around for him but saw only his father standing in Mertz's office, pouring whiskey into coffee cups.

Like a bolt of lightning, a brilliant idea came to me. I rehearsed my words, then wheeled the dolly to the door and took it outside. I pushed the dolly toward Eddie, wheels squeaking on the brick pavers.

"Thanks, Joe." He leaned against the truck, beefy forearms folded across his chest, like he'd been waiting for me. Even without smiling, his face was something to look at.

I forced out the words in one breath: "I need to make some extra cash real quick."

"Yeah?"

"You've seen how I can move these crates. You think your dad could use me on deliveries? I'm here for the whole month. I'm a hard worker, and only here at the hotel at night—"

He raised a hand to stop me. "Pop's got four sons and not paying wages to any of us."

"Oh."

So my idea hadn't been a lightning strike, after all. Only a worthless spark.

When I turned to go back inside, he spoke again. "Say, Joe, matter of fact, I *did* forget the dolly back in there. I needed to bounce out quick."

"How come?"

"I didn't want anybody reading my mind. Especially you." He lifted the dolly and placed it inside the truck, fastening the belts.

"Only a dumb game. Something we used to do back home for laughs."

"It was damn impressive."

"My cousin wanted to play a joke on his friend in there. Here, let me give you your dollar back, at least."

When he grinned, his dimples reappeared. "Keep it. You earned it fair and square. And you just now said you need it."

"It wasn't fair *or* square." I pulled a bill from my pocket. "Go on, take your money."

He glanced at the screen door, then lowered his voice. "Tell you what, Joe. Buy me a soda sometime instead. Or an ice cream. You can explain the trick then. You said you're here for the whole month, right? Maybe I could take you out and show you a good time."

. . .

"Answer me quick," he added. "Pop will be out here any minute."

"I—I don't have free time for socializing," I said finally. "And I'm saving every nickel I earn to send home."

"Add that to the things I admire about you already. Anyhow, Joe, the stuff I'd like to show you don't cost anything at all."

He winked, and then it was plain: This tough guy was queer.

Sweat flowed like the Illinois River down my back.

Before I could answer, his father burst through the screen door. He still had the invoice but not the hooch. He spit through his teeth, hitting the brick pavers near our feet, and then got into the truck without speaking. The engine roared to life.

I pushed the dollar back into my pocket.

Eddie pulled down the gate on the truck. "Now listen, Joe,

don't forget—you owe me one." Another wink, before he got in the truck.

On rubber legs, I returned to the kitchen. My face felt hot, fingers tingling. What had I said or done to encourage this stranger? Handsome faces had left me tongue-tied before, but no fellow had ever spoken to me so queerly. Another way people in the city behaved differently.

I took my spot on the milk crate and reached for the potato peeler, just as Bernie came over. He handed me a plate with two drumsticks, green beans, mashed potatoes and gravy. My first shift meal.

"Where'd you disappear to, kid? I saved this for— Jay-sus, your face is red as a tomato."

By the time we left the kitchen, it was nearly midnight. The hotels and skyscrapers glittered along Michigan Avenue; in the distance, a ghostly searchlight crossed the skyline. Even at that hour, the city bellowed the sounds of traffic horns, engines sputtering, streetcars screeching.

My feet were sore, my hands raw. I'd made it my goal to wash more dishes than anyone. I'd been so busy in the kitchen, they hadn't sent me up to the ballroom. My clothes reeked of bleach.

After crossing the bridge, we retraced our earlier route until we got to the monumental stone water tower and Bernie's neighborhood. The down-and-outs remained on every corner. We walked north past the grim cafés and tearooms with dirty windows; some were lit by candlelight, wax dripping onto the tabletops and then down to the floors. On every block, we heard music playing through open doors, "Blue Skies" and "Everybody Loves My Baby," numbers that were popular when times were easier.

"Swell work tonight," Bernie said. "And already you made two bills, just like I promised. Got your little *advance*. And those goons fear you now, which, trust me, is way more important than any of them liking you."

I slowed my pace to get his attention. "The thing is, two bucks isn't near enough."

"Sure, it isn't. You'll earn more, week by week. Maybe fifty, by the time you leave."

"No, see, we're sitting on dynamite back home. I'm telling you, we owe everybody. Feed store, the grocer, utilities. Plus back payments to the bank. Maybe you don't know how bad things are—"

"I know all about it. I thought the Fed was supposed to help out this summer, given the whatchamacallit. The drought."

"But they haven't. Not yet."

"Haven't you got those college savings from your grandparents? A fellow doesn't need Plato when he's working the horse-and-plow."

This was a sore point. My mother had already spent the college money in order to avoid selling land.

"Isn't my future for me to decide?"

"I understand completely," he said.

But my cousin didn't understand at all. He'd never been interested in farming or college. The April of his senior year, he ate half a jelly sandwich at school, walked out the cafeteria exit, and hitchhiked to Chicago. He hadn't even packed a bag.

"Listen," he said, "you made a fine impression in the kitchen tonight. Stayed busy and flew under the radar, that's just your

nature. In a town like this, a fellow like you can come in handy."
He stared me up and down, like he was measuring me for a suit.

"What, I got gravy on my face?"

"No, kid, you look terrific. In fact, I was considering that
there's nothing remarkable about your appearance at all. No scars
or strange marks, and you don't have a giant snoot or beady eyes
or anything. You've got brown hair and eyes, like half the men in
Chicago. You're the same height as me, and that's perfectly average."

"Average Joe. That's me."

Bernie grinned. "Mary Toomey likes you fine, according to
sources."

Another sore point. Mary's father had sat me down and offered
to send me to college, provided things worked out between his
daughter and me.

Just past the intersection of LaSalle and Elm, we arrived at
Bernie's brick building. The centerpiece of the weedy garden was
a bone-dry birdbath.

"Level with me now," Bernie said. "How much do you need?"

I wasn't sure how to price it. Enough to pay off the urgent bills
and maybe restore my college fund, too. "Five hundred?" I said.

His hand flew to his mouth.

"Don't look at me like that, Bern."

He glanced over his shoulder, as if even talking about money
that big could make us a target. Before I could start up the steps,
he fished something out of his pocket. "Here's a spare key. Now
listen, champ, don't lose any more sleep over it. We'll sort out the
money. Anyhow, I got an appointment."

"At this hour?"

"Can't be helped. Don't wait up!"

He continued limping his way north on LaSalle Street, going a remarkably fast pace after a long shift. I guessed he had a girl. Bernie always had girls. They showed him affection on account of his bum leg, and he took advantage.

I stood on the sidewalk, holding the key. The fresh night air had boosted my energy to the moon. Back home, my mother practically counted the sheep for me, but I wasn't anywhere near home tonight.

Once Bernie was out of sight, I doubled back over to Clark Street and headed toward the park. My cousin's warning flashed like neon in my brain: *pansy paradise.*

I was only curious. Eddie and his metal dolly had messed with my head. One minute alone together in that alley, and he had my number. I had to find out how.

Washington Square Park didn't take up much space, only one block on all four sides, with diagonal paths that led to a fountain. Garden beds were neglected and garbage littered the patches of grass. Even at that late hour, foot traffic was steady. Men of every age and background, both well-to-dos and derelicts. Some strolled, others loitered. A gay peal of laughter crossed the park as two figures greeted near the fountain. A trio of gals passed through as well; one smoked a pipe.

I viewed the action from across the street. Like watching the screen at a picture show, that's how far away I felt from those people.

I'd been dumb as an onion to my own feelings until high school, when two senior boys jumped me on the road near home. They wrestled me to the ground, pinning my legs and shoulders to the gravel. When one of the boys called me a pansy, I thought of the flower, that's how green I was. The excitement ended just as quickly. After a minute, they leapt to their feet and ran off, leaving me there. For them, it was horseplay. But for months afterward, I relived the scene in my head, imagining where the whole thing might have gone. I didn't quite know what *could* happen. I'd never seen the scenes I imagined described by anyone else.

I wouldn't set foot in the park myself. My work clothes stank, and my whole body needed a soak. For me, it was enough to stand across the street and watch. Nobody seemed to care about being seen. I didn't either, since I didn't know a soul in Chicago, except my cousin.

I wondered if Eddie spent time here. The thought of seeing him again at the hotel gave me butterflies. A part of me—the down-state part that pleased my mother by spending Sundays with Mary Toomey—wanted to avoid him completely. But another, brand-new part wondered what I might learn from a fellow who wasn't afraid to take a bold risk like that.

An older gentleman wearing a bowler approached. I hadn't seen a hat like that for ages. His gray suit looked old-fashioned, too, a size too big for him. He got close and stopped. "Good evening."

"Evening."

He showed me two dollars, holding them out for anyone to see. Then he offered to perform an unusual service on one specific part of my anatomy.

The trickling fountain in the park, the boisterous friends, the passing automobiles: Every sound receded into a dizzy darkness; suddenly, the man and I seemed far removed from the ordinary world. Far from the safe world I knew.

I managed to sputter, "I'm—on my way home. I'm expected there."

"A shame," he said, returning the money to his trousers. "Next time."

I stepped away quickly, pausing only to glance behind to make sure he didn't follow. My heart racing, I retraced the route back to Bernie's building, where my trembling hand struggled to get the key into the lock.

Anything could happen, I realized, if I wanted it to. If I wasn't careful.

THREE

SLEPT POORLY. A booming garbage truck outside the window woke me for good.

For three bucks a week, I had my very own slice of Bernie's room. He'd set up an army cot for me, next to the closet. The room was good sized, with bare walls. A single window faced the street. The corner sink was handy: I'd rinsed my work clothes and hung them in the room to dry. Bathtub and toilet were down the hall.

Bernie lifted his head from the pillow and waggled a friendly finger at me. Just before sunrise, I'd heard him return, when his toe kicked the tin ashtray on the floor next to the bed. The sound was loud as a gunshot. Ashes and butts still littered the floor.

"It's hot as blazes in here," I said. "I'm soaked."

He yawned. "Nah, it's fine." His bed was next to the window. The worn lace curtain fluttered from a breeze that never quite made the distance to me. "You're sleeping in the better spot, if you think about it. I put up with the street racket over here."

His arm fell limp to the side of the bed, landing on a stack of hardcover books. *Swan Song. Maid in Waiting. One More River.* Popular novels, all by John Galsworthy.

"You become a bookworm?" I asked.

When he didn't answer, I picked up *Swan Song* and opened to the title page. Signed by the author with a fountain pen. Blue ink, with a bold stroke.

"Hey, this one is signed. Might be worth money someday."

"Already is," he said. "They've all got signatures. I sell 'em on consignment."

"Neat-o. So you met the author?"

"Nah, he lives overseas," he said, swinging his hairy legs out of bed. "Merry old England or someplace. Let's get some grub, I'm starved."

✳✳✳

Breakfast was included with the rent. In the sunny kitchen, Bernie wolfed down a colossal bowl of Wheaties before I had taken two bites.

I stared at Lou Gehrig on the back of the orange-and-blue ccreal box. The photograph captured the Yankee slugger post-swing, powerful and perfect, like a Greek statue on a pedestal.

Delfina Tarantala, our hostess, gave us each a half a grape-fruit, served on bread-and-butter plates. Del was in her late for-ties, heavyset, with dyed auburn hair fixed with bobby pins that constantly needed checking. She worked the register most after-noons at a drugstore down the block. She wasn't permitted to sublet space in her apartment, so Bernie and I were instructed to call her Auntie Del when anybody else was around. Likewise, she would refer to us as her nephews.

Down the hall, a neighbor had a radio. Del told me I could join her whenever I liked. "I expect you enjoy *Skippy* and *Little Orphan Annie*," she said.

"I like *One Man's Family*," I said, because I didn't want her seeing me as a kid.

"Do you now?" Bernie grinned.

"Now if this isn't the saddest tale you ever heard," Del told us, holding up the *Tribune*. "This gentleman called Santiago—this widower in New York—he died while sewing his clothes."

"How's that, Del?" Bernie asked.

She fanned herself with her hand. "According to the story, this man Santiago fell asleep while darning in bed. He dropped the needle, which got wedged into the mattress. When he turned in his sleep, the needle pierced his heart and killed him. Poor man, I wonder if he even woke up to greet Jesus. How terribly sad for any man to mend his own clothes." Del stared out the kitchen with a worried expression, as if all single women bore some responsibility for Mr. Santiago's fate.

I went back to Lou Gehrig, wondering who had the pleasure of mending his clothes.

"And here's a young man in California," Del continued, "age twenty-one, who used a hatchet to kill his own mother and brother. How do you like that? It says here, 'The body of Mrs. Payne was nude. An electric light cord was looped tightly around her neck and her head was battered and gashed.' Think of it, a boy treating his own mother like that. They're calling him the Hatchet Killer."

Bernie dusted his grapefruit with sugar. "With your pleasant conversation, Del, it's a puzzle you haven't got gentlemen lining up to take you out."

"I'm only telling the truth here!" she said. "It's the way the world is now. Why, here's a story about a Texas man and his wife killed by a ranch hand. He crushed their skulls and burned their farmhouse to the ground."

"Jeez, that's not nice," I muttered to Bern.

He laughed, but Del only frowned. "The whole world has become hard as steel," she said, "and you boys are too young to know better. Ever since the crash, it's all sad news, every day. More tragedies, more bad luck. That's how I see it."

I nodded but only to be polite. I'd sure never known easy times, but I didn't like to think the world was hard as steel, especially not now, when I was getting my first real look at it.

✳✳✳

The humidity had kept my work clothes from drying properly overnight, and sweating didn't help. My trousers chafed my thighs as we crossed the river on Dearborn and cut over to State. The afternoon sun beat down as we weaved among businessmen returning from lunch. The Loop was the downtown area, circled by the elevated trains, where everything was hopping. I couldn't keep up with the signs everywhere: wood and canvas, the gold paint on windows, the theater marquees and neon signs, signs painted on the sides of brick buildings with letters five feet tall. A person needed a college degree just to keep up with all the reading.

ALL KINDS OF FLAT GLASS FOR EVERY USE

NEVER BEFORE SUCH AN OFFER

THE BEER THAT MADE MILWAUKEE FAMOUS!

TURKISH BATHS – PRIVATE ROOMS

CHIEF WASH CO. – SHIRTS ONLY 6 CENTS

SILVERWARE

GLASSWARE

CHINAWARE

"So, Bern," I said, extra casually, as we threaded through side-walk traffic, "how often do we get a liquor delivery?"

"Liquor, what?"

"I mean, at the hotel."

He shrugged. "Never really paid attention. Twice a week?"

"Oh."

"Put that outta your head now, Joe. I promised your ma I wouldn't give you booze this summer. Or let you smoke. Of course, there may be *special occasions* when you—"

I interrupted. "I only wondered if any of the delivery trucks might give me some hours."

"Anyhow," he said, "you did great yesterday with that trick. Played it cool, like you didn't want to do it. That was perfect."

"Hannigan sure fell for it," I said.

"Yeah, slow freight, that one."

"Slow freight?"

"Impressive train, but the tracks run real slow."

We shared a laugh at the big guy's expense, until Bernie said, "Forget about the hotel for a minute. I want to talk about the trouble you're in. I got a solid option for you."

I wanted to throw my arms around him. "I'll do anything."

"Okay then, it's very simple. You take a class for me."

"A class? That's all?"

He nodded. "Starts Monday and goes two weeks. Only twice a week. They do it at this cute little church over there on Dearborn. A ten-minute walk from Del's. Could not be more convenient."

"What kind of class?"

"It's a French conversation course for, like, people going overseas in August."

"Overseas? Who's taking big trips like that these days?"

"Plenty of rich swells are, dummy. Liners cross the Atlantic every day, loaded with folks. And when they get there, they want to visit all the fancy shops and read the restaurant menus. They love eating those snails in garlic oil."

"Ew, no thanks."

"I'm with you there. But these rich people, they need basic conversation skills, see? In this course, two short weeks, they get what they need."

"But, Bern, what do I need a class like that for? Besides, a course like that costs money."

"Nah, nah, we'll front you the tuition."

"You and who else?"

"A friend."

"Who? You got a rich friend here and didn't tell me?"

He laughed. "My pal Heinz is not rich, not by a long shot. We help each other out with jobs from time to time. Spoke to him last night, in fact."

"I don't get it. How does this make us any money?"

"Listen, just take the course. Four lousy classes, right? That's it. See how you like it, and you can tell me if the dough bothers you too much."

"Huh. And you and your friend Heinz, you're going to pay me to take the course, like, so I can speak French sometime?"

"Yeah, who knows? Maybe you'll take a trip yourself someday. You'll see the *Arc d' Tree-oomph* and whatever. Try those snails."

"And that's all I do? Learn some French?"

"Sure." He scratched his chin. "And find out their names, these other people, and when they're traveling. We need the travel dates. Couldn't be simpler."

"Travel dates?" Sometimes my freight was slow as hell, too. "Now wait a minute . . ."

"Bingo. Good boy. Later, say, when they get back from their travels and they find out something's missing—*if* they find out something's missing—no way do they link it back to the course they took at the cute little church. Most of the time, they probably never notice they've been took."

"How so? Rich people have eyes, Bern."

"These guys are pros. They take the stuff the dopes won't notice for a while."

"Like what? Jewelry?"

"*Never* jewelry. These high society dames, they notice when their ice is missing. They like to get it out and look at it. These ladies sit there in their *boo-drawers* in their big houses and count their jewels."

"So, like what? What could you take that they wouldn't notice?"

"Trust me, lots of stuff. You can pinch checks, for example, or even a key to a safe deposit box. Liberty notes. You don't worry about that part."

"But it's not right. To be part of something like that. Taking people's hard-earned money from them."

"Hard-earned money?" he said. "Says *who*? Listen, a long time ago I stopped believing this idea that wealthy people deserve every bit they got. You think they all made it honestly? Give me a break. Even the honest ones, they're not working too hard. They make their money off the backs of real workers, like us."

30

"You got something against rich people?"

"Nah, I'm for every man making a buck. But I don't think it's wrong to spread the dough around every now and then, if it's possible to do it safely."

We continued walking. State Street was dotted with gleaming new automobiles. Businessmen paraded the sidewalks in their crisp, shiny suits; at the same time, scores of down-and-outs sat idle, propping up the buildings at their foundations. The whole town seemed eager to prove my cousin's point. Nothing had ever been fair. And it didn't make sense that some people were so rich they wouldn't even notice getting took.

The job Bernie proposed seemed wrong, but the traffic hubbub made it difficult for my brain to reason why. Like he said, all I'd be doing is taking the class. In my circumstances, to turn down *any* job, no matter how small, seemed irresponsible.

"I never could break into someone's house," I said finally.

"Nah, nah, you're still not getting it. We leave all that to other people. *You're* not going into any stranger's house. *I'm* not going into anyone's house. We just need the names, addresses, and dates they'll be traveling. That's what we get paid for. A flat fee."

"How much?"

"Six hundred even."

"Quit pulling my chain."

"Honest to god, three hundred each. Fifty-fifty split. It's not what you asked for, but when you add it to your hotel wages, you're on your way."

If it hadn't been for the traffic, he might have heard my heart thumping. "Three hundred. That's some real money."

31

"For not much work, either. And we're not even doing anything illegal."

"I mean. That's only technically true."

"It's the truth! You're not stealing. You're not even *trespassing*. You just collect basic information."

"If it's so easy, why don't you do it yourself and keep all the money?"

"I did do it. Last winter I took German over at the very same church. I can't be going back again, how sketchy would that look? All I did was meet the people and learn about their travels. Every person there was loaded. I got the sense the society ladies take the class in order to know when their maids are talking shit about them."

"Did you learn any German?"

"I gave it a shot, Joey. Complete disaster."

I tried to see it his way. I wanted to believe it'd be okay to take things from people who would never miss them. Back home, we'd miss a spare shoelace if it left the house on someone else's foot. "But did you feel bad about doing it?"

He shrugged. "Honestly, I didn't. I never got to know those people. Like I said, they probably never missed a thing."

We walked for a while. "When would we get the money?"

"When the course is over. Or, a little after that. Heinz's people, they can't pay us before they know the information is good. It's better that way, anyway."

"Better how?"

"So we don't go *spending* what we oughta be saving." His hand rested on my shoulder. "So you'll do it? You'll help us out on this one?"

I couldn't get the figure out of my head. Three hundred in cash, guaranteed. Plus my hotel wages. Plus anything else I could scrape together. Even if most of it went to the farm, saving a quarter for myself might mean having a shot at college after all.

"You're sure it's nothing we could get in trouble doing?"

"I know so!" he practically shouted. "It's the answer to your prayers. Either way, we got to find you some better threads. You can't show up for any job in your farm rags. First thing tomorrow we pick up something new, got it? And not a word to anyone about this. That's not your role here."

"Got it," I said, and the conversation ended because we'd arrived at the hotel.

Inside the basement kitchen, Jackson handed me another peeler and pointed me back to the potatoes. "You seemed to enjoy yourself last night," he teased. "I could see it on your face."

I got to work. Every time the alley door swung open, I tensed up, waiting for more liquor to walk in. I tensed up for dairy, for ice, and for produce. But no liquor. It was for the best. Whatever Eddie had been offering me, I couldn't take it. I could never afford a risk like that, because if it went poorly, the cost would mean losing everything.

I put on my clean shirt, and Mertz led me upstairs to train me for banquets. Compared to kitchen work, serving was a breeze. The ballroom was air-cooled, and every guest got the same plate, so it didn't take a genius to hand them out. The only difficulty was carrying the tray in one hand (above the shoulder, palm in the center, the way Mertz preferred) and a tray jack in the other. The tray jacks were heavy as hell.

Mertz spat vitriol at me in the elevator: "Keep your *fingers* out of the *food*." He said it like I'd meant to dip my stupid finger in anyone's soup. "Keep the serving tray *far away* from your head. Do not *speak over* the food. Our guests do not want us to *breathe* on their *salads*."

Near the pastry counter, Jackson heard Mertz giving me the business. He pulled me aside. "He's like that with everybody, at first," Jackson advised. "Hannigan, too. Give it time and you'll be aces."

I went back upstairs and picked up the rhythm. Before long, sure enough, Mertz stopped spitting at me in the elevator.

"Getting the swing of things," I told Jackson later, "like you predicted."

With a nod, he slid me a slice of Boston cream cake. The slice looked like it lost a boxing match, but Jackson only smiled. "When the sides are busted like that," he said with a shrug, "we can't serve it."

I tore into it, the creamiest, most delicious cake I'd ever eaten. "It would be wrong," I said, "to serve this upstairs."

He reached for another slice, this one perfect looking, before destroying the top with a spoon. "Just couldn't do that to our guests."

With Jackson, I'd found an ally. Meanwhile, the other men in the kitchen gave me the cold shoulder. Whenever I passed by, they turned their heads, like they didn't want me going anywhere near their shameful thoughts.

FOUR

BERNIE MET A PAL FOR BREAKFAST, so Del had me all to herself. She read me a *Tribune* story about a family whose children died after eating spoiled pork from a peddler. Then she read about a three-year-old farm girl in Aurora who attempted to crawl between loose wood planks in the corncrib and was "guillotined."

With a sigh of wonder, Del folded the paper and set it next to her plate. She lifted her hands to check on her bobby pins. "Dear boy, your cousin said you lost your pa. How did that happen?"

"He died in 1918, during the flu," I said, which was true but misleading. I knew if I'd told her the real story, she wouldn't let up until she learned every detail.

"A nasty piece of luck," Del concluded.

She herself was the beneficiary of good luck. According to Del, she only got the job at Klein's Drug because of a chain of bum luck that had befallen other people, involving a broken clock, a rabid dog, and a childhood friend's gallstone emergency. "Luckiest day of my life," she told me cheerfully.

Listening to her stories, I wondered which kind of luck might be coming my way.

The only suit I'd ever owned was one my father had left behind. It fit like a glove, but it was heavy wool and out of style. I hadn't even brought it to Chicago.

Bernie took me to Benson & Rixon on State Street, where he picked out a linen suit in my size. Medium gray, with a silky pale blue lining. No waistcoat. It was on sale for ten dollars and fifty cents. I balked at the price, but Bernie reached for his billfold. "I got this," he said. "Think of it as an investment. You've got to look the part. If you dress in the rags you brought from home, no one will believe you're heading to *Milwaukee* this summer, much less to Europe."

At Marshall Field & Company, we purchased three shirts with attached collars, and a pair of trousers, less formal, along with two pairs of shoes: black wingtips and brown-and-tan oxfords. The mounting price tags left me queasy. I wouldn't have needed a new wardrobe to paint houses.

✳✳✳

At 10:45 on the morning of Monday, July 2, Bernie walked me to the first French class. We went east on Schiller Street, crossing Clark to the wealthier blocks beyond. The streets were quieter here, no car motors or blaring horns, nothing but the sound of birdsong and wind rustling the trees. There wasn't a speck of trash in the gutters. Closer to the lake, the air became noticeably cooler. I should have felt comfortable, but nerves soaked my undershirt.

At Dearborn, we stopped. Bernie said he didn't want to get any closer to the church. He socked me gently on the shoulder. "Relax, you're taking a class, not robbing a bank."

"These people are rich, Bern. Won't they see right away I'm not like them? Even the way I talk—"

"You talk like a goddamned prince! That's why you're perfect for this. Now go on, champ, and I'll see you back at Del's in a jiff."

The first sign of trouble was that the place was named for St. Chrysostom. I'd never heard of the guy, and I'd been going to Sunday Mass my whole life.

Behind the church, some flagstones led to a parish hall with gothic windows. The double doors were pulled open wide, as if welcoming any sap who wandered by. I passed through the doors into a dim hallway. The air smelled good, like beans cooking in a pot somewhere. Following the signs to the French language class, I reached a sunny gymnasium.

In the center of the basketball court, several card tables had been pushed together, set with pitchers of lemonade and paper cups. There were chairs for a dozen or so students, a fresh ditto at each seat. Several people, all women, were seated already, fanning themselves with the papers.

The teacher, Madame Monk, wore her gray hair in pressed waves, longer than most women her age, which I estimated to be fifty. She handed me a clipboard and pencil. "Here, please, you will write your name and address for your street? Merci."

My cousin had prepared me for this step. He'd told me to make up a name that sounded "high class." Nothing sounded more aristo-cratic to my ear than the name Charles. My favorite film actor was William Powell, who always appeared smooth and sophisticated in thrillers like *Double Harness* and *One Way Passage*. Combining the two, I printed my new name, Charles Powell, along with the phony address Bernie had provided.

These classes, I had decided, were like a game of pretend, no different than spending long Sundays with Mary Toomey and her parents. I'd had plenty of practice.

I returned the clipboard to Madame Monk and took a seat.

I remembered not to slouch. With my hands folded on my lap, I studied the ditto, which listed vocabulary words and common expressions we were expected to memorize for the next class.

Bonjour. Bonsoir. Bonne nuit. S'il vous plaît. Merci.

Below this, the sheet included more basic terms: Numbers. Days of the week. Months of the year. Morning and afternoon o'clock.

I smiled at the notion I might actually learn some French. Charles Powell seemed like the kind of fellow who *should* speak French.

When class began, most seats were filled. All women and girls, except for a blond fellow who arrived with his mother. He looked to be my age. The two of us were the only ones who removed our hats when we sat down.

Madame Monk smiled primly. Her accent was thick: "It will be very nice if we begin with the introductions, yes? Thank you. If you please will tell us who you are and why you are here for this class." She looked at me first.

Keeping my voice steady, I recited the words I'd practiced: "My name is Charles Powell. I'm visiting from downstate, near St. Louis. My parents and I are sailing to France later this month on Holland America. I'm here to learn some practical phrases."

I penciled the names at the top of the ditto as the others introduced themselves: Florence Shaw and her granddaughter, Evelyn; Maureen Feeney and her daughter, Lillian; Edna Palmer and her niece, Elsie; Kathleen Kenrick and her son, Raymond; Mildred Moore and her sister, Ruth.

My classmates didn't know one another, but everyone had plans to travel to France. They shared something else, too, a quality that reminded me of fine china. Different patterns, maybe, but pieces from the same factory. Compared to them, I felt like a coffee cup in some dump diner.

Was I slouching? I sat up again, but too late. The round-faced woman to my left, Mrs. Moore, was giving me the eye.

"Are you really here *all by yourself?*" Her tone suggested I'd abandoned my companion at the side of the road somewhere.

I faltered. Bernie should've warned me that everybody would be there in pairs. "I'm . . . well . . . I mean, my parents. They speak French already. I'm hoping to surprise them."

Mrs. Moore's lips pressed together like she didn't believe me. "Why are you taking notes? We haven't learned anything yet!"

"I'm no good with names," I explained quietly. "Hoping this will help."

I returned my attention to Madame, who led us through the terms on the ditto. She pronounced the words out loud, and we repeated them after her, over and over.

"Excuse me," Mrs. Moore interrupted again. "Mightn't it be better to teach us useful travel phrases rather than all these days and numbers? Is knowing how to say *Thursday* going to help me when I need to use the ladies' room at some café?" She smiled, as if the suggestion of humor might take the sting out of her criticism. Next to Mrs. Moore, her sister giggled loyally.

Madame folded her hands on the table, and the prim smile

remained. "Today we have the first class only, yes? Let us have patience with our learning."

During introductions, I'd snuck a few glances at Raymond Kenrick and his mother. Both good-looking, with golden hair and suntanned complexions. Raymond looked exactly like the kind of fellow boys back home would hassle, with his hair combed smooth and parted on the side, and a crisply ironed, lilac-colored Oxford shirt.

"Come to think of it," Mrs. Moore announced suddenly, "I'm afraid I do need to use the facilities. Or should I say, *Bonjour! Thursday!*"

Madame Monk nodded. "Thank you, yes. Then we will have a short break, five minutes, and take some of the citron pressé here."

At last, it was time to work. I'd always been able to get people to talk. Most people liked to talk about themselves, I'd learned. If I got the goods on one or two families per session, then by the end I'd have information on all five families, everything I needed. It should have been a piece of cake.

Mrs. Moore and her sister had gone to the lavatory, so I turned to Evelyn Shaw and her grandmother. The grandmother wore a large hydrangea on her white blouse, the tiny petals wilting in the heat. When she reached for the lemonade, her gem-studded fingers glittered in the sunny gymnasium. Now here was a woman who never worried about paying the power bill.

"And when do *you* leave for France?" I asked them, as if we'd been talking about it.

"We sail on the seventh and are back by September first," Mrs. Shaw said.

I nodded, both pleased and astonished that she shared the information so easily.

The granddaughter, who looked about my age, wore a floral

sundress with a white collar. "We go every August," she boasted. "Isn't it wonderful?"

Charles Powell, in my mind, had traveled widely by train but never internationally. My cousin and I had invented an itinerary for him, using newspaper ads. "This will be my first time on a liner," I told them. "We're sailing New York to Marseilles."

Mrs. Shaw's dark eyes sparkled beneath the brim of her plum-colored hat. "The sea air is divine, you'll see. You're young. You have loads of adventures ahead of you."

A voyage like that sounded like a dream come true, but it was only a dream for me. For wealthy people, it was plain old regular summer.

I felt a sudden pressure against my elbow. The blond boy, Raymond Kenrick, was standing to my left, his keister pressing against me.

"*Excusez-moi*," he said over his shoulder. His blue eyes were even more arresting up close.

"My fault," I said, withdrawing my elbow. "I'm blocking the drinks."

"*Pardon*," Madame Monk corrected.

"Excuse me?" Raymond and I asked at the same time.

"In French, when we knock rudely into another person, we say *pardon*, not *excusez-moi*."

Raymond spoke to me over his shoulder again. "*Pardon* for being rude."

"I forgive you in both languages," I said, which made him laugh.

He reached for the lemonade, pouring two glasses. Meanwhile, the keister barely budged. His clothes smelled like they'd been laundered in spearmint.

An ache formed in my stomach. Mrs. Shaw had handed me the

travel dates, but they were gone, forgotten, poured like Raymond's lemonade right out of my head.

They would sail on August tenth and return September first. Was that correct? Or sail on the first and return on September seventh? I couldn't blame Raymond's *derriere* entirely. My brain had a lousy habit of scrambling numbers at the worst possible times. Maybe this gig was no good for me, after all.

Mrs. Moore had returned from the lavatory and was giggling again. "Excuse me, are we going to do any learning today?" She pointed desperately at her ditto.

Madame Monk nodded and we began again.

Oui, s'il vous plaît. Non, merci. Enchanté. Adieu.

I felt like a dope for not getting the Shaws' dates, but I could ask them next time. In the meantime, Raymond Kenrick seemed like an easier target. The look he gave me over the lemonade suggested if I could get him alone, I could get anything I wanted.

After class, I waited for him in the gothic arcade, pretending to be engrossed in the ditto. His mother breezed by on her way out the door, but Raymond paused, holding his panama hat. His smile wasn't the least bit shy. "I hoped I'd catch you before you left," he said quietly, "seeing the two of us have something in common."

"Is that right?"

"I mean, as the only two fellows in the whole group."

"Oh! Yes, it's lucky we've got each other."

"If it weren't for you, I'd feel funny being here. I'm a hopeless case. Haven't got a head for languages. Which is strange, because I've taken piano lessons for years, and they say there's a connection between music and languages. People with a talent for one are said to be gifted at the other. But in my case, it's not true at all."

This sudden outpouring left me flustered. Where I came from, people were as frugal with words as they were with everything else. "Do you want to get together sometime and practice?" I blurted.

His face lit up. "I mean, of course. I'd be delighted to tickle the ivories with you. I can play just about any number by ear, even without the music in front of me. My absolute favorite to play is 'Stardust.' But I wouldn't force a song on you, nothing like that." His voice had a quick, clear cadence that sounded musical, too.

"I meant practice French," I said. "We could meet for a soda somewhere."

"*Bien sûr*, sounds terrific. But why don't you come to our house? We'll feel more confident with nobody watching. Trade cards?" He handed me a card with his name and address engraved in handsome geometric script.

I patted my trouser pockets, pretending to search. "Haven't got one on me."

"Our house then. Tomorrow afternoon, say two o'clock?"

I needed to be at the hotel by three. "I have an appointment in the afternoon. Would the morning work?"

"I'm never awake before ten. Let's say eleven, to be safe. We're just over on State Parkway."

I slid the card into my pocket, feeling conflicted. Meeting at his place would save me the nickel on a soda. But anyone could see this kid was good-natured, even sweet. If his family hadn't been rich, my conscience might have bothered me.

"Wonderful to meet you, Charles Powell. I mean—*enchanté*."

We shook mitts. "*Adieu*," I said.

Grinning, he turned and skipped down the flagstone steps toward the street.

FIVE

I FOUND BERNIE IN OUR ROOM, looking over the sports pages he'd pinched from the kitchen. My work clothes hung on the drying line that stretched from the window to the door.

He glanced up from the paper, a cigarette in his mouth. "How's tricks, hotshot?"

My brain hurt, trying to recall the Shaws' travel dates. My cousin didn't need to know how I fumbled the very first play. "I got all the names," I said. "And a fellow my age invited me over to practice French tomorrow. I'll get his travel dates then."

"Not bad for the first class. Don't forget the home addresses. We need that for everyone."

"Can't you look them up in a phonebook?"

"Some, maybe. But these how-de-do folks, they aren't always listed."

I kicked off my shoes and sat on the cot. I was determined to make as much cash as I could that summer, but I still felt jittery as hell. "The thing is, Bern, most of those people were very nice. Won't this whole thing weigh on our conscience?"

"Listen, it's normal to feel that way. I was raised the same as you. Same prayers at the supper table. Same church every week, too. You think I don't recall that?"

"I know you do."

"And I recall birthdays with no gifts. I recall Sunday suppers with no meat. I recall the time we picked you two up for church during a blizzard, and the grown-ups got into a shouting match over which of us would wear the snow mittens, because we only had the one pair. Remember that storm?"

I remembered like it was yesterday: Bernie sitting in the pew with those red, shiny hands. At home, any comfort that came my way meant a sacrifice for someone else.

He leaned forward, eyes wide. "Now then, pal, do you recall us ever going to Europe? Visiting castles in England and France, or tossing coins into the fountains of Rome? Nah, you can't. I don't recall any ocean liners, that's for sure."

He went to the closet, and when he returned he handed me an envelope.

"But I recall everything else," he said. "Count on that while you count this."

The envelope felt heavy in my hands. I opened it and looked inside. One thing I could not recall was the last time I saw so much cash.

"There's your *advance*," he said. "Down payment. We both get twenty now and the rest later, provided you make it through the course and get the information. Heinz will pay as soon as he knows the information is solid." He sat next to me on the cot. "You won't gum this up for us, will you?"

I was too busy counting the money to answer. Four fives, twenty ones. For once, my heart was beating fast because of joy, not fear. It was a long way from what I needed, but here it was, like a green sprout in springtime: the first sign of good things to come.

"I'll make it through the course," I said.

"You're a good son, Joe. Someone I can count on in a crunch. I'd want us to be friends even if we weren't family."

Sorting the money into two piles, I thought about the work ahead of me. Suddenly, the fifty-fifty split didn't seem very fair. When Bernie reached across my lap for his half, I grabbed his forearm.

"What now?"

"About the split."

"What?"

"The thing is, Bern, if I'm the one spending all my time taking these classes and getting the information from these people, then why do you get half?"

"You don't think I'm treating you fair and square? Remember, I'm the one who handed you this job. If it wasn't for me, there is no job, except for the other spot at the Lago Vista, which you *also* got thanks to me."

"That's true, and I'm grateful. But I'm the one putting in the time and taking these classes. It's my face they're seeing, my face they'll remember when their house is burgled."

He sneered. "Come on, they won't remember you. You're nothing to them."

"But you're only taking my information and passing it on to your pal."

"That's the arrangement. What, you getting scared now?"

It wasn't me being scared. Or, not only that.

"Bern, I'm only asking if the split should maybe reflect the true division of labor. More like eighty-twenty, I'm thinking."

"Ha! No way, José."

"Then what? What do you think would be fair?"

"Okay, don't soil your trousers. Jeez." He sighed heavily. "Sixty-forty. That's nearly four hundred for you by the end of the month. If you're not interested, that's peachy. I can call up some other kid to finish it up for a lot less. Any flunky could do that job."

I couldn't believe he had gone for it.

"Sixty-forty would be great, Bern." I took four extra dollars from his pile before handing it over.

He was staring at me. "The other way was fair and square, plenty of people would agree. But honestly . . . I'm impressed. You stood up for yourself here, and I'm proud of you."

"Gee, thanks."

"Listen, as long as we're on the topic of dough, this morning Del let on that having you here is costing more than she expected. She needs an extra buck a week. I already paid her the extra. She's giving us a square deal, I can promise you that. I wouldn't have mentioned the increase at all, except for you flippin' your wig about this money out of the blue."

Reluctantly, I laid an extra buck on his bed. "I understand. Besides, we've got the money now, haven't we?"

He grinned. "We will, just as soon as you finish that course."

I took my clothes from the drying line and got dressed for work. I wrote a quick note to my mother and put fifteen dollars in the envelope. I'd send more when I got my first paycheck. For now, fifteen would please her. I didn't want to give up all the money. Maybe I could even see a picture in one of those big palaces downtown. Nobody expected me to spend all my time working, did they?

"Is it safe to keep cash here in the room?" I asked.

47

"Hell no, it isn't. But it's no safer in any bank. You're not sending it home?"

"Not all of it," I said. "Not yet."

He gave me another funny look, as if he was seeing me for the first time. "Don't forget, you owe me for those new threads of yours. And given the new split, you can chip in for the French course, too."

"Sure. We'll square everything at the end of the month."

Bernie had an envelope for his parents, too, and we dropped them into a mailbox on our way to the Lago Vista.

The traffic honked and thrummed all around us as we made our way south. I liked knowing my cousin was proud of me. I felt proud, too. I deserved the bigger cut of the payout. I'd already put myself out there and made the acquaintance of those people. I'd even made plans to meet Raymond Kenrick outside of class.

Fleetingly, I recalled Raymond's expressive face, his musical voice. I warned myself not to dwell on him. He was only a mark, and an easy one at that.

✳✳✳

The kitchen that night was extra lively. Upstairs, we served dinner to an outfit of dentists who were all half in the bag before we served the London broil.

At one point, I stepped off the elevator with my cart and stopped dead.

Eddie, the liquor delivery boy, stood in the kitchen. He had his back to me, but I recognized him from behind, those solid shoulders and goofy ears. He was dressed in soiled trousers and T-shirt,

48

but didn't seem to be moving crates this time. Only chatting with the men on the line.

Like a reflex, I pulled my cart back onto the elevator so he wouldn't spot me. I wasn't sure what I was thinking. If I returned to the ballroom with an empty cart, Mertz would blow his top. But deep down I knew it was safer to avoid Eddie. I couldn't risk another bold overture. A queer gesture, even a lingering look from either of us, might be noticed by anyone, including my cousin. I dawdled upstairs for a few minutes, adding more dirty plates to my cart before heading back down. Sure enough, by then Eddie was gone.

Other than that near miss, everything was jake. All through the shift, my thoughts kept returning to the moment Bernie had tossed me that packet stuffed with bills. I could only imagine the look on my mother's face when she opened the very first envelope.

SIX

RAYMOND KENRICK'S CARD TOOK ME TO A GOLD COAST STREET lined with old townhouses, some with turrets and spires. There was still plenty of money on the block: gleaming wrought-iron fencing, elegant landscaping, and fresh-painted trim around the clean windows.

Compared to its neighbors, the three-story Kenrick residence was almost plain, red-brick with white trim. A privet hedge contained the tiny front garden. One of the living room windows framed a table set with a shiny white porcelain poodle. To the side of the front door, a narrow window was only a tease; all I could see was a fancy old pier mirror with an umbrella stand.

Bernie had insisted Charles Powell wouldn't hesitate to knock on any fellow's door, and neither should I. But I wondered what I might be in for. I told myself I'd do anything it took to acquire the travel information.

I straightened my shoulders and removed my hat. When I pressed the bell, I heard the sound of musical chimes from inside.

After nearly a minute, a young woman opened the door. Tall, with wispy blond curls that bounced freely around her face, like a dandelion ready to blow. Her gray uniform fit her snugly in what Bernie would consider "all the right places."

"My name is Charles," I said. "I'm here to see Raymond."

The housekeeper nodded without any friendliness. Could she spot a joker when she saw one? Although there was plenty of room for her to step aside and let me enter, she only cocked her hip to the left, forcing me to squeeze past her into the hall, our beaks nearly touching. She smelled good, nothing like any cleaning products my mother ever used.

A Hoover sat in the hall, with a cord that snaked all the way into the living room. The girl didn't take my hat or call Raymond for me. She had chewing gum in her mouth and didn't mind showing it.

Fortunately, I heard the bounce of feet on the staircase and saw Raymond waving over the bannister.

"Hello, Charles! Don't be a bother to Agnes. Come on up, why don't you?"

The Hoover wailed suddenly under Agnes's fingers, as I followed Raymond up the carpeted staircase. On the landing, I paused to observe the large window decorated with tree branches, birds, and fruit. I'd never seen stained glass in someone's house before.

Raymond's bedroom was large and sunny, with carved posts on the bed and matching furniture, all made of dark wood. The bedspread was so strikingly white I wondered if it was new. My mother washed our linens on a regular basis, but they never looked truly clean, not like this. Back home, I now realized, all the white linens had turned gray over time; somehow we hadn't noticed.

"The bed is terrible, I know," Raymond said. "You agree, I can tell by the way you're looking at it."

"No, I admire the old style," I said honestly.

"It's hideous. There used to be a canopy, but I took it off. At this point, I'm through with the whole gloomy set. I either want to have it painted white or burned for firewood."

Another first: a gramophone in a person's bedroom. Most families I knew, if they even had a gramophone, kept it in the parlor. A stack of records sat next to the console. I glanced at the top three. Ethel Waters, Connee Boswell, and Fanny Brice.

Raymond's physical appearance intimidated me less than it had in the church hall. He was good-looking in an ordinary way, not remarkably handsome. The most attractive thing about Raymond was the way he took care of himself, every bit of him groomed to the hilt, blond hair combed back neatly on the sides, and that easy, white-toothed smile. Used in magazine advertisements, a face like his could sell just about anything. He was wearing a cream-colored open-collar shirt with short sleeves that highlighted his suntanned arms, loose-fitting brown trousers, and white bucks with shiny rubber soles.

To stop my staring, I turned to the windows. Both were raised high, letting in a cool breeze from the lake. The back garden was smaller than I expected.

"Not much of a chatterbox?" he teased.

I'd been so seduced by the room, the gramophone, and Raymond, I'd nearly forgotten my purpose. I rolled up my sleeves, in both senses. "Got any brothers or sisters?" I asked.

"Only my sister, Millicent. Millie's eight, an absolute terror."

"That's quite a range between you. Seven or eight years?"

"I'll tell you the shocking truth. My parents separated for a while, before the crash. My father went bananas and ran off to London with a married woman from his office. It was a scandal all over the

parish, obviously, but with some urging from the cardinal, they rec-
onciled. Both couples did. Now my parents are crazy for each other
again, as far as I know. Mother's got him tied to an apron string."

"Your mother seems swell."

"Oh, she's terrific, especially when she's soused."

This remark made me laugh. I'd never known a fellow who
spoke so openly about private matters. At home, I'd be smacked
for telling juicy stories like this, even if I had any to tell. I'd been
taught to keep up appearances. But Raymond didn't seem con-
cerned with the impression he made. I wondered if this freedom
was like the white bedspread, another privilege of having money.

"So when do you leave for Europe? The whole family's going?"

He smiled and stared at the carpet. "The truth is . . ."

He didn't finish, so I prompted, "What?"

"We're not going to France this summer."

"You're not?"

"I'm afraid we've misled you. We're not going overseas at all."

I only stared at him. I couldn't believe it. "Raymond, it's fine.
In fact—"

"Yes?"

Just in time, I stopped myself from being careless. I needed
to stick to my story. My situation wasn't at all like Raymond's, no
matter what he might say next. I was only here on a job.

"Sorry," I said. "You were saying."

He laughed into his hands, as if to hide his face. "We're only
going to visit some family. *In Canada.*"

"I don't understand. Canada? That's—nothing to be ashamed
of, is it?"

He shrugged and shook his head. "When you and the others in the class spoke about your grand plans for Europe this summer, my mother and I played along. I'm embarrassed."

"No reason to be. You'll visit French Canada then?"

"Yes, Quebec City. This September, my mother's cousin is marrying into one of the oldest families in the province. Generations of timber and furs. The family keeps a ship on the St. Lawrence River. *Their own ship*, can you imagine? It sounds like a tall tale invented to impress people, but it's true because they brought the silly boat down to Chicago for the World's Fair last summer. Anyway, the wedding is going to be the event of the season there. The whole point of this summer reunion is so that we can meet the groom's family first. Mother thinks it will be good if both of us speak *a little* French. Dear god, I suppose she dreams I'll meet a lumber heiress for myself. Or even a mink tycoon for Millie. Now, Charles, don't judge us too harshly. Please tell me you come from a family of schemers, too."

"Yes, that's us to the core. Schemers."

He placed a hand on my shoulder, lightly, just for a moment. "Thanks for saying that. It makes me feel better."

"And so . . ." He was being so kind, it felt awful to ask. "When exactly do you leave on the trip?"

"July sixteenth. Two weeks from yesterday. At first, it was supposed to be only my mother and sister going, but then Father and I got roped in. We have train tickets for the day after Mother and Millie leave."

"When will you come back?"

He smiled, looking me up and down. "Why? Are you hoping I'll save you a spot on my calendar?"

His ribbing made me feel foolish. He didn't answer my question, so I didn't answer his. Instead I examined several newspaper clippings tucked into the frame of the mirror above his wide bureau. They were all of John Dillinger, the gunman the FBI called Public Enemy No. 1.

"I used to be a fan of *all* the outlaws," Raymond explained. "These days, only Dillinger. My Dilly. The new ones haven't got any style. When I was a kid, I was devoted to Vincent Drucci. Plenty rugged, and those intense dark eyes. For a long time I wore my hair slicked back like his. Poor Drucci, he met a sad end in the back of a patrol car."

I continued to examine the clippings, feeling tongue-tied. Putting on new clothes was one thing, but I doubted Charles Powell would ever speak as confidently or easily as Raymond could. Especially on the topic of handsome gangsters. This kid flustered my head.

"Where are you staying, anyway?" he asked.

"With my cousin, just for the month. Over near the park." I kept it vague, hoping he would fill in the blanks. "Say, I wonder if I could grow a mustache like Dillinger's this summer?"

"Which park? Grant Park? Lincoln Park?"

"Washington Square Park," I said.

He crossed the room to the gramophone. His feet hardly made a sound on the thick carpet. Another difference, I thought, between rich people and regular folks. At our house, when you crossed any room, you heard every step across the hardwood floor.

He flipped through his records. With a turn of a knob on the console, he played a number I recognized. "Moonglow" by Benny

Goodman. I wondered how much Bernie's contacts might get for a gently used gramophone.

"Washington Square Park, how fun." He took a seat at the foot of his bed, draping his arm around the carved bedpost. "I meet friends over there sometimes. Some of the dives I like best are on Clark Street." He lifted his pale eyebrows and stared, as if waiting for me to guess which ones.

When I didn't take the bait, he asked, "How are you spending your time in Chicago? Do you sail?"

"No."

"Do you enjoy riding?"

Until the eighth grade, I traveled to school on horseback. Then we sold the horse. "Not much," I said.

"Well, do you play golf or tennis? Or swim?"

Charles Powell, I imagined, would enjoy leisure activities like these, but I couldn't fake my way through the shallowest conversation about any of them.

Raymond was making an effort, so I offered an alternative: "I like the pictures."

He sat straighter. "Me, too! No matter what else I'm doing, I'd always prefer to be sitting in a theater somewhere with the lights down low."

The truth was, I hadn't seen a new picture in months. But my favorites burned brightly in my memory. I wished I could have told Raymond *why* I liked the pictures. The pleasure of being transported into worlds of glamour and danger. How men like Dick Powell, Clark Gable, and Leslie Howard made me feel whenever I watched them on screen.

There was only one chair in the room, the seat covered with magazines, neckties, and a hairbrush. I still held my folded ditto from the French class, and I lifted it to show him. "Madame Monk hasn't taught us how to say, 'Where should I sit?'"

"Join me over here." He patted the bedspread like Mae West. Still with that cheerful stare, those raised eyebrows. Anyone might think he was flirting.

I sat, leaving a foot of space between us. I felt an odd sensation, one I recognized from dreams, the feeling of standing too close to the edge of a balcony or a high open window. I lifted the ditto again. "Got yours handy? We can quiz each other."

He didn't move.

"Or lookit, let's take turns using this one."

He didn't answer. His silence seemed uncharacteristic.

I read aloud: *"Bonjour. Bonsoir. Bonne nuit—"*

Without warning, he reached over and gently brushed the hairs on my forearm. I stopped reading but didn't move, frozen in disbelief. His gesture was so brazen, I wondered if he'd had something to drink before I arrived. He let his hand rest there. My face burned from the nerve of him, and I jumped to my feet.

"What's that about?"

"What do you mean?"

"You—you touched me!"

His hand had moved back to his lap, but he didn't look at all sorry. "I suspect I have more experience than you, so that's my role to take. I'm discreet as a priest, if that's your concern."

First, Eddie at the hotel, and now Raymond, both acting so recklessly with a stranger. A fellow could be arrested for something like this. It was worse than confessing to a crime, because criminals, at least, could be rehabilitated. Maybe big cities afforded such recklessness to young people, or maybe only certain young people, like Eddie and Raymond, could afford it.

"What makes you think I'd be interested?" I asked.

"Honestly, I gained some experience when I was away at school last year. I guess I learned how to . . . pick up the radio signal."

"I'm sending out a signal?"

"Relax, please. Not a signal *normal* people would pick up. The way you looked at me, for starters. During class yesterday. I caught you, again and again. You're not very good at stealing glances. But I wasn't offended. I could tell you admired me. And those nerves when we spoke after class. Listen, I wouldn't take a risk like this if I wasn't absolutely certain. But I won't force you into anything, nothing like that."

The ditto in my hand was fluttering like a leaf. I had always worked so hard to blend into the crowd. But now, for the second time in a week, I faced the frightening possibility that my deepest held secret might not be much of a secret after all.

I needed to calm myself. "I'm speechless," I said.

The sound of a piano came from downstairs. The notes were played slowly, haltingly, but after a while I recognized the tune.

I'VE—GOT—THAT—JOY JOY JOY JOY—DOWN—IN—MY—HEART

WHERE?

DOWN—IN—MY—HEART

WHERE?

DOWN—IN—MY—HEART

"That's only Millie, my sister, practicing. She's terrible in any key. I'm the one who plays most of the time. Anyhow, did you really come here to practice French? Oh, I know! I'll play Lucienne Boyer for you. I have 'Parlez-moi d'amour' somewhere, so we can *hear* some French, at least." He went back to the record player, switched the records, and then returned to the bed. He moved with light, untroubled steps.

I could only stand there, watching. Even then, I wasn't sure if I should stay or rush out the door.

"I feel very strange right now," I told him. "Ill."

"Truly ill or just nerves?"

"Nerves."

"That's a relief. In my experience, nerves are a sign of good things to come. Walk over here, why don't you, and let's start with a cuddle. Kick off your shoes first."

That word, *cuddle*—that's what got me to stay. Also, Lucienne Boyer singing in French on the gramophone sounded gentle and sweet. Raymond didn't have a threatening bone in his body. The universe seemed to be telling me that Charles Powell could afford this risk, even if Joe Garbe could not.

I removed my shoes and joined him on the bed. We sat facing each other.

"I don't know what to do," I admitted.

"Be serious now. You said you go to the pictures, right?"

"Sure, but—"

He leaned close and kissed me.

I may have flinched when our lips made contact.

"Have you really never done this before?"

"Not much. Never with a fellow."

His hand moved to my shoulder, and I flinched again. "And you're how old?"

59

"Sixteen."

"I'm only seventeen," he said.

"I turn seventeen next month."

"Swell. Let me be the very first to wish you a happy birthday."

He kissed me again and this time I kissed him back. He pushed me against the headboard and we went on kissing there for a while. I detected no gin on his tongue.

I'VE—GOT—THAT—JOY JOY JOY JOY—DOWN—IN—MY—HEART.

WHERE?

I felt a strange combination of exhilaration and boldness. The experience was nothing like my times with Mary Toomey, polite, dutiful kisses at the end of her family's road. This was hungry, almost wild. "Is this okay?" I asked him at one point.

"Yes, you're doing fine. Ever since my first experience, a year or so ago, I've been on a kind of mission to help out other people in our situation."

"On a mission? Out of the goodness of your heart?"

He laughed. "But you understand, I know you do. It's such a relief to find someone who feels like we do. If you visit some of the pansy parlors in your cousin's neighborhood, you'll see for yourself. It makes you feel less lonely, seeing all those nellies in one place. Doctors and attorneys, schoolteachers, perfectly respectable men. Some even dress like girls. Plenty of rugged fellows, too, you wouldn't believe it. It's a tough situation to be in, and it helps to make a connection. You feel it already, don't you?"

"Feel what?"

"The connection between us. I expect I understand you better than anyone you've ever met. Don't you agree?"

Rather than answering, I kissed him again.

60

I wanted to agree. Yes, we had this one thing in common, and that felt like a miracle. I wanted to embrace that connection. But it was impossible to ignore everything else: the bright linens, deluxe carpet, the gramophone. It made perfect sense that a fellow like Raymond Kenrick could understand someone like Charles Powell, but my real life would be as familiar to Raymond as the surface of Jupiter. Raymond didn't know what it meant to be hungry or cold, or ashamed of your school clothes, or worried about losing everything.

"I love it when I'm right about someone," he said. "The moment I poured the lemonade in that gymnasium, I felt sure I'd be kissing you before long. And look at us now."

The gramophone had stopped playing. Downstairs, his sister had moved on to "Spinning Song," one of the relentless, cheerful tunes Mary liked to play on her family's upright to make our Sunday afternoons last even longer.

"Will you take me to one of the pansy parlors?" I asked.

"Someday, maybe." His blue eyes stared up at the ceiling. "They pretend to be strict about the age requirement. The performers are a hoot, Charles. They sit at the piano and sing numbers with the dirtiest lyrics. You'll scream your head off with laughter." He sat up on the bed. "We'll stay in touch after this summer, won't we? My goal is to keep in contact with every queer fellow I meet. I want to know them all. We should form a network. After all, we need to look out for one another."

Now this was an extraordinary thought: a network of pansies—a secret syndicate, like the mobsters.

"It sounds wonderful."

He kissed me again. "The way I see it, if I can put another fellow's mind at rest, why shouldn't I?"

61

Was my mind at rest? At the moment, I felt remarkably awake.

He stroked my forearm and then leaned down to kiss my hand sweetly. He rested his head on my chest for nearly a minute, as if listening to my heartbeat slowing to a normal tempo. Then he looked at me again. "Should we really practice some French, or—"

I silenced him with another kiss.

SEVEN

A N HOUR LATER, after Raymond showed me out, I strutted down
the sidewalk feeling like a different person. It wasn't just
the false name, I knew, or the fresh threads. I felt truly changed.
I'd connected with an ordinary fellow who felt the same as me.
Someone with experience, someone who gave me a glimpse of what
the future might be like.

Raymond was a mark in more ways than one. I wanted what
he had. Not just money, but his ease with a stranger, that same
openness, the same tolerance for risk. And didn't I deserve it?

I raced back to the apartment and found my cousin sitting on
the bed, clean-shaved, polishing his shoes. After I got changed,
we walked to the hotel together. Everything looked sunny, for
once. The sidewalk crowds parted ways for us, and the traffic noise
sounded like music.

Bernie seemed chipper, too. "So you spent the day with the
family, eh? Fast work, kid."

Faster than anyone could have imagined, I thought.

"I only spent time with the son," I told him. "He's my age.
There's a younger sister, too. I heard her practicing piano, but
never saw her."

"What's the house like?"

"The nicest house I ever visited. I wish you could see it. Raymond's even got a gramophone all his own."

"Yeah?"

"And the linens on his bed are so *white*, they nearly knocked me out. I can't recall a time when the linens back home looked so clean. And the carpet—"

"Hold the phone, Joe. You went to this kid's bedroom?"

Whatever he was suggesting, I waved it away with my hand. "We needed a quiet place to practice French. Raymond is very determined."

We walked for a while without speaking. Waiting at the river for the bridge to come down, he spoke again, but his tone was sour. "So that's his name then, *Raymond*? I bet he's stuck up."

"He's all right. I liked him right away."

"Forget about him. Your job is to find out when his family is going to Europe, and how long they'll be gone for."

"That's just it. They're only going to Canada."

"Eh, not ideal, but Heinz can work with that, so long as you get the precise dates they'll be gone. Can you do that?"

"Not a problem."

We were crossing the bridge then. To our left, the gleaming Wrigley Building called to mind the spearmint scent of Raymond's clothes. Even now, I felt the thrill of his lips pressed against mine, the joy it sparked, genuine pleasure rather than duty.

"Besides," I said, "if we need to leave one name off Heinz's list, who cares, right?"

Bernie's head spun to look at me. "*Who cares?* No way, pal. I already gave Heinz the list of names. Listen, these people, Heinz and his contacts, they have a very strict sense of fair payment. If they found out we left out any names, well, I don't like to think what they might do. To you or to me. I mean, I don't want to scare you, but things could get rough for us."

"Rough? Like how?"

"You don't want to know, and I'm not gonna scare you."

"Is your pal Heinz violent?"

"Didn't I just say I don't wanna scare you?" he hollered.

Too late. The hollering didn't help either.

"I never in a million years thought you'd spend time with men like that."

He shrugged. "He never laid a finger on me. Anyhow, it wouldn't be right, would it, if we didn't give them what they paid us for?"

I nodded. Some clumsy affection from Raymond was one thing. But his family had more money than I could ever dream of. Like Bernie predicted, the house was filled with things that could go missing without anyone even noticing.

"We'll get all the information we promised," I said.

"That's right, we keep things on the level. Now listen, I hear there's going to be someone new at work tonight. Working dishes with O'Malley. It's a chance to pick up another buck or two, maybe even from the others."

I nodded eagerly. "Let's show him what I can do."

✳✳✳

Sure enough, the new man, McGuire, was a dumb onion, and we made another three dollars each. Hannigan, the skyscraper butcher, took to calling me Nostradamus, with some respect. All in all, I felt like I stood a foot taller myself.

Jackson, the pastry chef, lost a dollar, too, but it didn't seem to bother him. He kept me busy and kept me fed. He looked out for me. I didn't feel right, taking his cash like that.

Later, lugging trash out to the alley, I was surprised to find the liquor truck idling. The motor sputtered and gasped like an old man's snore. Eddie stood next to the truck, alone this time. He was twice as good looking as I remembered, but I wasn't half as afraid of him. I credited my morning with Raymond Kenrick for that.

"How's tricks, Joe?"

I dropped the trash into the bin. "Another delivery?"

He stepped closer. "Naw, I made a little detour after my route. Came by yesterday, too, but didn't see you."

"They've got me serving upstairs now," I explained.

He kicked at some gravel. "So what's been keeping you busy? Other than this crummy hotel."

"That's it, just working."

"Really? Not making other friends, going out even a little?"

He made it sound so pitiful.

"I'm taking a French class," I said.

"Yeah, what for? You planning a trip to Paris?"

"I signed up to improve myself," I said, which wasn't a lie, exactly. "It's nothing fancy. It's in a church gym up on Dearborn Parkway in the Gold Coast."

He looked surprised. "Gold Coast? That's where you're staying?"

"No, I'm with my cousin. He's got a room on LaSalle in Towertown. The class isn't far from there."

"So, Joe, I've been thinking, couldn't I see you away from here sometime? Have a meal together?"

There it was again, that remarkable boldness. This time I considered it with admiration rather than fear.

"Like I told you," I said, "I'm saving all my wages."

"My treat, if that works better. Or hell, we could just go for a walk and get to know one another."

"Most days I have to get to work by three."

"I'd drive you here myself. Save you time and taxi fare."

"I never spend money on taxis. I have two good legs."

"I can see that."

I hadn't even been fishing for the compliment. This fellow wasn't out to test me or trap me. He was just looking to connect. Maybe I could be friendly to Eddie, the way Raymond was friendly to me. I recalled what Raymond had said about creating a syndicate, a queer fraternity. It could be useful.

"We could get together," I told him, "as long as it's free."

His face brightened. "There's the zoo in Lincoln Park. That doesn't cost a penny. Have you been there yet? Lookit, you're blushing like a peach. You want to say yes. C'mon, Peaches, say yes this one time."

The nickname made me laugh. A zoo seemed like a safe enough place to meet. "My French class meets Mondays and Thursdays. So how about Friday? Around noon?"

He stepped toward the truck. "Noon on Friday then. Want me to pick you up in Towertown?"

"It's better if we meet there."

He nodded, as if no explanation was necessary. "We'll meet at the corner of Webster Avenue and Lincoln Park West. Should I write that down for you, Peaches?"

"No, I'll remember. Webster and Lincoln Park West."

With that, he rubbed his hands together and got into the truck quickly, as if he were afraid I'd change my mind. The truck pulled forward, motor roaring, and disappeared down the alley.

The day kept surprising me. I felt proud to have screwed up the courage to accept Eddie's offer.

As I got back to work, I reflected that making connections with Raymond, Eddie, and other fellows like me would make returning home painful; now I'd know what I was missing. Then again, if I were successful in my work, if I collected every bit of information Heinz needed from these families, maybe that would add up to a future where I could visit Chicago now and again, just to see what the big city had to offer.

EIGHT

DEL GREETED US AT BREAKFAST WITH A GRIM PREDICTION: "One hundred people will die in auto accidents today. On account of the holiday."

Bernie scraped jam onto his toast. "Good morning to you, too, Betsy Ross," he said.

"It's only what the statisticians at Travelers' Insurance say in the paper. Read it for yourself if you don't believe me. You boys need to be careful."

Bernie looked at me. "Some pals and I are heading to the beach to watch the fireworks. Wanna tag along?"

"Thanks, I'm meeting a friend later to practice French."

"Who? Kenrick?"

When I nodded, he only said, "Do what you have to."

Del turned from the sink. "Practice French?" she exclaimed. "On Independence Day? Oh, nuts to that, Joe. I'd rather you be out playing games. Sack races or egg-tossing contests. A ballgame in the park even. It's always been that a boy can find other boys for horseplay if he looks hard enough."

The Kenricks' housekeeper slouched against the doorframe, her arms folded.

"Call Raymond for me, please?" I asked again.

"Didn't no one ever tell you it's a national holiday?" she said. "Families spending time together, ice cream cakes, all that?"

"Raymond expects me."

Her eyebrows were drawn on so close together, they nearly met. As she pulverized her chewing gum, I wondered if she recognized something phony about me. Could she see I was closer to her level, socially speaking, than Raymond's?

"Wait on the sidewalk," she said, before closing the door.

I moved to the curb. A ribbon of festive bunting decorated the Kenricks' doorway, and tiny American flags poked out of flowerpots on the stoop.

Ever since Raymond and I had kissed in his bedroom, my brain was like a scratched record, repeating the desire to *kiss him again, kiss him again, kiss him again* . . . For once, the fantasy wasn't only a fantasy.

Finally, the door opened and Raymond appeared, holding his panama hat. He wore a bright blue shirt that complemented his eyes and cream-colored trousers. His smile looked relieved.

"Charles, you've saved me. Mother's gone completely bananas. If she has her way, we'll be marching down State Street in costume, playing fife and drums."

"Has your family been celebrating all day?"

"We had a barbeque lunch with people from the parish. Later they'll all go watch the fireworks. We can go, too, if you like. Oh, I cannot stand this heat!" He fanned his face with his hat. "Say, let's go see a picture, could we? All the picture houses downtown have cool air now."

I didn't like the idea of spending money, but I hadn't seen a picture in ages. The cool air sounded swell. Plus, when Raymond's family went to the lakefront later, the house might be empty. Maybe we could generate some fireworks of our own.

"You always make me do the talking," he said. "Tell me all about your family. Absolutely everything. I know you haven't got any siblings, but talk about your parents, grandparents, all that."

He already knew the fictional biography I'd invented for class. I'd stolen my grandparents' background to use for Charles Powell: a family history of farming, five hundred acres of corn. In truth, the property had shrunk down to sixty acres even before I came along. I felt a funny pride in giving Raymond a sunnier picture of farm life.

"I see a stately farmhouse," he said. "A graceful front porch and a wicker swing for summer afternoons. Am I close?"

"Right on the nose," I said, feeling wistful. In fact, there had been a porch, decades ago. But porches need upkeep, and upkeep costs money.

Downtown, we bypassed the houses playing *Registered Nurse* and *Hold That Girl*, and finally stopped at the Orpheum at State and Monroe for *Tarzan and His Mate*.

"You probably saw it when it came out," Raymond said. "Kid stuff, right?"

While I'd scrutinized every photo of Johnny Weissmuller in magazines at the five-and-dime, I hadn't seen either of the Tarzan movies. I shook my head. "Have you?"

"Three times." He grinned. "Let's go in."

To my surprise, he paid for both tickets. He spent money as easily as he made conversation.

As promised, the picture house felt cool as an icebox. As soon as we took our seats, I placed my foot against Raymond's. Our knees touched, elbows pressed together on the armrest. Between every show, the organ played "The Star-Spangled Banner" and everybody stood, hands pressed against their hearts. The picture was over in no time. We enjoyed watching Mr. Weissmuller and Maureen O'Sullivan swimming underwater so much, we stood for the anthem twice and sat through Disney's cartoon *The Big Bad Wolf* just to watch the swimming part again.

"There's a pool I can take you to," Raymond whispered, "where Johnny swims when he's in town. All tiled in blue-and-gold mosaic tiles. The walls and ceiling, too." The suggestion thrilled me, in part because I'd never been swimming indoors, but Charles Powell could never confess that fact to Raymond.

✳✳✳

Afterward, outside, the air was soupy, the sky nearly dark. The whole sparkling city was there, waiting for us to explore it. Bernie and Del didn't expect me back anytime soon.

"To the lakefront?" Raymond asked. "Fireworks will be starting soon."

I pulled Raymond out of earshot of sidewalk traffic. "Actually, I'd like to see one of the pansy parlors you told me about."

He shook his head. "We're too young. They won't let us through the door."

"But you've been to them before. You told me—"

"Only twice. Both times, I was with someone older. Besides, you shouldn't get your hopes up about them. There's a rumor Mayor Kelly wants to shut them all down. Part of his war on corruption and vice."

"Oh no!" In my mind, the nelly taverns already seemed like an essential part of my future. "But now I have to see one before they all disappear. Please."

He only groaned. "Forget I ever mentioned it. We are *not* going."

✳ ✳ ✳

Twenty minutes later, on Chicago Avenue, we approached an establishment called Vi's Little Grapevine, the one and only spot, Raymond claimed, where we had a shot at getting in.

"Try to look mature," Raymond said. "Shoulders back and show some confidence. In case anyone speaks to us, we'll use false names."

"Is that necessary, Ray—"

"It's a matter of safety. And all part of the fun. So let's see, you can be . . . Chad? Yes, Chad. It's easier if you use the same first letter as your own. I'm Ricardo."

I almost laughed. Raymond looked as much like a Ricardo as Warner Oland looked like Charlie Chan.

"Are these the right clothes?"

"It doesn't matter, because we have the double advantage of being young and adorable."

Vi's was located just west of the famous water tower, only six or eight blocks south of Del's building. No sign outside. Royal-blue velvet draping covered the windows inside, thick as a theater curtain; romantic grapevines decorated every corner of the windows, drawn onto the glass with shiny gold paint. From the sidewalk, we could hear a combo playing "Night and Day."

As expected, the goon at the door balked at our youth, but Raymond flashed a smile and, to my surprise, an Argentine passport issued to "Ricardo Leon." Inside, the place was dark, lit with shaded sconces on every wall. The smoky air reeked of cologne and sweat. Musicians played on a stage up front. We squeezed our way through the crowd. Forget about grabbing a seat; the place was mobbed, fellows of all ages and races mixing. It was the noisiest place I'd ever been to.

Raymond leaned close to my ear. "High time for something wet. Want a beer, Chad? You can have a beer in a place like this, nobody cares."

"Sure." I tried to hand him some change, but he just smiled and pushed his way toward the bar.

I couldn't help staring at every fellow who passed by. While some were handsome as film stars, most looked remarkably ordinary, wearing suits and neckties. Anywhere else, I would have guessed they were husbands and fathers. Some were eating, some dancing, but most were just laughing and acting slaphappy, as if they were glad to be together. The sight overwhelmed me, and my eyes filled with tears. I wished I could record every detail to memory.

Raymond had returned with the drinks. "My apologies, I ran into some ridiculous people I know near the bar."

"Thank you, Ricardo."

"What's wrong? Oh, I know, this crowd. There isn't room to breathe!"

"No, it's a revelation. All these people. I'm stunned. The world is more open-minded than I ever knew."

"Let's not go overboard. Every fellow here has a secret that could ruin him."

I must have looked surprised, because he pressed close to my ear again. "If you think the world is open-minded, take a look at Hollywood. Supposedly the most open-minded and *sinful* place on earth, according to the papers. But look at William Haines's film career."

I blinked away amazed tears. "I don't understand. What about William Haines?"

"Queer as a pink carnation."

"I don't believe it."

"Four years ago, a major star. Have you seen him in pictures lately? Someone told me Haines got careless about bringing his 'dear friend' out with him in public. When the studio boss, Louis B. Mayer, asked him to cool it, Haines told him to go kiss a duck. So much for Haines's film career."

The room continued to fill, until bodies pressed against us from every side.

When the musicians took a break, a tall brunette appeared on stage and sat at the piano. Her black-sequined gown emphasized her broad shoulders. In a husky voice, she sang a slow-tempo version of "Happy Days Are Here Again," but she'd rewritten the lyrics. She had to pause frequently, waiting for the howls and cheers to subside.

TOWERTOWN IS QUEER AGAIN.
SO, PANSIES, DRINK YOUR CHEER AGAIN.
WE FAIRIES HAVE NO FEAR AGAIN.
TOWERTOWN IS QUEER AGAIN!

DROP YOUR PANTS AND TAKE A BOW.
GLANCE AROUND, DEAR FRIENDS, WE ARE THE CAT'S MEOW.
WE'RE NOT BACK HOME WITH YOUR DADDY'S COW.
TOWERTOWN IS QUEER AGAIN!

Ray and I stood shoulder to shoulder, watching. Some fellows sang along, in booming voices. Next the performer sang "Yankee Doodle Pansy" and "God Save the Queen," before the combo took over again, and the clamor resumed.

I told Raymond I'd buy us another round, and this time he let me. For once, I didn't think about the cost. I didn't want the night to end. The beer made everything sparkle even more, like stepping out of my own life and onto a movie screen. Even though I knew I'd return home at the end of the month, back to the farm and chores and Mother and Mary, now I had this tantalizing alternative to take back with me: this night and these songs, and the knowledge of a secret, sordid, glittering world out there for the fellows like us.

With an expression that looked both serious and hopeful, Raymond leaned close to my ear. "If you want to kiss me tonight, right now may be your best and only chance."

So that's exactly what I did.

NINE

MORNING RAIN GAVE THE STREETS AN OILY SHEEN. I went walking after breakfast to clear my head. Raymond and I had lingered at Vi's until it closed. Our voices strained from singing and flirting with complete strangers, we parted ways on a busy sidewalk corner with nothing more than a firm, heartfelt handshake.

Now I observed the early commuters with a fresh awareness, considering the countless fellows making their way across town, heading to office buildings, factories, schools. Passing undetected, living productive lives. Somehow, surely, I belonged in the city with them. I imagined parties and dinners where people could relax together and be their silly selves. I might become someone who could step into Vi's on any night of the week and greet half a dozen friends. I only needed my syndicate.

From down the block, Del called from the window: "Joey Garbe, a letter for you came in the morning post!"

Upstairs, I took the envelope to our room. Sitting on the cot, I pressed the notepaper to my cheek, hoping I could smell a bit of home on it.

My mother had stuffed the envelope with clippings from the local paper. The length of her note surprised me, two full pages, like she wanted to get her money's worth from the postage. The cash I'd sent left her "weeping, but not for sadness." She planned to take some of it to the grocery store that very afternoon. "That way I can brag to everybody I see shopping that it's thanks to my own hard-working Joe." She said she prayed to keep Bernie and me safe and to "give thanks for you, my son."

I read the letter twice, soaking up the words. It had been years since I saw this side of her, using words like *grateful* and *hopeful*. Her pride in me felt strange.

Just as quickly, my spirits sank. The past twenty-four hours had exposed the dismal truth: My mother and I had sacrificed for years, gone hungry, sold our treasures, and drained my college fund—all to save sixty acres I had no interest in inheriting. Something had to change.

And it could change, if I made a necessary adjustment. Of the money I made that summer, I would give half to my mother and save the rest for me. With my future at stake—a future I was just beginning to see glimpses of—all my mother needed to know was that I'd send more money each week. And at the end of the month, I'd surprise her with more cash than she'd seen in ages. I'd make up a story about painting houses or landscaping, something.

After changing into nicer duds, I hoofed it over to the church for the second class. My body was exhausted, but my spirit was optimistic. I had warmed to the idea that I wasn't personally going to rob anybody's house. Already I'd seen how Raymond spent cash without counting it first. If this job would help me so much and hurt other people so little they wouldn't even feel it, was it even a crime?

Once again, the ladies arrived dressed in tailored summer suits with matching hats. Their powdered skin fragranced the air with scents I recalled from early childhood: jasmine and rose, carnation, vanilla. The scene outraged me in a new way, maybe because of the letter I'd opened earlier. I thought of my mother at home, wearing a simple dress sewn from cotton flour sacks, and whose only Christmas present had been a bar of Lux soap.

Across the table, Raymond greeted me with a weary smile.

Madame Monk had set the table with lemonade again. She stood with her clipboard, calling out names for attendance, then distributed new dittos that featured vocabulary we might encounter on a menu, in a hotel, and in a shop—at least fifty terms, sorted into categories. The endless list made me question whether I'd have enough time to get all the information I needed.

"To begin, we will review the very important terms from last time," Madame said. "The numbers, as well as the months. Shall we share our birthdays?"

"Birthdays will be fine"—Mrs. Moore ugly-giggled—"but I won't admit my age in any language!"

"How about travel dates?" I suggested. "Less personal? More practical?"

"Oh, but birthdays are fun," Mrs. Kenrick insisted.

I would never win the argument, I realized, since Raymond and his mother didn't want to admit to the group they were only traveling to Canada.

So we circled the table, revealing our birthdays, and then Madame led us through common traveler phrases: *What does this cost? Where are the facilities for ladies? What time is the church service in English?*

Every now and then, my eyes met Raymond's, and I felt an electric current pass through my limbs.

Est-ce qu'il fait très froid?

Non, il fait très chaud.

When class ended, he waited for me near the exit. "Listen, Mother's taking me to lunch at the Cape Cod Room at the Drake tomorrow. She'll take you, too, if you'll practice French with us."

I would have given anything to join them at the famous Cape Cod Room, but I'd made plans to visit the zoo with Eddie. "I wish I could join you," I told him. "But I have plans tomorrow. How about Saturday?"

"Noon?"

"Eleven o'clock?" I asked eagerly.

"Noon is better," he said. "We'll meet by the fountain at Washington Square Park."

We sealed the deal by shaking mitts, before he raced after his mother.

On a table against the wall, I noticed the clipboard Madame used to take attendance, its attached pencil dangling on a string. The paper on top was the one we had completed at the first class, with every student's name and address. Half the information I needed, right there waiting.

Madame was folding the wooden chairs and stacking them against the wall. I jumped in to help, wondering how to distract her. If I simply stole the paper, she might catch me red-handed. Even if she didn't catch me, she'd soon see it was missing.

"See you Monday, Charles," she said, when we finished.

"I guess you know Paris very well, madame?"

Her smile was proud. "Paris is the city of my heart."

"May I ask a favor then?"

"Of course."

"Will you please write down the names of some of your favorite cafés? Close to the shops and Notre-Dame and everything?"

"Yes, well, many of them are quite famous." Removing a composition notebook from her canvas bag, she tore out a blank sheet. She bent over the table to write. "Les Deux Magots, Café de la Paix, near the opera house, La Closerie des Lilas . . ."

"Thank you, madame. Please list as many as you can, and I'll make a quick visit to the washroom."

With her attention diverted, I removed the attendance sheet from the clipboard and hid it under my hat. I went to the hallway and looked both ways. There was a curving stone staircase on one side, near a door that read WC. I went to the washroom, closed the door, and turned the lock. I pressed my own ditto against the rough wall, and one by one, I wrote down all the addresses. The uneven surface made my handwriting practically illegible, but I could recopy it before giving the information to Bernie.

When I had double-checked my work, I went back to the gym. I had hoped to return the sheet to the clipboard, but Madame stood waiting by the table, facing me, bag over her shoulder. She handed me my list of cafés.

"Thank you, madame." I showed her the attendance sheet. "This was on the floor in the hallway. Do you still need it?"

Her eyes opened wide. "You found this in the hallway?"

I nodded.

"But how did it get there? Did it fly?" She gave me a grave look, until I saw her first-ever genuine smile. "Did a pigeon carry it away for his lunch?"

"Yes, that," I said with a laugh, "or maybe it fell off the table when the others were leaving. See you Monday."

"Merci, Charles!" she called after me.

$$***$$

At the hotel that afternoon, Jackson piped flowers of pink icing atop two dozen chocolate-frosted cupcakes. When he moved them to serving platters, he must have noticed me staring. "Hey. Need to speak with you, Joe. Need your help with something."

"I want to talk to you, too," I said. He'd been so decent, I promised myself I wouldn't take any more of his money. It wasn't right to take from hard-working people, and now that we had the down payment from Heinz, there wasn't any reason to, either.

Jackson led me over to the pastry cooler where we could speak in private.

"All right," he said quietly. "You go first."

"Jackson, I can't read anyone's mind, or tell anyone's fortune. That mind-reading trick is only a trick. A game we've played since we were kids. I always know what the correct answer is because Bernie points at something *black* before he points to the right object. A cast-iron fry pan, say, or the oven grate. It's simple, so I always know."

"Is that right?" He smiled and scratched his chin.

"That's all it is, a dumb trick. I shouldn't have done it. I should be cutting grass for rich people, or painting houses . . ." I reached into my pocket and handed him a few dollars, the same amount he'd put in so far. "Here, take this back. It's only fair."

Nodding, he took the cash. "Fair and square. I appreciate it."

I felt better about coming clean, but still wanted a chance to make it up to him. "You said you needed help?"

He only laughed. "Not anymore I don't!"

"What do you mean?"

"The fact is, I needed your so-called *ability* with this policy game I play. But never mind that now."

"What's policy?"

"You know, a policy wheel." He stared, as if surprised I didn't know. "Local lotteries. They have wheels in neighborhoods all over town. There are a few popular places near Thirty-Fifth and State. You never heard of the Lucky Strike or the Tia Juana? Those wheels are famous. I play one out of a candy store down on Forty-Third."

"But how does it work?"

"It's a guessing game. You pick three numbers from one to seventy-eight, and they draw twelve. Sometimes they use a wheel, or just draw the numbers. If your numbers get called, you win. One-hundred-to-one payout. I hoped you'd help me pick the numbers, but never mind that now."

"Does it ever pay out?" I asked.

"You think I'd play if it didn't? Every single night, someone wins."

Just then, Hannigan passed the cooler on his way to the washroom. The door shut behind him, followed by the clatter of the hook-and-eye latch. The moment he'd spotted us, the clock was ticking. We couldn't let Hannigan catch us standing there when he emerged.

"How do you know the policy games are fair?" I asked. "Who runs them?"

"It's done in plain sight. In some places, a child draws the numbers. There may be more dependable ways to make cash, but none easier."

With another glance at the washroom door, he turned to go back to his station.

I followed right behind him.

"Can I go with you to the candy store and play?"

He stared like I was the biggest fool he'd seen in a while. "At your age, looking like you do? Come on, Joe, put the idea out of your head."

I did not put the idea out of my head. For the first time in a long while, good luck seemed entirely possible. I felt hopeful: about coming clean to Jackson, about seeing Eddie at the zoo the next day and Raymond on Saturday, about the windfall of money that would come from the French class. In all the areas that mattered to me, it looked like the hard times were finally coming to an end.

TEN

I COULDN'T WAIT TO SET EYES ON EDDIE AGAIN, away from the hotel this time, so we could talk more freely. But I worried over how to dress. While there wasn't any reason to put on airs with Eddie, I didn't want to wear clothes from home either. I chose a lemon-yellow Oxford shirt and gray light-flannel trousers. My new bucks had finally become comfortable to walk in.

At noon, I found Eddie standing at the corner of Webster and Lincoln Park West. He was dressed in twill trousers, a blue-and-white button-up shirt, and a bowtie. I never saw a fellow who could fill out clothing as well as he could. His shirtsleeves were rolled up high, but he was sweating, same as me.

"What's the score, Joe?" he asked. Just like that, he gave me a big bear hug. His strong arms felt good, as he squeezed me for about five seconds. "Gee, you clean up real nice," he said, rubbing his hand against my back. "Ready to spook some sleepy animals?"

"Sounds swell," I said, even though I felt weak in the knees.

It seemed like half the town had showed up to gawk at the giraffes and the wrinkly rhinos. I'd never seen exotic animals in real life, only in books. Eddie led me to the Primate House to see the famous Bushman. I stared into the gorilla's black eyes and felt a strange kinship with him, both of us so far away from home. I sure knew what it was like to feel things that couldn't be discussed with anybody.

With Eddie, I didn't need to invent a whole story. Standing there, I told him about our farm and the trouble we were in.

"I've faced hard times, too," he said. "Made some bad mistakes. But I've learned from them."

"Learned what?"

For a moment, he only gazed at the powerful black gorilla sitting behind the bars, silent and still. "Not to let anyone take advantage of me."

"And how do you manage that?"

"Choose your pals wisely, that's my advice. Better yet, take after Bushman here and forget about pals."

"Sounds lonely."

"Lonely?" With a grin, he draped his arm around my shoulder. "At present, lonely is the furthest thing I feel."

Eddie lived on the South Side with his parents, three brothers, and two younger sisters. The liquor business was still new, and everybody was expected to help out, even if it meant missing school—something my mother never would have allowed. He shrugged it off with a laugh. "Only so much you can learn in school. Anyhow, we skip less than we used to."

He had coins in his pocket and seemed eager to spend them on me. He bought scoops of ice cream in paper cups from a park vendor. "Time to fatten you up, Peaches. You're skin and bones." We sat on a bench to eat, watching families pass by on the trail.

"Been to the Century of Progress yet?" he asked.

"Haven't gone near the fair. It must cost a bit."

"Naw, you gotta see it. People back home will ask about it, don't you think? It'd be a shame if you missed it."

"Like I told you, I'm—"

"Saving every penny. I understand, I really do. But, Joe, there's a whole city waiting for you to explore it. You're here now, aren't you? You should take advantage of everything while you can. I can help with that."

We finished our ice cream, exited the zoo, and walked south. Eddie kept so close, his shoulder knocked against mine occasionally in a way that wasn't accidental. Riders on horseback trotted past us on the bridle path, heading to and from the stables in Lincoln Park.

We walked a long while, gradually moving toward the water, until we faced the most crowded beach I'd ever seen. The water, bright and shimmering, stretched to the horizon line. The famous Drake Hotel stood to our right, with a ribbon of yellow taxis surrounding it.

"Oak Street Beach," Eddie said. "Boy, look at that crowd. On hot weekends, that mile of sand gets busy like you wouldn't believe. Forty or fifty thousand people." I must have looked skeptical, because he added, "It's true! Let's come swimming, if you want."

A strapping young man passed us, wearing nothing but his bathing suit and bright white canvas shoes. Eddie nudged me again. "And the fellows take care of themselves. As you can see."

Even after spending time with Raymond, it felt remarkable to speak to someone openly about this. Eddie had raised the subject, so I felt I could go further.

"Can I ask a personal question?"

"Ask 'em all, if you want."

"The other day in the alley, when we were unloading the crates, you took a risk with your directness. And then you came back to see me. What made you think I'd be interested?"

He smiled, almost shy. "You said you could read minds, Peaches. I figured you knew."

"But I told you, that's only a dumb trick."

"Your face went pink each time we spoke. If you wasn't interested, you wouldn't give me the time of day. Now let me ask you a personal question. Is Joe your real name?"

I nodded, but now he was the one who looked skeptical, so I removed the Peoria Public Library card from my billfold. The library was ten miles from our farm, but the card was one of the few items I ever owned with my name printed on it, along with my birth certificate and my junior high diploma. "See for yourself."

He handed it back. "Thanks. Appreciate you showing me that."

"Now you've got me wondering. Is your name really Eddie?"

"Edmund," he said, "Zambriskie. I don't have any fancy library card, though, so you gotta take my word for it."

"Do you know a lot of fellows . . . like us?"

"No one like you."

"But you do know *some*?"

He folded his arms, as if thinking about it. "I mean, Chicago's a big town. A fella can't go a week without running into one someplace. Seems to me they jump right out of the woodwork."

This only made sense. Even the most discreet person might take chances around someone who looked like Eddie.

"But nobody hassles me," he clarified. "Who's gonna mess with a fellow my size? I feel perfectly safe, no matter where I go."

"Do you ever go to the pansy parlors over in Towertown?"

He shook his head. A firm no.

"Why not?"

"Who needs it?"

"But you talk with a lot of confidence. Do you have much experience?"

He gave me a playful shove. "No more than you do, I bet. You probably got a different squeeze for each night of the week."

"Nothing like that."

"But you got a steady?"

I shook my head, feeling sheepish. I shouldn't tell Eddie about Raymond without Ray's permission. And I could never tell Raymond about Eddie, because Ray would ask to meet him. And they couldn't meet, of course, because I'd given them two totally different names. So much for my syndicate of queer fellows.

In order for Eddie to become a genuine friend, I needed to show him he could trust me. Based on what he'd hinted about people taking advantage, that would take time.

I checked my watch. Nearly two. "I'm working today. Need to go back to my room and change."

"I'll wait for you and give you a lift downtown."

We spun around and walked north again through Lincoln Park. Eddie led me to the liquor truck, which he'd left in an alley. "My pop's got contracts in a few of these places," he bragged. "I can park wherever I feel like it."

The passenger-side door screeched wildly from hinges that needed oiling. The seat was littered with delivery receipts, pencils, a restaurant matchbook, a 3 Musketeers candy wrapper, and other trash. With a single gesture, Eddie swept it all off the seat and onto the floor. I scrambled in. The interior stank of cigarette smoke and gasoline.

I gave him Del's street address, and he drove for a while. Before we got there, however, he steered abruptly into another alley and slammed the truck into park behind a warehouse. The building didn't have any windows, and Eddie didn't kill the motor. "This won't take long," he said.

"Why are we stopping?"

He didn't answer and didn't need to. A second later, he slid across the seat and pulled me toward him. His lips were warm, rough stubble around his mouth. He kissed me so eagerly, I was afraid he'd leave my own lips raw. His mouth pressed so hard against mine, the back of my head knocked against the window frame. We kept at it, and I was happy to grasp his solid shoulders and feel his strong hands on me. I ran my fingers through his close-cropped dark hair. I wanted to touch every part of him.

Before long, we heard honking behind us.

Eddie cursed and slid behind the wheel again. He wiped his mouth with the back of his hand and then shifted into drive. We pulled forward to the street.

"For a minute there, I was worried," he said. "I thought, What if I don't even get a kiss out of him? I was scolding myself for not buying you a sandwich."

I felt almost light-headed. I wanted to laugh. It wasn't right to compare people, I knew. And there was no comparing Eddie and Raymond. They were alike as coffee and Coca-Cola. I enjoyed both. But I'd never felt this way from a kiss before.

"Buy me a sandwich another day," I said.

ELEVEN

O N SATURDAY, I met Raymond near the fountain at Washington Square Park. It was already noon, and I had to be at work by three.

Even before I could make an excuse to cut it short, he said, "I can only take a walk today. I don't have a dime on me. I've lost my wallet."

"What? When?"

He shrugged. "I had it with me when we went to Vi's the other night. It's a real tragedy, because I'd just cashed a check from my father. The money was meant to carry me through the summer."

"Did your folks give you hell for it?"

"I haven't breathed a word to them. Oh, how they love to lecture me when I make any little mistake. I hate to admit it, but this was hardly the first time I've lost a wallet filled with cash."

We walked along Michigan Avenue, window-shopping and commenting on the handsomeness of strangers. In a sense, this was all I could dream of: a fellow to go walking with, see pictures with, flirt and make jokes with. But with Raymond I was Charles Powell, and this wasn't the genuine dream. I needed his travel dates.

"You must be looking forward to your trip," I said. "It will be cooler up north."

"Yes, except it will mean not seeing you."

"Which day do you come back, exactly?"

"Sunday, July twenty-second. You'll be off to France by then."

"Yes. Terrible timing."

"But we'll write to each other—"

"What about Agnes?" I asked, because I'd been wondering about the difficulty of burgling a house with a live-in housekeeper.

"What about her?"

"She'll take the week off, I suppose. Go and visit family."

"Not a chance," he said. "She'll stay put all week. Agnes never sees her people."

"Why not?"

"No idea. She mentioned once that she's the black sheep. She didn't explain why, but, I mean, you've *seen* her. It must have to do with a fellow. Every time she runs to the market, she's practically got men buying tickets to carry her grocery bags. My guess is, she got mixed up in some ridiculous scandal in her town, and late one night she packed a suitcase and never looked back."

If Agnes remained at home every day while the Kenricks were in Canada, it would make it difficult for Heinz and his team to burgle the house. It might even be impossible. Well, good luck to them. Not my job to worry about it.

"Gee, that story put a smile on your face," Raymond said. "Don't tell me you're bewitched by Agnes, too."

"No, I only share your fascination for other people's dirty laundry."

"We're so much alike, Charles."

Raymond was the only fellow I'd ever known who wanted to talk about the same things I did, like motion pictures and popular music. He seemed eager to hear my take on anything at all. He made me feel smart. As long as I remembered I was Charles Powell around him, I could be myself in a way I never could be with fellows back home.

Near Huron Street, we passed a stationer's shop. Raymond said he needed a new address book. "I can't buy one now, of course. I'll wait awhile and then ask Mother for the money."

Must be nice, I considered.

"There's a fellow at my school," he added, "who uses a code in his address book. He puts the letters M.D. next to the names of his pansy friends. M.D. stands for *marvelous deviant*, but if anyone snoops in the book, it will only appear he's well known at local hospitals."

We both laughed. Raymond pressed a hand against my shoulder for support as his giggling increased. "He uses D.D.S.," he said, between gasps for breath, "for certain friends."

"Not dentists?" I said.

"*Deviant*," he whispered, nearly in tears, "*devoted to sex!*"

I was more amused by his silly sputtering than by the remark itself. I never dreamed of being able to laugh about the subject of so many sleepless nights. I could only hope to be as carefree as Raymond; maybe after I solved my money trouble, I would be.

When his giggles subsided, he said, "What a tragedy that our travels will spoil our summer fun. But I'm keeping you in my syndicate. Once I learn to drive, I'll borrow the car and come downstate to visit you."

Of course, we couldn't stay in touch. I'd lied to Raymond about my name, my background, practically everything.

"I'll write to you first, Dr. Kenrick," I said, "since I already know your address."

93

"Joking aside," he said, "I want to study psychoanalytic science in college. I plan to be a doctor. Already I can see myself with an office in the Loop someday, a window with a view of the lake. Can't you picture it?" He took me by the arm. "Now listen, I have a serious question, and I want you to be honest—*brutally* honest."

"About what?"

He lowered his voice: "Are you more attracted to fellows who are more masculine than you or more feminine?"

"I—I don't know. It's never been my habit to think of fellows like that, divided neatly into two groups."

"Every man goes for one type or the other," he explained. "Let's try it this way. Name some of the film stars you dream about. Give me a long list, and I'll tell you which camp you belong in. This will be fun."

We walked for another hour, appraising each other's cinema crushes and howling with laughter, until I had to beat it. "Family visiting," I told him. I regretted telling another lie, but Charles Powell would never serve plates of pork medallions to the Illinois Meatpacking Commission. I was scheduled for a double shift on Sunday. I would have preferred to spend the whole weekend with Raymond.

TWELVE

BY MONDAY'S CLASS, listening to the ladies boast about which French shops and brasseries they planned to visit, I felt no apprehension whatsoever. My classmates weren't pieces of fine china, after all. They were clay plates at a carnival shooting range. I only needed to hit them all so I could collect my prize.

I had gotten the names and addresses, but still needed the travel dates. Two classes remained, only four households left to question. The goal was within reach.

I aimed to be the very last person to arrive, so I could choose who to interrogate. Only trouble was, Raymond had arrived before me, and he waved me over as soon as I entered the gymnasium.

"I won't sit with you today," I whispered, tapping my throat. "I feel a tickle this morning."

Instead I took a seat between the Palmers and the Moores. Mrs. Moore whispered loudly to her sister, "If Charles is feeling poorly, he might better have spared the rest of us and stayed home."

Madame distributed a sheet with short sentences and common expressions.

C'est magnifique. C'est formidable. C'est parfait.

Each time it was my turn to repeat the phrase, Mrs. Moore made me feel like the slowest horse on the track. "Listen to the rest of us, Charles," she declared cheerfully, "and it's very possible your pronunciation will improve."

I had decided early on that Mrs. Moore was the classmate whose burglary would bother me least of all. When we reached a break, I turned to the Moore sisters and pronounced my words extra carefully: "Tell me *all* . . . about . . . your travel plans."

Mrs. Moore seemed happy to brag about the details. "We sail for Arles on July eighteenth and return to New York on August ninth. We expect to see many dear friends during the visit, including—"

"How delightful," I interrupted.

This time I was prepared. I'd been doodling in the corners of my class worksheet, and I hid the dates inside the pencil swirls and hatchwork. No need to rely on my memory this time.

Next I turned to the Palmers, Edna and her niece, Elsie. "And you?" I asked. "When will you go abroad?"

The Palmers were the true chatterboxes in the group. We always knew how the temperature was affecting them, where they had purchased their clothes, what they had eaten for breakfast, and which picture they planned to see that afternoon. So it came as no surprise that, upon hearing my question, their travel dates spilled like lava from Vesuvius.

Finally, I'd gotten the hang of this. I only needed two more. It had occurred to me that I might choose one of the girls, Lillian Feeney or Evelyn Shaw, and ask her out for a soda.

However, when class ended and I rose from my seat, Mrs. Moore blocked my path.

"Now, Charles, a summer cold is nothing to ignore. The best remedy is hot tea and *rest.* If your nose feels congested, add some baking soda to warm salt water . . ."

She then described a procedure in such vivid detail that by the time she had finished, I no longer needed to pretend feeling ill. Worse, both Lillian and Evelyn had left the gymnasium.

Raymond, however, had waited for me near the door. Together we retrieved our hats from the wall hook.

"How are you feeling?" he asked.

"Never better," I said, and we left the parish hall arm in arm.

I wasn't scheduled to work, so I had the whole afternoon and evening free. Raymond still hadn't found his billfold, so that day he took me sightseeing. We visited the Tiffany ceilings at Marshall Field's department store and the Chicago Public Library. In both places, we stood back-to-back, gazing up at the shimmering mosaic domes.

Raymond said he was determined to "educate" me. He taught me that if a fellow walked along State Street outside Marshall Field's wearing a red necktie, another fellow would approach him for a date. He said it would happen in Bughouse Square, too. But there were only certain days of the week when it worked.

"I don't own a red necktie," I told him.

"Don't look at me. I won't lend you one."

"What if someone is wearing a red necktie by accident? I guess he gets the surprise of his life."

"Among other things," Raymond explained, "it would teach him that he should never dress in any clothing *by accident*."

I soaked up everything Raymond taught me, thrilled by the new information: the secret signals and coded language, all the ways to make connections. With his guidance, I might finally learn how to live my life.

Next he said he wanted to take me to see Buckingham Fountain and the rose garden at Grant Park. "We can pop into the Art Institute, too. Ever since the crash, they've waived the entry fee."

"Ray, what I'd really like is to visit another of the queer places. Can we do that?"

"Tonight, you mean?"

"Is there a place we can go to now?"

"At this hour?" He glanced at his wristwatch, frowning. "It's not even three o'clock. And I don't have a cent on me."

"A café, then, rather than a tavern. I'll treat you to a Coca-Cola."

At Chicago Avenue, we boarded the streetcar. I paid the seven-cent fare for each of us, while Raymond found us seats. Even with all the window latches unlocked, the heat was intense. We headed west for many blocks, along an endless commercial stretch, and the streetcar kept stopping every block or two, so people could board or step off. We continued past the river, farther than I'd ever gone, to Halsted Avenue.

I followed Raymond off, and he led me down a block of tall brick buildings, factories and machinery plants, the sidewalk clogged with workers.

"Over here we're not likely to be seen, but pull down your hat a bit," he instructed.

Quite happily, I pulled down the brim of my homburg, as he did. The secrecy of queer places felt romantic, shrouded in mystery and invisible to society at large. These were the safe places, intended for fellows like us.

We turned down a quieter block and finally stopped in front of a yellow-brick corner tavern with all the windows painted black. A round wooden sign above the door identified it as the Up-and-Up.

"You've been here?" I asked.

"Only one time," Raymond said. "Once we're inside, I'll get the drinks. Sit anywhere you like. But keep your hands on the table, got it? And promise you won't speak to anyone."

I gave him a coin for the drinks. "I promise, Ricardo."

The Up-and-Up consisted of one long room, the air laced with smoke and the odor of a stale kitchen fryer. There were a dozen or so small tables and a humble bar against the back wall. A radio behind the bar was playing "I Guess I'll Have to Change My Plan" by Rudy Vallée.

Most tables were occupied. Two lonely floor lamps with torn shades—one at each side of the room—gave off a somber yellowish light that left nearly everyone's face in shadow. It took about five seconds before I realized that Raymond and I were the youngest people in the room by at least two decades. Still, I was struck again by the ordinariness of the men. They might have been anyone.

I took the closest open seat and rested my hands on the wobbly tabletop.

Raymond returned with two bottles of Coca-Cola and two glasses with ice. He removed his hat and smoothed his hair, before speaking very quietly: "We must stick to the rules here. No holding hands. Certainly no kissing. Now that we've taken our seats, we're stuck. No moving around, no talking to strangers." He pulled a pack of Chesterfields from his trousers, but I waved it away.

"Why so strict?" I asked, pouring the drinks.

"Cops. They love to come looking for trouble, but they won't find it here."

"But at Vi's—"

"Vi's has deep pockets. You saw how it was there. Vi's can pay off the cops. A dump like this can't."

"So it's only harassment then," I said, a statement so obvious that Raymond only shrugged and knocked a cigarette out of the pack. I leaned forward, eager to light it for him like they did in the pictures.

He inhaled deeply. "You never smoke? A single cigarette cools the skin by nearly ten degrees. That's science. I read it in the paper. Grab me an ashtray, will you? Make it quick, so we don't get scolded."

I grabbed a tin ashtray from the table next to us. Now the radio was playing "Life Is Just a Bowl of Cherries."

"Have you got a girl back home, Charles?"

A frowning Mary Toomey, with her confused and frustrated eyes, flashed before me.

"Nothing serious," I said inaccurately. "Have you?"

"I'll take a girl out now and then, just to keep my hand in. I attend all the formal dances at school. Keeps my parents happy. I suppose it's the same for you."

I nodded, although it wasn't the same at all. I thought of all the afternoons I'd spent on Mary's porch swing. The earnest conversations on the walks home from school. Making polite small talk with her parents on Sundays. The whole thing was a mistake, but I could never see my way out of it.

"Hands on the table," he reminded me.

Obediently, I laced my fingers around my Coca-Cola. On the topic of Mary Toomey, I realized, I could be honest with Raymond. It was one of the few areas where there was absolutely no difference between Charles Powell's life and my own. "There's one girl I spend time with back home," I told him. "Mary, her name is. I've known her since the first grade. She's about the kindest girl I ever met. Caring and thoughtful, quiet by nature—"

"What does Mary look like? Which film star, would you say?"

"Oh . . . I don't know. Billie Dove, maybe? Her face is round like that. And her eyes—"

"Billie Dove! My god, she was hilarious in *Cock of the Air.*"

"Yes. Anyway, Mary and I spend a lot of time together. I suppose her family has expectations, and my mother has expectations. And it feels lousy to consider that I'm not, you know, suited to be a good husband."

"No, you sell yourself short. I mean, it's true I've only known you a little while, but I think any girl would be very lucky to marry you."

"That's nice of you to say. I'm grateful to have someone to talk about it with. It feels very difficult, you know?"

"I know it's difficult. You don't need to explain it."

But I wanted advice on how to navigate it all. "How do I—"

Before I could go on, the Up-and-Up's front door swung open with force. Every head in the joint turned toward the entrance, eyes squinting in the sudden daylight. Except for Jeanette MacDonald singing "Love Me Tonight," the room went silent.

Two policemen appeared, searching in opposite directions with brisk determination. Both were young, slender, buttons gleaming on their uniforms. Neither cracked a smile, but anyone could tell they enjoyed the sound their boots made as they weaved among the tables, pointing their straight batons menacingly in the face of every patron. It wasn't until they reached the bartender that conversation resumed.

"Let's beat it," I whispered.

Raymond didn't move. "Let's finish these Cokes. Bolting right away looks bad. You can bet they've got friends waiting on the sidewalk. Say, when we're done here, how about we take a taxi to the Loop and see a picture?"

"Another picture?"

"It's been almost a week since I treated us to *Tarzan*. Now that you've brought up Billie Dove, all I want is to sit in a cool theater."

In my head, I added up the cost of the sodas, the taxi, and the movie tickets. While I was frugal on my own, I didn't mind treating Raymond now and then. Every time Charles Powell paid for something, my feelings of guilt lessened a bit.

He set his empty glass on the table. "We'll sit in the balcony this time." Daringly he pressed his knee against mine.

I jumped out of my seat, eyeing the cops. "Please, let's go," I said again.

"Lead the way."

***

Later that night, I sat on the cot in Bernie's room and copied the dates I'd saved in the margins of my ditto. "Big leap forward at today's class," I told him.

"You're a natural at this, Joe," he said. "Where've you been all day?"

"After class, I went to the pictures with Raymond Kenrick. We saw *Fog Over Frisco* and then ate at Thompson's."

He made a face. "Doesn't Kenrick got some girl to take out rather than you?"

"We haven't talked about it."

"I don't know why you're even spending time with the dope. You already got the info we need."

"I'm allowed to have some grins this summer, aren't I?"

"Here, grin at this instead." He handed me a brown paper bag. "Maybe it'll remind you what we're doing this for."

The bag contained forty in cash. Another installment.

I removed twenty-four dollars and tossed the bag onto Bernie's bed. "Thank Heinz for me."

"One not-so-good thing," he added. "Del approached me again, complaining about the cost of groceries. She got the water bill this morning and showed it to me. She hadn't taken it all into account."

"Tell her we haven't got any more. She doesn't know about this money, does she?"

"How would she? She's only asking for another buck."

"In other words, two dollars more than we agreed upon before I came."

"She wouldn't chisel us, Joe. She's good people. Anyone can see that."

I highly doubted Del was the one who was chiseling me. But I wouldn't argue with Bernie. Hell, I was learning from him. I might as well pay for the lessons.

I sat on the cot and wrote a letter to my mother, with another fifteen dollars tucked inside the envelope.

I considered writing to Mary, too. Before leaving home, I'd promised her I would send my address in Chicago, but I kept putting it off. Ever since talking with Raymond, however, my conscience was weighing on me. The whole thing with Mary felt like a grand deception now. I set aside the pen and stared at the ceiling, feeling lousy as hell, until my brain clocked out.

THIRTEEN

E ACH TIME I VISITED THE KENRICKS' PLACE, I tried to predict what Heinz and his crew might pinch. The fancy porcelain watchdog in the front window would be missed, but the place was loaded with shiny trinkets that wouldn't be. Sterling silver thingamajigs. Cut-crystal doodads.

Meanwhile, at our house, there wasn't a single item left worth taking. At one time, we had an heirloom cookie jar; now we didn't even have cookies.

On Tuesday, Raymond and I found Mrs. Kenrick at the dining room table, looking over pencil drawings on sheets of typing paper. The aroma of bacon and eggs lingered in the air, and a dozen or so dirty cups and saucers had been abandoned at the center of the table. My eyes settled on a nifty salt-and-pepper set that would fit in anyone's pocket. I wondered what they were worth.

Mrs. Kenrick looked smart, as usual, in her matching jacket and hat, dark green with white piping along the seams. "I finally have a grand vision for the garden," she told us. She beamed at me, her lips done up in a bright coral. "I don't expect you know much about growing things, do you?"

"On the contrary, Mother, Charles's family owns thousands of acres downstate."

"Not thousands," I corrected. "We have some land near St. Louis. I'm used to having dirt under my fingernails."

Mrs. Kenrick lifted a sheet from the table. The paper was filled with handwritten boxes and clouds, a map of the layout she'd planned. I sat next to her, praying the aroma of the breakfast wouldn't make my stomach growl.

"It *all* needs to be redone," she said. "I hosted a breakfast lecture this morning. Our speaker was Mr. Thomas Church from the University of California. He wants our gardens to represent nature. Spontaneous, wild. No more stuffy symmetry and order."

The arrival of her husband interrupted the speech. Mr. Kenrick entered with the day's newspapers folded under his right arm. His only arm. His left shirtsleeve was pinned neatly at the elbow. How strange, I considered, that Raymond had never mentioned this fact. In most other ways, Raymond took after his father, the long angular face and blond hair combed back with oil.

"Good day, all," he said in a gruff voice, only glancing at me. He let the papers drop to his place at the table.

I rose from the chair.

"Harry, this is our new friend, Charles Powell," Mrs. Kenrick said. "The three of us are learning French together."

Mr. Kenrick and I shook mitts, and he nodded. "*Bonjour*, I'm sure," he said. "What's this little meeting about?"

Raymond rocked impatiently on his heels. "Mother's only telling us about her exciting scheme for the garden."

"I don't know what's wrong with the garden you put in every year," his father said. "Petunias and snapdragons look swell to me."

Mrs. Kenrick shook her head. "According to Mr. Church, the time has come to replace annuals with hardy perennials, which come back every year. It's insensitive to spend a fortune on flower gardens every spring, when so many families struggle to make ends meet."

At once, I saw a chance to get a better look at the rear of the house, as well as some extra time with Raymond.

"I can help," I said. "Raymond and I could do some of the work ourselves. All we need is a shovel, some good soil, and whatever you want to plant." I pointed at the garden sketch. "If you don't want this privet anymore, we could dig it out this week."

Raymond only glared, as if the last thing he wanted to do was get his hands dirty outside.

"Awfully kind of you to offer," Mr. Kenrick said.

Mrs. Kenrick gave me a warm smile. "We think the world of you, Charles. I would like to meet your parents when they come."

"That'd be nice," I said. "Unfortunately, we leave for Europe before you get back from your trip."

"Then I'll call your mother and pay her a compliment. What's the telephone number at your house? Write it down for me, will you?" She tore off a scrap of paper and handed it over.

Like most people in my town, we didn't have a home telephone. Most folks used the payphone at the general store, and I couldn't very well give Mrs. Kenrick that number. No one there had ever heard of Charles Powell.

"You can't call my folks," I said.

"Why not?"

"They're replacing all the telephone lines near us this month. A big storm knocked them down."

"How long have you been without service?"

"Since . . . June?"

Mrs. Kenrick fell back in her chair. *"Since June?"*

"Very early June."

"You poor things!"

"We remember what it was like"—her husband grinned—"not so long ago."

"Yes, but we didn't know any better then. My goodness, Charles, it must feel like living in ancient times. Like when everybody used a privy, too!"

"Exactly like that," I said, before turning to Raymond. "Say, didn't you want us to . . . learn those new verbs for class?"

Finally, he smiled. "Your dedication inspires us all. Let's go upstairs."

✳ ✳ ✳

We lay together on the bed, fully dressed. We'd been kissing for ten minutes, first him on top, then me on top, when I pulled away.

"How did your father lose his arm? Was it in the war?"

He hesitated before nodding. "The Second Battle of the Marne. That's all I know. He never talks about it. It's our family's greatest tragedy."

I almost pointed out that worse things could happen, including what had happened to my father, but I didn't want the issue to be a competition between us.

"The greatest tragedy," he repeated. "He lost the whole forearm, but it's never stopped him from working."

He spoke these words in a rush, like he'd said them many times before. I wondered if the missing arm was something Raymond felt embarrassed about when he was younger, or something he felt proud about now. He added, "Let's not talk about gloomy things."

We kissed again for a while.

I stared at his flushed face, his swollen lips. "Raymond, do you think we could ever try . . ." I stopped, unsure of how to say it. I'd been thinking about my first night in Chicago and the geezer who made the shocking proposition in the park.

"Try what?"

"Something . . . more," I said.

"More? Are you sure?"

I nodded. "You said you wanted to educate me, remember?"

"Well, then, handsome, no time like the present."

"Really?"

"First, take off your clothes. Set them on the chair."

I got to my feet clumsily and pulled my shirttail from my trousers. I took a deep breath. Was I dreaming? Without warning, my hands were shaking so hard I could barely maneuver the buttons through their holes, and my eyes wandered to the door. "What if someone comes looking for you? Your mother or your sister?"

"This isn't a public thoroughfare."

"I guess not."

"Hurry up and get undressed."

✳✳✳

The lesson that followed covered the subject area thoroughly, emphasizing skill and rigor. Afterward, we lay in the tangle of those bright white sheets.

"Stop trembling," Raymond said. "It's warm in here, and you're shivering like we're on some ice floe in the Arctic."

"I can't help it. My body is going haywire. Where did you learn to do that?"

"Away at school. There were nights in the dormitory like something out of the Wild West—don't look at me with those scandalized eyes, Charles. The important thing is, now you're a *marvelous deviant*, too!" He said it with a laugh, but I wanted to talk seriously now. He was the only person I could ask.

"Do you think God will punish us?"

He squinted. "Punish us—for this?"

"Do you ever worry about it?"

"Honestly, I think God will *reward* us, after putting us through something difficult as this. I never asked for my lavender heart, did you? That was God's choice. Same as my eyes or the color of my hair. Listen, when we write to each other this fall, we can discuss religion all you like. But we should get dressed now, before somebody comes knocking."

"You said this isn't a public thoroughfare."

"I am sometimes wrong."

"Kiss me again first."

"You are far too romantic for this world," he complained, and he kissed me anyhow.

If it hadn't been for the threat of visitors, as well as my job, I might have stayed in that bed kissing Raymond for the rest of the day. Next to him, I felt happier than I could remember feeling for a long time.

But he was wrong about one thing. I couldn't afford to be romantic. I could only be practical. I couldn't forget or ignore the scheme that had led me to his front door. The two of us would never exchange letters, never meet again to discuss our summer fling.

I would finish the job for Heinz, collect the final payment, and leave both Raymond Kenrick and Charles Powell behind, on the road to something better for Joe Garbe. Nothing could get in the way of that, least of all my feelings.

It was July tenth already, and my time in Chicago was nearly half over. The only trouble was, even if everything went according to plan, the money I'd make from the French class wouldn't be enough to see me off the farm. The University of Illinois was free for state residents, but room and board cost about three hundred each year. Missouri's state university charged much less for room and board, but fifty dollars tuition for out-of-state residents. Plus, we faced a mountain of bills at home. I needed a hell of a lot more than four hundred dollars.

FOURTEEN

JACKSON WAS PREPARING DOUGH FOR THE PARKER HOUSE ROLLS the next day when I stopped by to ask a favor: "When's the next time you're going to play that policy game?"

He only shook his head over the big mixer. "Put it out of your mind. I told you, I can't bring you along."

"Couldn't I give you two dollars to play for me?"

"Can you afford to lose it, Joe? People do win, game after game. But it's more common to lose. I don't want to mislead you."

"It's worth the risk. I've told you how we're sitting on dynamite back home."

He transferred the dough into a bowl and covered it with a linen cloth. He sighed. "I'll play this weekend."

I wanted to dance around the kitchen, I felt so hopeful. I chose the numbers based on my father's birthday (three, fifteen) and my age (sixteen). I gave Jackson two dollars and he slid them into his pocket. "You'll remember?" I asked.

He nodded. "If you're so keen to earn money, stick around here. August is quiet, but bookings pick up after Labor Day. You could even finish school here in Chicago and work at the hotel at night. On slow shifts, you could do your homework in an empty ballroom upstairs."

The offer was tempting. Mertz had warmed to me, and the twin novelties of steady pay and savory meals never wore off. I could only dream of living in a place where I could manage my own schedule, chart my own course.

"My mother expects me home at the end of the month," I admitted. "And Bernie wouldn't like me staying with him forever."

"You're nothing like your cousin."

"He's a good egg, once you get to know him."

"I know something about eggs—" he said, but then stopped. I never heard Jackson speak ill of anyone.

Lots of people didn't like Bernie, I knew. They didn't appreciate his cockiness or nerve. But they didn't know how much he'd had to overcome, either. There were certain things only family understood.

✱✱✱

There were also things family would never understand.

I was rinsing the mixing bowls when Eddie came in from the alley, bringing another liquor crate. His red cheeks were as shiny as the amber bottles he carried. He set the crate on the floor near Mertz's office and got Mertz to sign off on the delivery. Invoice in hand, he signaled silently for me to follow him outside.

That signal gave me a thrill, but someone on the crew was always watching. I couldn't even smile. I took my time drying the bowls and returning them to the shelves before I joined him in the alley. The truck held plenty more crates to bring in.

"It's Wednesday, Peaches," he said. "Our visit to the zoo was *five days* ago. You ready for another good time?"

I needed a minute to think it through but didn't want to get caught goofing. "Let's get these moved. Which ones are ours?"

He pointed. I grabbed a heavy crate and carried it inside. I went back for more, dropping one after the next near Mertz's office.

Of course I wanted to see Eddie again. It wasn't just the way he filled his clothing, either. He understood how it felt to struggle, to go through hard times. Eddie might be the genuine friend I needed to begin my syndicate. The two of us could keep in touch after the summer.

Meanwhile, in less than a week, Raymond Kenrick and his family would leave for Canada and I'd never see him again. I wanted to spend every free minute I had with him before he left town.

When I returned to the alley for the last crate, Eddie blocked my path. "Well, how about it? How's tomorrow?"

Once Raymond left for Canada on Monday, I'd be free as a bird.

"I've got my French class tomorrow," I said. "Besides, payday's not until the end of the week. Next week I'll have cash in my pocket."

"Naw, forget about money. Neither of us busted our piggy bank at the zoo, did we? I'll come see where you're staying. If you have the place to yourself, we could spend the afternoon together. That wouldn't cost a penny."

I pictured Eddie and me in Bernie's bedroom, doing what I'd done a few hours earlier with Raymond. Was it possible for a fellow's brain to spontaneously combust just imagining? But I couldn't risk Del or Bernie catching us.

"Or we'll go to the beach, cool off in the lake." He lowered his voice. "You haven't seen me in my bathing suit yet, Peaches."

I laughed, feeling my face flush.

He rested his shoulder against the back of his truck, giving me those sandy brown eyes. "C'mon, Joe. Haven't you been thinking about me?"

"Sure I have. Just give me some time. How about next Tuesday?"

"Tuesday? That's almost a week!"

"Be patient, please. That's all I'm asking."

He stared more closely. "You got someone else?"

I shook my head, almost by reflex. "Nothing like that."

"Just tell me if you have."

"No," I insisted. "I'm working some extra jobs this week and don't have any free time. You understand, don't you?"

He didn't speak, just turned around and closed the gate on the truck, locking it with quick, impatient hands.

"Guess I'll be seeing you," he grumbled. He moved to the front of the truck and reached for the door handle.

The last thing I wanted to do was discourage him. I couldn't let him drive away without a plan to see him again.

"Eddie, please. I do want to see you. *Tuesday*, I promise. I'll be free then. We can drive around and you can show me whatever you want."

"Guess I'll take what I can get."

"You can take everything," I said, hoping it sounded risqué. "Tuesday."

"I heard you."

"Will you pick me up at noon? You remember where I'm staying?"

He nodded.

"Okay, see you then." I waved for him to get in the truck quickly.

The motor roared to life, the truck lurched forward, and I was back inside the kitchen before anyone came looking for me.

FIFTEEN

B Y THE FINAL FRENCH CLASS ON THURSDAY, I only needed travel dates from the Shaws and the Feeneys. Before I even made it inside, however, Raymond greeted me on the sidewalk.

"Charles, I'm stealing you away!" he announced, extending his arms. "It's too fine outdoors to be stuck in that gymnasium. Mother's already gone inside, and Agnes took Millie downtown to buy a new bathing suit for our trip. We'll have the house to ourselves for at least an hour before anyone returns."

I was *this close* to getting everything I needed—everything I had to deliver—for Heinz.

"It's our last class. I want to go," I said.

He raised his eyebrows. "Why, what have you learned so far?"

. . .

"Just as I thought. Now let's breeze off."

"No, Ray, I paid good money for these lessons. I want to get something out of it, if possible." I stepped past him, knowing he would follow.

Miraculously, inside, the chair between the Shaws and the Feeneys was free, and I nabbed it.

Madame Monk distributed a list of common verbs and began the lesson.

To like. To give. To win. To live.

I listened, making more doodles in pencil, preparing hiding spots for the dates I would collect.

Evelyn Shaw and Lillian Feeney were both close to my age, so I felt more confident about speaking to them. In particular, Evelyn was warm and unguarded. I suspected she made friends as easily as I peeled spuds.

"I wonder if we'll be in Paris at the same time," I said to her during the break.

"We leave the seventh of August, and we'll be back . . . September first? I think that's right. But we won't be in Paris at all. Our tour is keeping us in Saint-Tropez and Cannes. Are you really making the trip all the way up north?"

"Sounds swell," I said, ignoring her question.

Until that moment, it had not occurred to me that travelers to France might not go to Paris. I wouldn't know where to find Paris on a map.

Time was running out, so I turned to Lillian Feeney. She and her mother were pale redheads, slender, with tiny hands protected by white gloves. Their matching sundresses were pressed so carefully I could almost smell the Faultless starch on them. I always imagined the Feeney women sleeping under domes of glass.

"I'm sailing on Holland America in two weeks," I told them. "New York to Marseilles. How about you?"

Mrs. Feeney took a sip of her lemonade before murmuring, "We're sailing on the *Champlain* on the first of August."

"How nice. A tour?"

"A whole month!" the daughter declared. "We won't be back until September."

I didn't need specifics. If Heinz's prowlers needed an open window, "a whole month" would serve just fine.

"This will be my first time in France," I said.

Lillian scooted her chair closer to Evelyn Shaw and me. She lowered her voice. "Ours, too."

"*Really?*" Evelyn exclaimed, as if Lillian had admitted to never tasting ice cream.

"My grandparents—we share an apartment with them—they're sending Mother and me on this trip. They surprised us with the tickets."

"Lucky you," I said.

"More like tough luck, honestly," Lillian said. "My grandparents' shoe-repair shop had a fire last winter. They lost everything. Rather than reopening, they used the insurance money for our tickets." With a smile, she reached gently for her mother's hand before turning back to me. "A once-in-a-lifetime adventure for us, I suppose."

"You don't *know* that, Lil," Mrs. Feeney said. Her tone implied they'd had this conversation before.

"I'll have a job waiting at my uncle's coffee shop when I get back," Lillian added.

"How fun," Evelyn said unconvincingly.

So the Feeneys were not like the others, I realized. I wondered if the grandparents would be at home when Lillian and her mother were traveling. Before I could ask, Madame began the lesson again.

I hid the dates inside the other random notes on my ditto. At last, I had all the information. My part was done. I should have been tickled pink, but I only sat there. I couldn't listen to the final minutes of the lesson. For the first time in a while, the guilt pestered me like a housefly. It wasn't right that the Feeneys could lose whatever they had left. Maybe Heinz's men would see the Feeney residence wasn't grand like the others. Maybe I could leave a note on it, so Heinz would skip it altogether.

I made a beeline for the Kenricks after class.

"Free this afternoon?" I asked Raymond.

His mother answered for him: "I'm afraid we're in a terrible crunch the next two days, Charles. Haircuts, packing, and errands all over town."

Raymond nodded, looking sad. "That's why I hoped you'd skip class with me today. Will I see you Sunday? You can come by and help me pack."

Today was Thursday, and Sunday felt like ages away. I realized I could only see Raymond if I convinced his mother. "Say," I told her, "I meant it when I offered to help in the garden. Want to start before you leave? I could come by for a while on Saturday."

"Mother and Millie leave on Sunday," Raymond interjected.

I suspected Raymond was only trying to avoid yard work, but Mrs. Kenrick bit her lip hopefully. "I suppose I would like to get things rolling . . ."

"We could clear out everything," I suggested. "That way, it will be ready for planting just as soon as you get back. Ten o'clock? Before it gets hot?"

Mrs. Kenrick nodded. "It's a date!"

Raymond stood by, looking unhappy. Of course, this wasn't how he wanted to spend his Saturday. But I had seized upon a double opportunity: more time with Raymond, plus a small way to atone for my part in Heinz's scheme. If the Kenrick family remembered Charles Powell after the summer, they would recall only a helpful, hardworking young man. Nothing else.

Back at the apartment, Bernie was in bed with another stack of hardcovers. This time the titles were all the same: *The Good Earth* by Pearl S. Buck. He must have gotten a deal on them.

I copied out my notes, before handing over the full list of travel dates. "That completes the picture. Everything's there. Names, addresses, and travel dates."

"Nice work."

"So when do we get the rest of the money?"

"Give it time."

I sat on the cot, facing him. "What do you mean?"

"I mean, give it time. It wouldn't make sense for Heinz and his crew to pay us before they know the information's good. A dishonest person could make things up. Heinz needs to see you're on the level."

"The information is good. You *know* me, Bern. Can't you ask him?"

"Nah, that's not how it works. We can't rattle Heinz's cage right now, not when we're so close. His temper is nothing to fool with, see? Now relax, you did your part. Handled the job like a champ."

I lay back on the cot, staring at the ceiling cracks. "How's he going to do it? Some of these houses won't be empty. The Feeneys share an apartment with the grandparents. The Kenricks have a live-in housekeeper. She's not traveling with them."

Bernie and his fountain pen returned to Pearl Buck. "Even housekeepers take days off. That's for someone else to lose sleep over. Besides, you're only feeling anxious because you made a pal of that goofy *Raymond*."

"Goofy? You never laid eyes on him."

"Remember, nothing that happens will make the slightest difference to the Kenricks or the other hotshots you met in that church gym." He shook his head. "You're coming into some real money soon, Joe. For you to be anything but *happy* right now? I mean, I'm sorry to say it, but it's practically certifiable. Lookit, a letter came for you."

The envelope was another doorstop from home, stuffed with more clippings, prayers, and praise.

"Painting houses—good for you!" my mother wrote. "Honest young men always can find ways to earn money." She reminded me to "save every penny" I earned and to avoid any "glittering spots" Bernie might take me to. "Keep your free time truly free!"

I folded the letter, thinking of the money I'd already spent on new clothes, and pictures with Raymond, and Jackson's policy game.

"Hurry up and change," Bernie said. "Hightail it out of here, or you'll be late."

"Not working tonight?"

"Not me, pal. I plan to unload these books, and then I got a date later."

"Good for you." I went to the closet and took out some of the worn-out clothes I'd brought to Chicago with me.

"Whaddaya need those old rags for?" Bernie asked. "That's not who you are no more, Joe."

The trousers did look awfully rough. What made me think I'd have any use for them in the city? I wasn't the same person who stepped off the train three weeks ago. Nothing about me was the same.

"I'm helping the Kenricks with some gardening Saturday."

"What, giving them free lawn care now?" Bernie lay back against the headboard and groaned.

"What?"

"You know I love you, buddy, but you are such a sap sometimes."

SIXTEEN

THE FOLLOWING NIGHT, my fingertips wrinkled from dishwashing, I punched out and left the hotel through the alley. The hotel kitchen had been steamy, so stepping out into the night air felt like plunging into a swimming pool. I recalled Johnny Weissmuller moving forcefully through the water, up and down the screen, in *Tarzan and His Mate*.

Then I saw Eddie. Standing at the corner, slouched under the lamppost in this tough-guy pose, he glanced over my shoulder, as if making sure I was alone.

"Eddie—are you waiting for me?"

"Got plans?"

"Aren't we seeing each other Tuesday?"

He flashed those dimples. "I wanted to see you tonight."

"It's close to midnight. My clothes are soaked, I stink of bleach—"

"I won't take you to a nightclub, Peaches. C'mon, take a walk with me. Not a cloud in the sky. I want to show you something, and it won't cost a dime. And when we're done, we'll come back here and I'll drive you uptown. Sound good?"

He seemed so eager and looked so handsome, I couldn't refuse. We walked about six blocks, heading south on Michigan to

Cermak. To my surprise, he pulled open the door of the Lexington Hotel and waved me in.

"You keep a room here or something?" I joked.

"Naw, but Al Capone did, a while ago. He practically lived here for a few years." When I didn't respond, he shrugged. "It impresses some folks. Anyhow, that's not why we came."

The lobby had wood-paneled walls and a handsome chandelier, a dozen lights hidden under tiny black shades. A putting green made of artificial grass took up the center of the lobby. Two men stood with golf clubs, shaking the ice in their glasses as they considered their putts. I felt out of place in my kitchen clothes, but no one gave me a second look.

We got onto the elevator. Eddie pressed the button for the tenth floor. Top story. Even the Lago Vista only had eight. Mirrors lined the three walls of the elevator car.

Was he taking me to a hotel room? The notion beat all. I'd never slept in a hotel before, much less done anything else. All the fatigue in my body suddenly disappeared.

"Your family has a contract here?"

"Working on it," he said.

When the elevator doors opened, he led me down a long corridor lit by elegant sconces. I'd delivered plenty of room service meals in hallways at the Lago Vista, but here the carpeting was thick, the wainscoting fresh-painted.

At the very end of the hall, Eddie pulled back the heavy brocade curtain at the window. "Take a gander," he said.

The Century of Progress exhibition spread out before us, heading north and south along the lakefront, lit up like a swirling map made of dazzling, colorful electric lights. The World's Fair buildings looked sleek and futuristic, like a kingdom you'd find on Neptune. Steel towers, a mammoth arena, and bridges that connected fairgoers to island attractions.

"Golly."

I'd seen black-and-white photos in the papers, but I hadn't appreciated how much ground the fair covered. From this height, I could take it all in at once. The most incredible view I'd ever seen.

"You said you haven't visited the fair yet," Eddie said, knocking his elbow against mine. "Up here, you can see it for free." He removed a handkerchief from his pocket, unfolding it to reveal black licorice chews and saltwater taffy in pink, orange, and blue. "Have one," he said.

I selected the orange taffy. It was soft and easy to chew, warm from being in his pocket.

He pointed out some of the fairground landmarks: the Time and Fortune Pavilion, the towering Hall of Science, the Chrysler Motors complex. End to end, the boulevards teemed with visitors, what looked like rivers of tiny people walking.

"It doesn't even look real," I said, "all lit up like that."

"That's because it's powered by starlight."

"How's that?"

"Honest, they used light from a star. Arcturus, one of the most powerful stars in the sky. Some scientists converted light from Arcturus into an electric current and sent it to the Adler Planetarium over there on Lake Shore Drive. Then they used that same current to light the opening of the fair last year."

"I don't follow."

He laughed. "Me neither. Here, have another taffy. It's your first visit to see the fair, after all."

I took the blue one. Peppermint.

The stuffy hallway smelled like my filthy work clothes and the citrus from Eddie's Brylcreem. As if reading my mind, he bent forward and lifted open the window high. All at once, we were bathed in fresh, cool air. I was glad when his arm circled my waist. The window was so high up, nobody could spot us. I never in my life expected to see a view this beautiful while standing with a fellow as handsome as Eddie.

"Lookit now, the lagoon." He pointed to the fountain, which had erupted suddenly into a burst of splashing colorful light, high arching plumes of green, red, amber, blue, and white. The center of the fountain resembled a glass bowl turned upside down, spilling over with water. Several cauldrons surrounding the fountain shot spectacular fiery-looking water high in the air. "That's the Fountain of Light. It's not something you get to see during the day. That fountain is like a secret the city keeps to itself. The tourist dopes miss out."

"I'm lucky to see it then."

He pulled away. "I'm not griping about tourists. Good for my pop's business. I recall what you said about the farm and your parents having hard times."

"My father is dead," I blurted. "He had an accident with a team of horses. So it's just my mother and me."

Eddie glanced back toward the elevator, as if to make sure the corridor was clear, and then grabbed my elbows and kissed me. He was taller by a few inches and stronger, someone who could take control of most any situation. Kissing him made me feel light-headed, and I didn't mind the feeling.

He pressed his nose against my ear. "Your pop got a bum deal. A man shouldn't die when he's only trying to provide for family."

"I'm not asking for sympathy. I was still a baby when it happened, so I'm used to it by now. I wanted to tell you the whole story, for some reason."

"I'm awful sorry about it."

And then we were kissing again, hands grasping at each other, breathing heavy. Our mouths tasted sweet like the taffy.

We stood at the window kissing for several minutes, until we heard the elevator bell. A family stepped out and filled the hallway with their voices and suitcases. Five children in all. They came running to look at the view, calling their parents to come see.

Eddie lowered the window quickly, and we beat it. In the elevator mirror, my lips looked red and swollen. The skin on my neck was blotchy. Outside, as we walked back toward the Lago Vista and his truck, we kept sneaking glances at each other, smiling and shaking our heads, as if neither of us could believe our dumb luck. Before that month, I hadn't kissed a single fellow, and now I was juggling two. *All part of the fun*, Raymond might have said.

On the ride back to Del's, Eddie rolled down his window and grinned at the oncoming traffic. "See? How much did that cost you?"

"Not one penny. I'm glad you came by tonight." I felt so happy, I squeezed his knee. "Can I ask a question?"

"I told you before, ask 'em all."

"I'm leaving town at the end of the month. I hope we can exchange letters. Could we do that?"

Now he looked almost bashful. "I'm no writer, Peaches."

"Nothing formal," I clarified. "I don't care about spelling mistakes, nothing like that."

He shifted in the seat, looking uncomfortable. "The thing about letters," he began. "My family might hassle me about exchanging letters with a fellow. Not to mention, something we put in a letter could get us into trouble—"

I stopped him. "We'd only write about general things. Work or school, or even about the weather. You can trust me. And we wouldn't write often, just every once in a while. Wouldn't that be swell? It's important for fellows like us to stay connected. We can look out for one another. Make sense?"

He drove for a while without answering.

"What? Tell me."

"Nothing," he said. When he smiled, I could tell it was forced. For once, I wished I truly could see inside a man's head.

We rode in silence most of the way uptown. I didn't understand his reluctance, but I didn't want to nag him. Still, the long stretch of quiet felt unbearable. I was relieved when we got to Del's building, and Eddie stopped at the curb. The sidewalks were empty under the lampposts.

"Listen, Peaches," he finally said. "I took a shine to you the first day I saw you. That's obvious, right? I feel like we're out of the same can. And I want to spend time with you. As much time as we can, before you go back home. We can have fun together."

"But you don't think we can write this fall? What's the problem?"

He gave me another weak smile. "We'll figure it out later, right? I'll see you here at noon on Tuesday. Like we planned."

I nodded. I wouldn't give up on him. The surprise trip to view the fair had been swell. I didn't want to spoil it now by acting greedy. "Tuesday."

"All right then."

I squeezed his knee and waited until I got a genuine smile from him, before getting out of the truck.

SEVENTEEN

"**B**LACK-EYED SUSANS WILL RUN ALONG HERE," Mrs. Kenrick said, pointing, on Saturday morning. "Coneflowers over there. We'll plant when we get home, so I can be here to water." She was dressed in a pair of men's trousers, the bottom cuffs folded up.

Raymond wore a pair of dark, stiff-looking dungarees, which he claimed made him look like a scarecrow. Meanwhile, my own shabby clothes had grown tight from all the shift meals and pie I'd eaten at the hotel. I prayed the seams wouldn't split.

The back garden was private but puny. It was remarkable to see rich people with so little land to show for it.

Mrs. Kenrick was handy with a pitchfork. Working together, we tore out an entire line of privet. Each time she used the pitchfork to overturn the roots, I grabbed hold of the branches and pulled them onto the canvas tarp. We left ugly trenches in our wake, which Mrs. Kenrick said would be filled with new grass or shrubs in no time.

"Oh, I can't tell you how happy this makes me, Charles. Already I feel accomplished, don't you?"

Raymond had been circling the yard uselessly with a rake, and I called him to help me tear out another two bushes near the back door, leaving another rectangle of overturned soil. Then we removed a fat evergreen shrub from under the kitchen window, exposing a smaller basement window, too. This pleased me, secretly, because it meant those windows could be seen by neighbors now and were therefore less useful for anyone who attempted to break in from the back of the house.

The day was a scorcher, and we didn't talk much. We'd been working over two hours when Mr. Kenrick came through the back door, bringing a glass of iced tea for his wife.

"Don't even look!" Mrs. Kenrick said. "We've made a mess of things."

His gaze moved from one ugly furrow to another without comment.

"Did you get to the bank?" Raymond asked.

"Yes." His clipped tone suggested he didn't care to discuss the topic.

"The garden will be shipshape in no time," I told him.

"I'm sure it will be."

"It's already beautiful," I added. "How fortunate to have private space right in the middle of the city."

My comment was meant to be cheerful, but for a long moment afterward, we heard nothing but the breeze in the elms at the back of the garden.

"Fortunate, Charles?" Mr. Kenrick said finally. "Is that the correct word for it?"

. . .

"I wonder if you mean lucky," he prodded.

Raymond stretched out his arms. "Look at us, Father, toiling out here like dirt farmers. We don't need a vocabulary lesson. How about some cold drinks for us, too?"

"I assure you, luck had nothing to do with it," Mr. Kenrick added. "I *earned* this. I didn't inherit my money. My father was a laborer. I went to college and worked hard. I still work hard."

Where was this coming from? I glanced toward Raymond, whose wide eyes told me not to pursue it.

"Oh, I needed this sweet tea," Mrs. Kenrick interrupted. "How considerate to bring it out, dear."

Mr. Kenrick's glare remained fixed on me. "You were saying?"

My neck felt suddenly itchy. "I only meant, I guess, that lots of people work hard and don't have a garden like this. Especially these days."

"You're saying I should feel guilty about it?"

"I only said it was fortunate. Honest, I didn't mean anything by it."

He hummed. "Sounds like you did."

Raymond stepped forward. "Father, please. That's not fair."

"You know, Charles, a man came to our church recently and said something that stuck with me. He claimed he'd read the New Testament cover to cover and could not find a single reference to Jesus Christ saying anything against a man making a profit—"

Raymond cut in loudly: "*Charles is helping us.* He didn't come for a lecture."

The silence was unbearably tense. I felt like I'd been dragged into the principal's office without knowing what I'd done wrong. With no answers or directions, I took the rake and began smoothing over the dirt nearest me.

"I believe I *will* get you boys some cold tea," Mrs. Kenrick said, and she led her husband back into the house.

I waited a moment for Raymond to explain. When he didn't even try, I grabbed the evergreen shrub by the base of its rough trunk and dragged it down the sidewalk past the garage to the alley. When I came back, I lingered near Raymond. I'd never seen him look so downtrodden, his mouth shut tight, eyes staring across the yard.

"I'm sorry I upset your father."

"No, the old man's temper has nothing to do with you."

"So what's he so steamed about?"

"Me, of course." He fanned his face with his hat. "The steam is usually about me."

"But about what?"

He sighed. "It's a long story, one I wish I didn't have to tell you. But I should."

"So tell me."

"Oh, Charles," he murmured. "Something terrible has happened. The worst possible thing."

"What?"

He wiped his brow with his forearm. When he spoke again, he faced the garage. "Not here, where he can see us talking."

"Who—your father?"

He nodded.

"Let's take a walk then. I've got time."

"No, it's not smart. I should go inside now, and you should beat it, please. Take the alley, and I'll explain to Mother. Meet me tomorrow?"

"Yes, I want to see you before you leave for Canada. But Ray, are you okay?"

He was the picture of misery, but he only nodded again. "Lunch then, tomorrow. Do you know the Ranch? It's on Oak Street, just across from the Drake. I'll meet you there after Mass. Say, twelve thirty? I promise, I'll tell you everything."

✳✳✳

I hoped that when I saw Raymond for lunch, I would be carrying the winnings from Jackson's policy game in my wallet. A story like that would lift anyone's spirits. I didn't want our last day together to be unhappy.

But when I saw Jackson in the kitchen later, bent over a tray of strawberry-rhubarb tarts, he only shrugged and shook his head. "Told you it wasn't reliable, Joe."

"Worth the risk," I said. "We need to keep playing, in case it's our turn to be lucky."

Grinning, he broke off a corner of one of the tarts and slid the plate toward me.

EIGHTEEN

THE RANCH DIDN'T SEEM LIKE RAYMOND'S TYPICAL KIND OF PLACE. Western decor, with a wood-beamed ceiling and heavy dark furniture. Two imposing longhorn mounts dominated the wall behind the bar; the men serving drinks wore cowboy hats and leather vests. The interior was so dim, it took me several seconds to see Raymond waving from a back-corner booth.

"*Bonjour, mon ami.*" I slid into the seat across from him. Now that the classes were over, French felt like something we shared in common, our own language.

He was leaving for Canada the next day. The mood was somber, even after we ordered. "This was a mistake," he said. "I can't find my appetite."

"Ray, what did I say to offend your father yesterday?"

"No, no—I already told you, it's between him and me."

"What happened? You promised you'd tell."

"Yes, but I couldn't yesterday. Couldn't risk my father watching out the window. It's a story I've dreaded telling, but you need to know. For your own safety."

I did not see how my own safety figured in to it, unless he'd lost his mind completely and told someone about us. About me. "Go on."

"Turns out my wallet got stolen the night we went to Vi's Little Grapevine. Probably when I was chatting at the bar. You remember all the people squeezed into the place."

"That's why your father was upset? He found out about the money you lost? Or about us going to Vi's?"

"We haven't even discussed the money. No, listen. On Friday afternoon, a stranger appeared on our doorstep, asking to speak to Father. Mother and Millie were upstairs packing. I'm grateful for that—"

The waiter arrived then with the fried chicken lunch platters, piled high with golden drumsticks and thighs, mashed potatoes, and slaw. I dug in, but Raymond only frowned.

"Who came to see you?" I asked.

He pushed his plate to the side. "A man I never saw before, this skinny little punk. He didn't give his name. He told Father he knew *all about* me. 'Your pansy son.' Said he had my wallet and evidence. Threatened to tell everyone we knew if we didn't pay up. This punk stood on our doorstep, presenting an extortion plot with utter calm, as if he's done it a hundred times. Probably has. He explained exactly how much money Father needed to pay him."

So this explained why Mr. Kenrick had been so rude in the garden. Did he assume I was the same as his son? That I had corrupted him? Would he try to contact my family? I lost my appetite, too. "So your dad paid him?"

"There wasn't enough cash at the house. The man said he'd come back and Father needed to be ready. I'm telling you, this punk was too scrawny to take seriously. It would have been hilarious if it weren't so frightening."

"Did you call the cops?"

"Charles, please. This is Chicago. The crooked police would extort us *themselves* if they had the same information. You saw how they taunted us at the Up-and-Up. No, Father just needed to pay and be done with it. He told the man to come back yesterday, at exactly four o'clock, when Mother and Millie would be at the hair salon. Sure enough, the man returned at four, Father paid him, and he left."

My heart was pounding. "How awful, Ray."

He nibbled at the chicken, finally, but didn't seem to enjoy it. "Now it's done."

"I don't understand. You had the fake passport—"

"But I had my wallet, too, with my school ID and my library card. That's how that goon got my true name. Any flunky can find a person's street address."

Considering how difficult it had been for me to get all the addresses in the French class, this remark cut a bit.

"Why didn't you tell me your wallet had been taken at Vi's?"

"Before Friday, I didn't know how I'd lost it. I hoped I'd misplaced it at home."

"You said the man had evidence. What kind?"

Raymond lifted his hands to hide his face, embarrassed. "Never mind that."

"Tell me."

"It's so *ridiculous*. One of the boys I spoke to at the bar that night—a kid named Rick—slipped me his name and number. I didn't give him the time of day, because I was eager to get back to you with the drinks."

"It's fine, Ray. All part of the fun—"

"No, listen, I didn't give him a second thought. But that note was in my wallet."

"Why was a name and telephone number *evidence*? It's the kind of thing anybody might have on them."

"Not exactly." He leaned forward to whisper, "Under where he'd penciled his name and number, Rick made a charming little drawing for me. Two silly stick figures. Anatomically complete."

"Oh my."

"It struck me as funny then, but now it's humiliating. My father is avoiding me. That train ride to Canada will be *endless,* neither of us saying a word. Pretending none of it happened."

"Give it time," I said. "It'll be okay."

Even I heard the hollowness of those words. Things would never be the same again between Raymond and his father.

"I won't tell him about you," he promised. "He thinks we're just pals."

I nodded gratefully.

With a sigh, he reached for another drumstick. "I feel better, honestly, now that I've told you. We've both learned something. We have to watch ourselves in those places, look out for each other. Another reason I'll miss you when I get back."

I glanced at the big clock hanging between the longhorn mounts. Already past one. I hoped we'd have a little time, at least, to fool around at Raymond's house before I raced back and changed for work. "Ray, we need to finish up here quickly. I'm due some-where by three."

"Really? But I hoped you'd spend the day with me. Help me pack for Canada."

"I can't. I'm sorry."

"What's with you? Why are you never free to spend time together?"

"How can you say that? We've seen each other nearly every day."

"I mean in the evenings. We went to Vi's, and to the pictures last week after the Up-and-Up, but those are the only two times. We never went to Riverview amusement park. And I wanted to take you to the World's Fair. You've been here all these weeks and we never saw Sally Rand's scandalous act."

I waved for the waiter to bring the bill. "You have other friends."

Concern darkened his face like a cloud. "You've been keeping something from me, too. I've suspected all along. Have you met a girl?"

At first, I didn't speak. I didn't want to tell another lie. More urgently, I didn't want to say good-bye. I knew we wouldn't be able to write after the summer, but was it possible I could see him again, even for a short time, after he returned from Canada? It felt worth the risk. But I needed to start with some kernel of truth.

"The fact is, Ray, I've found a job. It's temporary, but it's why you hardly ever see me in the evenings."

"A job?" He squinted, as if trying to understand. "That's all—a job? Please don't look so crestfallen. You've taken a job. I mean, so what?"

"You don't care?"

"Honestly, it's another feather in your cap. My whole family knows you're not a lightweight, the way you rolled up your sleeves and helped in the garden yesterday."

"Gee, that's a relief."

"An *evening job*," he marveled. "At one of the theaters?"

"No, a hotel. An old hotel you've probably never heard of. South of the Loop, off Michigan Avenue."

He looked as if I'd said something sordid. "Well, now I feel sort of silly. What are you doing in a hotel? Are you"—he gestured with his hands, as if grasping for options—"a *concierge* of some kind? Do you work the front desk? I know you don't play in the orchestra."

He didn't need to know about the peeling or dishwashing. "I'm a waiter," I said. "I serve hundreds of identical meals to guests in the ballroom. Parties, weddings, a different event every night. Anyhow, that's why we don't see each other as often as I'd like."

Our own waiter had finally brought the bill. I took a buck ten out of my pocket and set it on the table.

Raymond sat quietly for a long time, staring at the money.

"But I don't understand," he said. "Why have you taken a job, when you'll be sailing to Europe next week? You can't expect whatever wages you earn in this hotel to make a big difference when you're in France."

"That's the thing, Ray. And I feel lousy about not being truthful. I'm not going to Europe this summer. I was never going to Europe."

At this, his shoulders drooped forward, almost comically. "But the French class?"

I couldn't tell him the true story. I never could. "I'm from a farm town, remember, where we don't have courses like that. Courses people can take for fun. When I saw the sign posted at the church, I signed up on a whim. It sounded like something I could do this summer to improve myself." In a way, this part was true. The money I earned from the class would improve things for me considerably.

He pressed his hands against his cheeks and stared at the table, as if in complete shock.

"I apologize for lying. I understand if you're angry." I braced myself, in case he jumped to his feet and stormed out.

Instead, he lifted his eyes and smiled. "On the contrary. It's a *relief!* If you're not going to Europe, I hope it means we can spend time together when I get back from Canada."

"I hope so. I'm relieved, too. I felt foolish lying about it."

"It's simply the best news I've heard in ages. The truth is, your job and you taking these classes to improve yourself are only more things to admire about you. Not to mention your foxy secret-keeping skills!"

I laughed. "I'm glad. Come on, we should get moving or I'll be late for work and lose that job you admire so much."

Leaving the restaurant, as we walked north on Lake Shore Drive, I was flying high and feeling free. Now I wouldn't need to make up excuses and he wouldn't take it personally whenever I had to rush off.

We turned on Division, then walked along Astor Street, admiring the fine old townhouses. Many looked neglected, a few beyond saving, but because of my mood, I saw new potential in all of them. "Maybe someday," I said, "our pansy syndicate will take over an entire block somewhere. We'll all be neighbors and throw excellent parties on weekends, and we'll come and go as we like."

"That's only fantasizing," Raymond answered. "I expect we'll keep things safe behind closed doors. Having a wife will help."

I knocked against him, still giddy. "A wife? Raymond, you never told me. Congratulations!"

He looked serious. "I won't marry any time soon. But every man should have children, don't you think? Father swears he won't do business with a man without any children."

"Yes, but I've been thinking lately," I said, "that fellows like us probably shouldn't marry."

"Of course we will. Someone, say, like Miss Feeney from the French class. Don't you admire the way she dresses? She's no Mae West, but I think she's flossy."

I stopped walking. "Stop joking for one minute. You shouldn't marry Miss Feeney or any other girl."

"Of course I will. And so will you. Maybe even the sweetheart you told me about. The one you bragged looks like Billie Dove."

"I didn't *brag* about her. I was only answering your question."

"I shouldn't speak for you, Charles. But I intend to be married. It's what's expected, and it will keep us safe from those rumors we'll need to avoid."

Frustration welled in my chest. "Yes, it's expected for both of us. But I mean . . ." I started to walk again, but struggled to articulate, with care, what seemed so obvious. "My feeling is . . . given our character, Raymond . . . our desires . . ."

He glared as if I'd said something I shouldn't.

How could I explain it? I'd never said any of this out loud before, although I'd been thinking about it. "Before I came to Chicago, I didn't know how I would manage it all. A traditional life, with a marriage and family. But now I see we need to invent our own path. Maybe in another place, or another part of the country. We could find work in Florida or California. Buy a house, make a life. Create a community with other fellows like us. Can you imagine something like that?"

He only grimaced. "Florida? Have you been there? So much of it is swampland, and you spend all summer sweating like a racehorse—"

"*Stop, please,*" I interrupted. "Forget I mentioned Florida. We could live anywhere. We could go to a place where nobody knows us. My point is that it's up to us to figure it all out."

"You talk as if I could give up everything I have here. Family support, business connections. That would be—not only impractical, but reckless."

"Compared to you," I admitted, "I have less to lose if I leave the Midwest—"

"My whole future is here."

"But I'm asking you to consider a different future. You and me, we shouldn't go along with what's *expected.* Can't you see that? For either of us, a marriage would be a terrible mistake. It would be dishonest, and cruel to both parties involved."

He stopped walking, looking exasperated. "Listen, you'll do what you want. I am speaking from the heart now, with total sincerity. I don't have a choice."

"But, Ray, you do! Why choose a life that makes you the perfect target for the kind of dirty business that happened this week?"

He recoiled, as if my words had stung him like a bee. "If you enjoy arguing so much or making judgments about people, maybe you should have lunch with other friends."

"Ray, don't—"

"I need to go home and pack," he added. "Alone."

"Really?"

We'd reached an intersection. We had so much more to talk about. Depending on how things went with Heinz, I might never see Raymond again.

"I apologize, Ray. I wasn't judging you. I only wanted—"

"Didn't you say you needed to rush off to your hotel job?"

I stood there, feeling helpless. We'd made no plans to see each other upon his return. "Have fun in Canada. Good luck with your dad—"

"So long!" he said with false cheer. He turned and walked in the opposite direction.

My stomach was churning, not because of the greasy chicken. First there was Raymond's terrifying story, then my confession, and now this abrupt good-bye. I hated to leave things like this.

I'd been arguing with myself, I realized, as much as with Raymond. Why did I continue to devote so much energy and worry to preserving a life that was expected for me rather than for a life I truly wanted?

The long road that lay ahead had always felt like a mystery, even dark, but my time in Chicago had provided two clear signposts: My future could not be on the farm. My life could not include a wife.

Back at the apartment, Bernie was waiting, ready for work. I changed clothes and then asked him for a sheet of writing paper and an envelope.

"What for? You sending the rest of the cash home?" he asked.

"Nope. Give me ten minutes."

Before I could lose my nerve, I sat down and wrote Mary Toomey a long-overdue letter.

NINETEEN

I KEPT THE LETTER BRIEF.

Something unexpected has happened, I wrote. *Something wonderful. I've met new people.* I spared Mary the details. *The important thing,* I explained, *is that this time apart has shined a light on our time together.* I explained how it wasn't right for *people like us* to make *sweet-sounding promises* to each other or anyone, and that I would hold her *in highest esteem* for as long as I lived. I reminded her of our *mutual respect as we remained friends forever.* I signed the letter using the affectionate nickname she'd given me: *Always-a-Gentleman Joe.*

I didn't explain a word of it to Bernie. He wouldn't understand.

On our way to the Lago Vista, we passed three corner mailboxes before I found the courage to drop the envelope into the fourth. I felt proud and excited, even a little afraid. But it was the right thing to do, a kindness to her and a kindness to me. And then it was done.

Hannigan declared it "too goddamn hot" to use the kitchen ovens, especially for a Sunday, so he set up charcoal grills in the alley.

He and his sweaty crew stood in a smoky line, icy towels from the freezer draped around their necks.

I stayed inside, plating tomato aspic onto beds of lettuce. The aspic had to be cut from large tin molds. The upside was carrying the ice-cold tins from the cooler to the prep table.

I hoped keeping busy would take my mind off Raymond, but it didn't. On one hand, I felt relieved to have told him about the job and pleased that he had responded so favorably. It felt like a wall between us coming down. Still, his remark about getting married was only another example of how different our lives were and always would be.

I carried a tray of salads back to the cooler, where Jackson was pulling out sheets of chocolate cake.

"We got that anniversary party up in the ballroom, Joe. Need your help getting this onto plates."

I was only halfway through the aspic, but the ballroom was air-cooled. Nodding, I swapped my soiled apron for a clean one.

Jackson put on his white jacket, gloves, and toque, as he did whenever he went upstairs. We loaded pastry carts with the chocolate cake and raspberry glaze, one of the hotel's signature desserts. The sweet fragrance filled the elevator.

On the third floor, we pushed the carts to the Empress Ballroom. The air temperature dropped twenty degrees. The guests filled a dozen round tables, as big as some weddings. At one end of the ballroom, we found two tables set with rows of dessert plates.

Holding a tray for Jackson, I whispered, "When are you playing policy again?"

He set the slices on the plates one by one. "Not for a few days."

"Whenever you play, count me in."

"I've got a little problem, Joe."

I thought he meant with the cake. "Need me to run to the kitchen?"

"Not that kind of problem." He turned his head, as if to make sure no servers were giving us the ear. "I've got this lady friend, Gertrude. Nearly three years for us already."

I had no idea where he was going with this. Already I was out of my depths.

He slid an empty tray onto the cart. "I'm nearly twenty-two, see? High time I settle down and get married. And Gertrude's the best that ever was."

"Married? That's swell, Jackson."

"Swell? I've got to make some coin. Gertrude and me need to get hitched quick."

One of the waitresses shot us a glance to lower our voices.

"Where's the fire?" I asked.

"She's tired of waiting. Three years means more to a lady than it does to us, see? Trouble is, if we don't do it next month, when the bookings are slow and I can get away, we'll have to wait until *next* August. Gertrude says she won't wait that long. She says she'll go back home to her folks."

"That's no good."

"We both want to get married, but I haven't got the cash for a nice ring or the honeymoon. And it's the *only* reason I'm playing."

"Couldn't you do something more certain? Paint houses maybe? Or cut grass for rich people?"

His eyes looked desperate. "You got a mower I can use?

Thought you understood. You and I both need money fast. I won't let Gertrude down. Not after three years. I can't."

I felt bad for him. Clearly he was nuts for this Gertrude. Plus, Jackson couldn't bear the idea of things not working out for anyone. He only liked happy endings. In this sense, he was the polar opposite of Del.

Given my quarrel with Raymond and the letter I'd sent to Mary, I felt ill prepared to weigh in on matters of the heart.

Our task finished, we pushed the dessert carts back to the service elevator. There were a few slices of cake left, but Jackson seemed too miserable for me to raise the subject of digging in.

"Wish I could help—"

He waved his hand to stop me. "It's fine, Joe. You're too young to know what I'm talking about. Hell, you've probably never even *been* in love."

The remark hung in the air between us like a challenge.

"Well, have you?"

All I could picture was Raymond and how lousy I felt about how we'd left things.

"You *have*!" he said, pointing. "I can see it in your eyes."

"If you see anything in my eyes, it's only the blues at your policy wheel not paying out. Like I told you, I want in again."

I reached into my pocket and handed him two more dollars. When the elevator doors opened, I grabbed my apron and returned to my aspics and orange gelatins.

I could hear Hannigan holding court at the grills in the alley. Bernie passed through the kitchen on his way to the washroom, paused at my counter, and belched like a cow on corn.

Assembling more cold salads, I wondered if Jackson had come closer to the truth than either of us realized. I'd never had a better friend than Raymond. He would leave for Canada in the morning. To have any hope of seeing him upon his return, I couldn't let our last memory be an argument.

TWENTY

BERNIE WAITED UNDER THE ELEVATED TRACKS ON WABASH while I stopped at a cigar store to use the payphone on the back wall. I dialed the number at the Kenricks'. No one picked up. I needed to see him anyway.

Outside, clouds blanketed the sky and the air smelled like coming rain. Heat lightning flickered in the distance, as Bernie and I walked along Wabash, then cut over to Michigan Avenue past the river. The beacon light atop the Palmolive Building guided our way.

When I told Bernie I needed to stop over and see Raymond, he said, "At this hour? Look at you now, kid, staying up late with the grown-ups."

I couldn't explain without telling another story made up mostly of lies, so I didn't even try. Soon enough, at the old water tower, my cousin peeled off onto a side street toward Del's, and I continued north by myself.

For several blocks, I debated the judgment of ringing anyone's doorbell at this late hour on a Sunday, especially at a residence dealing with the tension Raymond had described. I talked myself out of it, then opted to let fortune decide. Maybe Raymond would be gazing out the front window when I came down the street. Better yet, sitting on the front steps smoking, as if waiting for me, so we could talk and make up.

State Parkway was as quiet as I'd ever seen it, nearly every house dark and nobody on the street. At Raymond's, the porch light was turned off. The living room drapes were drawn, but lamplight showed through the cracks. Someone was awake.

I climbed the steps, intending to give a soft knock, when I heard the unpleasant crunch of glass under my shoe. Looking down, I saw the glint of shards strewn across the step. Not many. But then I looked up again and noticed all the glass missing from the narrow window to the side of the door. Moreover, the door itself stood very slightly ajar.

I froze. The house had been burgled.

Raymond and his father hadn't left town yet.

Had we given Heinz the wrong date? No, I was certain I'd been clear: Mrs. Kenrick and Millicent were leaving Sunday, the fellows on Monday. Why would they rush the job when they had a whole week?

I waited on the step, listening to the sound of men's voices inside. All I could make out was the tone, angry and sharp.

It was one thing to have passed on information for a burglary, but another to think I might be responsible for Raymond or Mr. Kenrick assaulted, tied up. Or worse.

Like a fool, I pushed open the door and went in. Broken glass littered the floor in the hallway, announcing every step I took.

Mr. Kenrick hollered from the living room, *"Stop right there!"*

"It's only me! *Charles.*"

I stepped out of the shadows, so they could see.

In the big room, only one table lamp was turned on. It looked as if Agnes had quit in the middle of cleaning. Nearly all the tables and chairs had been pushed to the walls. The Persian carpet was rolled up in the far corner. A Chicago telephone book sat on the floor in front of a chair, like a child-size footstool. The white porcelain dog had been removed from the table at the front window, but I didn't see it anywhere.

Raymond gasped at the sight of me. His whole appearance was disheveled: face flushed, hair a wreck, shirttail hanging out. His cheeks were shiny with sweat, as if he'd been moving the furniture. Or fighting a prowler.

Mr. Kenrick held a cocktail glass near his chest. At this hour, on a Sunday night, I hadn't expected him to be awake, much less having a drink. Like Raymond, his clothes were unruly, shirt unbuttoned and hanging open.

"I saw the broken glass," I said. "Have you been robbed?"

Raymond shook his head, but he looked like he might cry.

"Are you both all right?"

"We're fine now, Charles," Mr. Kenrick said. "But you should go."

Fleetingly, I wondered if their argument had turned physical.

"Raymond, I hoped we could talk."

"No, no—it's too late. Can't you see?" My friend's voice sounded so agitated, it felt like meeting a stranger. Did he really not want to see me again? It wasn't clear if he was upset about our argument or that I'd been lying about the job and the trip. I only needed to explain.

"Sorry about the time," I said. "I called a short while ago, but nobody answered."

For five seconds, nobody moved. The tension in the room felt palpable.

Then Raymond's face softened and he moved closer. "Charles, listen—"

"I'll push off," I said. "Ray, we'll talk when you get back from your trip."

He reached for my arm. "The thing is," he continued, "you have arrived at a spectacularly bad time. Something *horrible* has happened. Tonight a man—"

His father interrupted. "Raymond, let me tell it. Charles, I need you to brace yourself. You're old enough for me to say this directly. Tonight, in our home, a man shot himself. I'm sorry to put it to you straight like that, but it's the truth. He died here in this room."

The sound of Raymond's breathing increased, and he sank into a velvet armchair, crumpled like a flower. He was crying.

I stared all around, unsure how to respond. The room felt very hot with the windows closed. Now the disarray made some sense, at least.

"How . . . how awful," I managed.

Mr. Kenrick nodded. "I'm only grateful my wife and daughter left for Canada earlier. We can't let them know."

"Who was he?" I asked him.

"Stanley Marks. He worked under me at the Mercantile Exchange for nearly two years. Last fall, he tried to embezzle from us, and I let him go. I should have called the police when I had the chance, except he hadn't been successful and I was too soft to want to punish him further."

"The police?" Raymond cried. "Yes, *if only.* You should have called them when you had the chance."

Mr. Kenrick spoke with utter calm, almost from a distance. "Marks didn't give me the slightest trouble when I fired him. Seemed embarrassed more than anything else. I assumed he left the city with his tail between his legs and started over somewhere else. But then he showed up on our doorstep tonight with a head full of booze. When I wouldn't open the door to him, he broke the window and forced himself in. Said he wanted me to see what a ruin his life had become. As if he blamed me for his misfortunes. He stormed around the room, ranting like a lunatic, waving a gun. He only stopped when Raymond came downstairs."

"I'll never forget it," Raymond whimpered, a balled fist pressing between his eyes. "The blood—*everywhere.*"

Mr. Kenrick set his drink on a table, where I noticed an expensive-looking Kodak camera and a pair of diamond-and-pearl earrings. The sight conjured a bizarre image in my head: Stanley Marks posing for a photograph before removing his earrings and taking the gun from his jacket.

"The cops came already?" I asked.

For a long moment, I heard nothing but the ice settling in Mr. Kenrick's glass.

"Charles, the man's goal was to punish me. He promised he'd put my name in the papers with this action tonight. He tried to hand me a scandal. I'll be damned if I take it from him."

"But what did the cops say?"

Raymond got back to his feet. "Don't you see? We didn't phone the police. We couldn't."

"As I said," Mr. Kenrick went on, his voice still calm, "there are other factors to consider. In families like ours, a story like this can't leave the house. You understand that, surely. We must take care of it ourselves."

I should have been flattered by the way he included me in "families like ours," but I wasn't. The whole situation seemed unreal.

Before I could ask, *Where is the body?* Raymond took me by the arm and pulled me across the room, the bare floor groaning underfoot. He pointed at the long rolled-up Persian carpet. It looked like a monstrous brown snake that had swallowed the biggest catch of its life.

We both stared, Raymond's hand still resting on my arm.

I always found it difficult to tell when someone was lying, but had less trouble knowing when two people were. None of this added up. Especially given the story Raymond had already told me about the extortion plot. And those diamond-and-pearl earrings on the table. Anyone would put those away before traveling.

"Where's Agnes?" I asked.

"It's her night off." Again, Raymond addressed his father. "My god, we haven't even talked about how lucky that is."

Mr. Kenrick shrugged. "We'd have handled it. I would've given her a stiff drink and enough money to keep her mouth shut. She would've understood."

Would I be given cash, too, to keep my mouth shut? Mr. Kenrick probably felt I'd be offended by an offer like that. Maybe families like the Kenricks helped each other when they got into scrapes. Whenever needed. No questions asked.

I glanced again at the carpet, wondering which part of the story was a lie. Was Agnes herself inside the carpet? Raymond had once mentioned his father's philandering. In an instant, my mind leapt to a scenario in which Raymond's mother had caught her husband and Agnes in a cozy position, and Mrs. Kenrick had reached impulsively for a gun. Was she, even now, listening from the top of the staircase?

Or what if someone from Heinz's crew had removed the camera and earrings from upstairs and got caught red-handed on the way out?

"We need to move quickly," Mr. Kenrick announced. "We'll take the body somewhere far away, and—and we'll dump it."

"Dump it?" I repeated. "But when someone finds him, and his death is discovered, what then?"

Mr. Kenrick waved this threat away. "It's been a year since I've had anything to do with Stanley Marks."

"He may have told someone he was coming here," I said. "Like his wife?"

"He wasn't married," Mr. Kenrick said. "No wife, no children. He was a lone wolf. If the police identify his body, they'll assume Marks got mixed up in some nasty business that has nothing to do with my office or me."

"But—"

"Charles, I owe Stanley Marks nothing. He's the one who tried to cheat my office. He chose to come here tonight to end his life."

All I could think was that this shocking turn of events made my own crooked scheme with Heinz feel small, almost child's play.

"I need to leave," I said. "Right now."

Raymond clutched my shoulder with strength that surprised me, considering his tears and trembling earlier. "Wait, don't go, please. We need your help. Agnes will be back soon. Even if she's soused, she'll notice . . . all this."

"Raymond can't carry the carpet by himself," Mr. Kenrick said. "And I need to clean up this mess before Agnes returns. We'd been wondering who we could call—"

"And then *you* arrived," Raymond interrupted, taking my hands. "To save us."

I shook away his grip. Nausea had crept into my throat. "Are you serious when you say you're not going to tell the police about this? Never?"

"We've already told you," Mr. Kenrick said sharply. "The police would either sell the story to the papers for a handful of cash, or they'd shake us down for even more. We're men, aren't we? We can take care of this."

"Wait," I said, unsure how to express what seemed so obvious. "I mean, for one thing, won't Mrs. Kenrick notice the carpet's missing?"

"She will," Raymond said. "We'll tell her we purchased a new rug to surprise her."

His father nodded. "First thing in the morning, I'll order a new carpet from Field's. We'll have the front window repaired. Those aren't things to worry about now."

They both made it sound so simple, inventing it as they went along.

"So if I help you get the carpet outside and into the car, that's it? Then I may go?"

Raymond gave me a pleading look. "Can you drive an automobile?"

I didn't answer. I was still trying to make sense of it all. My choices over the past weeks flashed before my eyes, like stepping stones across a creek. All I'd done was take a French class. Played

155

a game of pretend. Made a new pal. Now I realized with a kind of horror who Charles Powell really was: someone who got involved in messes like this. I'd thought I had it all figured out, but I was never prepared to take it this far.

I needed to speak honestly for once, as Joe Garbe: "I've only driven tractors. And we have a '27 Chevy dump truck on the farm."

"Only a different breed of horse," Mr. Kenrick said. "Let me get some rags."

When he was gone, I said, "Ray, wait. None of this is right."

"I know, I know," Raymond murmured, crouching down at one end of the carpet. "It's like some terrible dream."

"But we can't—"

"*Charles, please,*" he cried. "We'll talk later."

"Ray—"

"Can't you see? I can't do this alone."

"Yes, but—"

"I am begging you now. *Please help me.*"

I never saw a more pitiful or frightened expression on a human face.

Kneeling, I picked up my side of the rug. It must have weighed nearly two hundred pounds. We had to carry it five feet at a time, in short bursts of energy. I couldn't believe Raymond could lift his side at all. Mr. Kenrick reappeared with a handful of rags, mopping up blood from the floor. I thought I'd be sick.

We struggled to get the carpet down the service stairs to the mudroom and the back entrance.

"Hurry up, boys," Mr. Kenrick said. "Agnes may be home at any moment."

"*Shut off the yard lights!*" Raymond hissed from the door.

Mr. Kenrick hit the switch, plunging the garden into darkness. "This next bit needs to go quickly," he warned.

In fewer than sixty seconds, Raymond and I half-carried, half-dragged the carpet roll across the muddy lawn, all the while staring up at the window curtains of the neighboring houses. The moon was still hiding behind clouds.

Inside the garage, Mr. Kenrick turned on a bulb that dangled from a ceiling cord. The family owned a dark blue Packard convertible. In an impressively fluid movement, Mr. Kenrick pulled down the top so that Raymond and I could wrestle the carpet into the back seat more easily. Then we raised the top again and locked it into place.

Raymond and I stood for a minute, catching our breath. My clothes were soaked with blood and sweat.

"Now where?" Raymond asked his father. "A lagoon, or what?"

"Too shallow," he said. "Same goes for the beach. You'll drop it in the river."

"Not the Loop," I argued. "There's traffic at all hours."

"No, west of here," he said. "The north branch. Use the bridge at Fullerton. Better yet, the old steel bridge off Clybourn. You'll turn left on a little street called Cortland. Do you recall where that is, Ray?"

His son nodded woozily.

"Good. At this hour, no cars will be anywhere near there."

"Shouldn't we wait until later?" I asked. "Until there's no chance of seeing *anyone*?"

"It's plenty late, Charles," Mr. Kenrick said. "You don't want to be the only car on the street. That attracts the wrong kind of attention."

I pointed at the license plate. "What about the numbers?"

The dark brown plate showed the yellow numbers as 8916.

"Mud," I said. I went and grabbed handfuls of dirt from the garden where we'd worked only the day before. Astonishingly, my mouth could form spit. While they stood watching, I applied quick dabs onto the numbers so that they now read 3316. The plate wouldn't fool anybody who gave it a second look.

"Wipe some on the fender, too," Mr. Kenrick said. "Front and back. Make it messy, as if you've driven through the woods or somewhere rough."

Like a servant used to performing outrageous tasks, I went back to the garden and returned with more dirt. I spat again and smeared the mud generously on the fenders and tires.

"It'll do," Mr. Kenrick said, handing me an oil rag from the shelf to clean my trembling hands. "There won't be much traffic at this hour anyway. Let's pray you don't cross paths with a patrol car."

He cracked the barn-style garage door to make sure the alley was clear, before pushing it open wide. "I'll be waiting here when you get back, with a well-deserved drink for each of you. God knows you've earned it."

Raymond already had climbed in from the passenger side, so I slid behind the wheel. I tried to make sense of the controls and the dashboard. It all felt strange and wrong. For starters, the steering wheel had been outfitted with a rubber knob to accommodate Mr. Kenrick driving one-handed.

"You really can't drive?" I asked Raymond again.

"Will you look at me shaking? I'm in a terrible state. Even if I knew how, I'd steer us into a lamppost."

I told myself that the sooner we got going, the sooner I'd be back at Del's, and I could put this nightmare behind me forever.

I pumped the accelerator once and pressed the starter. The engine howled, as if awakening. Compared to our dump truck at home, it sounded like music.

"Twist the steering wheel all the way to the left," Mr. Kenrick said. "It needs to be turned all the way to get the car out."

I backed the automobile slowly into the lumpy brick alley, turning sharply so I didn't hit the telephone pole on the opposite side. Then I shifted forward.

"Good work, Charles," Mr. Kenrick said. "Slouch low, Raymond, so your face can't be seen."

Raymond slid down on the seat, his knees pressing against the glove box. At the end of the alley, he told me to turn left onto the street, but I only went half a block before I pressed the brake.

"This is a terrible idea, Ray. Not just terrible, it's criminal. We need to drive straight to the hospital and explain what's happened. Go get your dad."

Lifting his filthy hands to his face, Raymond began to sob again.

I'd lost patience but spoke gently: "Listen now, the longer we wait, the worse it will be. Where's the closest hospital? We'll take the body there. The hospital staff won't be able to save him, but maybe they can make things right with the cops."

"*But we can't,*" he cried. He breathed deeply again, hands still covering his face. A sustained cry prevented him from speaking.

"Why not? Spit it out. You've pulled me into this mess. Have the decency to tell me what's going on."

He lowered his hands. His eyes were red from the tears. "It's not Stanley Marks in that carpet at all."

TWENTY-ONE

"**T**HE LAST TWO HOURS HAVE BEEN AN ABSOLUTE HORROR," Raymond said, through more tears.

"But what happened? Pull yourself together and tell me."

He pressed his hand against his chest, as if it would slow his racing heart. "Drive and I'll tell you. You've got to trust me now, Charles. Drive forward, please, and turn left at North Boulevard. You'll go right at Clark Street soon after."

I lifted my foot from the brake. "Okay, we're moving. Tell me everything. The little punk came back, didn't he?"

He nodded. "I hoped the whole thing was behind us. But late tonight, he came back, soused and slurring his words. And demanding even *more* money. Father reminded him that he'd already paid, and it was the very last dollar he'd get from us. He slammed the door in his face."

"He didn't leave?"

"No, he just stood there in his drunken daze. But then I did something very stupid. I grabbed our camera and took the man's picture through the window. It wasn't planned. The camera was simply sitting out, ready for the trip. But the gesture only enraged the thug. He broke the window with his fist and forced himself in. Charles, it was terrifying!"

"So your dad *shot* him? Or you did?"

"No, it's difficult to explain . . ."

"You better try. Practice for when you tell it in front of a jury."

"The man attacked Father in the living room, pulling him to the carpet, hands around his neck. It wasn't a fair fight, so I rushed to help. All three of us rolling around, our teeth bared like wolves. I couldn't believe how strong he was, given his size and the smell of whiskey on him. I'll be covered in bruises tomorrow. All I could think was, *This lunatic is about to kill my father, or me.* That's when the phone rang—it must have been you!"

"So what happened?"

"Finally, I broke free and grabbed the Staffordshire dog from the table near the window. I threw it but missed, and it broke in big pieces on the carpet. So I ran to the hall and grabbed the heaviest thing I could find. The telephone book. I aimed for his face. I didn't miss that time." He looked up, suddenly alert. "Turn here, left onto Armitage."

"And that . . . killed him?"

"No, it only stunned him but long enough for Father to pull free and roll away. Unbelievably, the man scrambled to his feet. Swaying back and forth as if he couldn't decide which of us to take on. He lunged toward *me,* but Father tackled him from behind and they went down together. We were determined to hold him this time, arms behind his back, his face to the floor. For a while he struggled, gasping and gurgling. That's the most sickening part . . ."

"One of you was choking him?"

He shuddered visibly. "No, I thought he was *snoring.* Like I said, he was drunk beyond belief. We didn't realize it until he stopped moving, but he'd fallen right where the broken dog lay on the floor.

One of the jagged shards pierced his neck. When we rolled him over, we saw the blood spilling out of him."

"Be honest, Ray. Did one of you stab him with it? Slash his throat?"

"No, *it was an accident*. We might have stabbed him, if we had to—if it had come to that. Would you have blamed us? He was trying to kill—"

"And you didn't call an ambulance."

"It was too late for that. The first thing Father said was that we'd need to dispose of the broken dog. Bury the pieces in the garden, or leave them in a garbage can across town. We'll need to destroy the camera film, too."

"Hold on, there wasn't any gun at all?"

"Of course not. Neither of us has ever fired a gun before."

Another lie.

"You told me your dad was in the war."

"Oh, I only said that because I wanted him to appear dashing and heroic. He never fought in any war. He's never been in a fist-fight, as far as I know."

"How did he lose his arm then?"

"One winter, when he was twelve, there was a terrible acci-dent. A rusty toboggan in Baraboo. It left him ineligible to join the military."

"But that's batty as hell, Ray. Why lie about something like that?"

"I can't help it if my nature is to make life sound more exciting than it really is. Can you blame a person for wanting his father to sound like a hero?"

"Forget about that. We should have called the cops tonight."

"Before you judge me again, imagine calling the police in *your* town and telling that same story. Any part of it. How would that go over?"

I didn't answer. I could not imagine it. I would never make that call.

"Don't you see how it is, even now?" he added. "For fellows like us?"

"Why did your dad tell me the false story about Stanley Marks?"

Raymond only shrugged. "I guess he didn't want you to know the true story."

"But you'd already told me. Why didn't you stop him?"

"Charles, I promised I'd protect you. I won't let him know about you, too. Maybe by now he's guessed. I don't know what's worse for him: a death like that, disposing of a body—or a son like me." He leaned forward in the seat, fingers pressed over his eyes.

"Please listen now," I said. "Don't you read the papers? When the man's body is found, they will identify him. Next week, even months from now, because of his teeth."

"His teeth?"

"Dental records, I mean."

He took another deep breath. "Who cares if they identify him? We have no connection. I never saw the man before Friday afternoon. Anyway, we're going to dump this carpet in a place nobody will ever find it."

"What if this man's people show up, asking questions?"

"If that happens, we'll tell them we paid the man on Saturday and he left. That's the truth. I swear, after tonight, you'll have absolutely nothing to do with any of this. You'll walk away with nothing but our gratitude. Hold on now—turn left here, then take a quick right."

I followed his directions, turning onto a narrow street called Cortland, until we reached an old steel bridge over the river. The cage-like girded iron beams and trusses were painted black. In the moonlight, the curving geometry called to mind an amusement park roller coaster. But I hadn't taken this thrill ride voluntarily. Had I?

The bridge lanes were divided, and there was a car following behind us. Raymond told me to drive forward and turn around on a cross street, so the other car wouldn't see us stop. Upon our return, I stopped the car near the center of the bridge and killed the engine. Warehouses occupied the land on either side of the river, including a steel mill with enormous coal piles. The only bright lights we could see were miles away, downtown.

"Hurry up, Charles, let's be through with this part before I fall into hysterics again." He got out of the convertible and pulled down the heavy cloth top.

Grabbing hold of my end of the carpet, I felt an awful churning in my stomach and a throbbing pain between my eyes. Could I believe what Raymond was telling me? Maybe both stories they'd given me had been designed to cover up something more sinister. Given the absurdity of the situation, anything could be possible.

"Pay attention now, Charles. *Lift*."

We carried the load to the side of the bridge, but I stopped. "Wait."

"Why?"

"I'm afraid it might float."

He groaned as we dropped the carpet onto the pavement. "The carpet's solid wool. Won't it sink like a stone?"

"I don't think so. Especially not . . . with a body inside it." I glanced back at the Packard. "What can we use to weigh it down? Something from the trunk?"

"Do I strike you as someone who spends time poking around the trunk of an automobile?"

I went back to the car. The trunk was filled with assorted items, including tennis racquets and a wicker picnic basket.

"Lookit," I said, lifting the picnic basket. "Are those snow chains?"

We took out the chains and slid two onto each side of the carpet roll. The snug fit worked in our favor and would hold the carpet together in the water, too. But now the combined weight was so heavy the two of us could barely lift it at all. I paused at the railing, until Raymond nodded. In a single motion, we heaved the carpet over the iron handrail and let it drop. It made a tremendous splash when it landed, then disappeared under the dark current. If it resurfaced a hundred feet down the river, we couldn't see it. I prayed it would sink to the bottom, or get lodged in the thick marsh and stay there for months.

Just then, I heard another vehicle approach from the west. The yellow headlights lit up the bridge like a spotlight.

"Keep your back to it," I called. "We can't let anyone see our faces."

The vehicle slowed as it crossed the bridge, the driver surely wondering if we were having engine or tire trouble. To my relief, it moved along without stopping.

"This bridge, my god," Raymond said, lifting his hands from the railing. "All the spiderwebs."

Suspicion still nagged at me, my head pounding. "When I saw you tonight, it looked like the place had been robbed. Like you'd fought a burglar."

"But I've already told you what happened. Why don't you believe me?"

"I saw some earrings on the table. Whose were they?"

He said nothing at first. "Mother's, probably. I have no idea. We found them when we were rolling up the carpet. Now let's beat it before another car comes along."

We returned to the Packard just as it began to rain. The first drops struck the pavement hard. We struggled to close the heavy cloth top of the car, pulling it together until it clicked into place. We scrambled into the car and rolled up the windows.

Raymond swore under his breath: *"Jesus, Mary, and Joseph!"*

It was the first time I ever heard him say my real name.

We took the same route back, passing few automobiles on the street. It wasn't nearly as bad as the ride with the carpet, but the journey felt endless, slowed by the weather. Raymond only stared out the window, wiping tears from his cheek.

Blood streaked my sleeves. It would never come out. On top of everything else, I realized furiously, I would need to spend money on a new work shirt.

"Is this *all part of the fun*, Ray?"

"Don't you see?" he cried. "I wish we could have called the police, too. I wish things were different, same as you."

Except for Raymond's directions, we didn't speak again during the ride back to State Parkway. In the alley, we found Mr. Kenrick waiting where we'd left him, smoking, the eaves of the garage protecting him from the downpour. After I pulled the car in, he closed the garage doors and set the board in place to secure them. I used an oilcloth to wipe the steering wheel and the door handles. Any spot I might have touched. Meanwhile, Ray cleaned the mud from the license plate.

"Forget about that now," Mr. Kenrick said. "I'll have the automobile cleaned tomorrow, top to bottom, someplace where they need the work and won't ask questions. I'll sell the damn car and buy another one when we get back from Canada."

Inside, Raymond's father gave us both tumblers with Scotch and ice. "Drink up. I expect it's the only thing that will help us all sleep tonight."

"I'll never sleep again," Raymond murmured.

"Did Agnes come back?" Part of me still wondered if she was in the carpet.

Mr. Kenrick nodded. "Shortly after you drove off. Pie-eyed as a sailor and fast asleep by now. Raymond, go upstairs and get Charles a fresh shirt. He can't go home looking like that."

Ray set his tumbler on the piano before disappearing up the staircase.

The first sip burned unpleasantly as it went down my throat. I set my drink on the piano next to Ray's and didn't touch it again, aware of my fingerprints on the glass.

Mr. Kenrick poured himself another. "I owe you an apology, Charles. Not just about tonight. I gave you a hard time in the garden yesterday. You didn't deserve it. I was in a foul mood, and I regret taking it out on you. I can see now, you're a true friend to us."

"Sure I am."

The lie burned my throat like the Scotch. I had never been a friend to Mr. Kenrick or his family. The only reason I met them in the first place was to make them vulnerable to a burglary. And if I hadn't insisted Raymond take me to Vi's Little Grapevine that night, his wallet wouldn't have been stolen, and none of this would have happened.

Mr. Kenrick had absolutely no idea what I meant to his family, specifically what I meant to Raymond. I recalled Ray's question in the car about which of the two things might upset his father more: a violent death in his living room or a pansy son. Either way, we would never understand each other.

"Anything you ever need," Mr. Kenrick went on, "a business contact or a character reference, you name it. I will help you."

"I don't want a character reference for what I've done tonight."

"You know what I mean. We owe you—"

"Money," I interrupted.

The word startled me, but Mr. Kenrick didn't look surprised at all.

"I'll take everything you have on you," I said.

For the first time all evening, I saw things with clarity. The events of prior weeks had not led, like stepping stones, to a body in a carpet, but to this moment now, and this opportunity to make choices for my future.

Mr. Kenrick only gave a calm nod. "If that's what it takes." He removed all the bills from his wallet, before showing none remained. "Two hundred, more or less. It's what I planned to take to Canada."

I could see once again that Bernie was right about these people. In the morning, Mr. Kenrick would go to the bank, take out another two hundred, and never miss what he had given me.

"You earned it," he said, handing me the cash. "No hard feelings. But let's agree, Raymond won't see you again when we return."

"We agree."

At last, Raymond came downstairs, looking like he'd washed up. He carried a light blue dress shirt, maybe the same one he'd worn to our first French lesson. "Give me yours," he said, "and we'll have it laundered for you."

I took the clean shirt. "Throw it away, for all I care."

"Yes," Mr. Kenrick said. "Early tomorrow, I'll take our clothes to the dump, where they'll never be found."

I was slightly bigger than Raymond, but the new shirt was loosely tailored and worked fine. When I finished with the buttons, I felt ready to leave that house forever.

"Charles, you will always be welcome here," Mr. Kenrick lied.

With Raymond watching, I shook mitts with his father for the last time.

Raymond walked me outside. It was nearly two in the morning. The rain had ended. Even the houses looked like they were sleeping. We couldn't linger. If we were seen by anyone at this hour, we'd be remembered.

"Good-bye, Raymond."

"No, don't say it like that," he whispered. "When we come back from Canada, I want to see you right away. All right? We can get past this horrible night. We'll have some fun."

I chose not to answer. After so many lies between us, it was too late for any of this.

His eyes searched mine. "You were right, earlier today. I see that now. We can go away, far from here, where nobody knows us. We'll invent our own path for how to live. I can't be married. Of course, I shouldn't be."

That argument seemed so distant now, seventy years ago. How Raymond might choose to live his life was up to him. After all, I'd known it from the first day we met: He could play no part in my future.

"More than that," he went on, "I'm truly grateful. This has been the worst night of my life. I've never been so frightened. When I fell apart, you didn't run. You helped us. That means everything. After what happened tonight, our lives are linked forever. How could they not be? I must keep you in my syndicate. As a special friend, or whatever way you'll have me. We need each other, don't we? Come on, Charles, say something."

I could only stare at him. The novelty of that expressive face had never worn off. A face I would never lay eyes on again.

"My shirt," I said.

"What?"

"My shirt. Give it to me."

He looked down, as if he'd forgotten he was holding it. He surrendered the shirt without protest.

I didn't trust the Kenricks for a second. The shirt could pin me at the scene. I couldn't leave it behind or take it back to the apartment. I would stuff it into a garbage can on the way home.

Raymond's eyes looked pleading. "I've just told you how much I care about you. How much I need you."

"You don't care about me," I said. "You don't even know me. My name isn't Charles."

And then it was my turn to walk away. There wasn't a sound on the street. He couldn't call out, and I never looked back.

TWENTY-TWO

WHEN I GOT BACK TO DEL'S, the room was pitch-black. Soft as a whisper, I closed the door behind me and crept toward the closet. My stupid foot kicked the metal ashtray on the floor. It sounded like cymbals crashing. By the time I got the light on, Bernie was frowning and stretching his shoulders.

"Sorry, Bern."

"Nobody told me it was New Year's Eve." With both hands, he gave his head a vigorous scratching. "What's the damage? You been to a party?"

I sat on the cot and pulled off my muddy shoes. I would need to scrub them with a brush and soap. It all felt like a dream, but the mud was proof: It really happened. The thick wad of cash in my pocket was proof, too. "Go back to sleep," I said.

"Back to sleep? Hell, I've been waiting up for you. I was worried. Do you know what your ma would do to me if you—"

"I said sorry. Listen, I need a hot bath."

"What? Nah, your bath night's not 'til Wednesday."

"It's an emergency."

"You can't take a soak at this hour. Makes too much of a racket. Del won't like it."

"Look at me, I'm filthy as a pig. I—I helped out a friend with car trouble."

Now he sat up with a big smile. Nothing pleased Bernie more than when bad things happened to rich people. "Your pal Kenrick had car trouble, huh? It broke down or what? That's juicy. What make of tin can do they drive?"

"None of that matters now. I'm completely through with that family."

"Yeah? See, I told you how those people are. Didn't I warn you? Now I got to hear everything."

"There's nothing to hear, Bern. I've decided it's time I beat it. I'll take the first train home and surprise everyone."

"Go home?"

"That's right. When you get the money from Heinz, you can mail me my half."

"What? No way, we're not trusting the postal service with cash like that. Think clearly for half a second now. You can't *up and leave* halfway through the visit. How will you explain all the dough to the family?"

"I've already told my mother I've been painting houses with a friend from the hotel. I'll tell her we worked hard and finished the job sooner than expected. She'll understand."

"Sure, she will. And if the pay is so damned good, she'll ask why you didn't keep painting houses for as long as possible. You think she's going to grin on you quitting work early and putting up your feet? Level with me now, Joe. You quarrel with Kenrick?"

I pulled off my socks, still trying to calm my nerves. "Something like that."

"Who cares? You hardly knew the kid!"

"You don't know the half of it."

"So tell me half."

How could I begin to tell him? Even if I told him half—that Raymond Kenrick was being extorted for being queer—then Bernie might use that information himself to blackmail him. Or sell the information to someone like Heinz. I couldn't tell my cousin any of it.

"I don't want to discuss it. I only want to wash and go to bed."

"You can't go back home. Now listen—"

"No, Bern, you don't understand. I've become involved in something that's just no good. After the night I've had, I don't want to think about it."

"Give me the headline, at least."

For a moment, I couldn't speak. I only pictured the bloody carpet, and Raymond's tears, and his father handing over cash like a bank teller to a bandit.

"Simplest way to explain it is, I don't like what I've become this summer."

"What you've become? Come on now, Joey. You're one of the few decent fellas I know. Everybody who meets you thinks so."

"I *want* to be decent, of course. But taking that class for you was a mistake."

"Yeah, well, wait until you've got the cash in hand. That mistake is going to set everything up for you."

"That may be so, but I've realized that the only way to fix things is to get out of town. It's the only solution."

With a big sigh, Bernie swung his bare legs off the mattress and got to his feet. He came and sat next to me, his voice gentle: "I get it, kid. Really, I do. Listen, if something's gone wrong that you don't want to talk about, that's jake. I won't ride you on this one."

"Thanks."

"But you need to listen now. If what you're saying is true and you're in some kind of hot water, then you've got to keep steady for now. Does this trouble involve cops? Because even if it does, it's not the end of the world. Cops in this town can be paid off. Is that what it is?"

When I didn't respond, he held up his hands.

"Never mind. Don't answer. I'm not giving you the third degree. Bottom line is, if you change your schedule out of the blue, it looks bad. If you fly the coop, it's even worse. It's a sure sign you're up to no good. You've got to stick around a while longer."

"How long?"

"I don't know what kind of jam you're in, but I'd stick around for the full month. It's only two more weeks. Act like nothing at all has happened. Keep your nose clean and work your hotel shifts like a good boy."

"I won't stay that long. I can't."

"And I'm telling you, leaving's not smart."

I got up and went to the window, because I didn't want him to see me cry.

He did have a point about the mail. "I'll only stay until we get the cash from Heinz," I said.

He shrugged. "Right, then you can go. Or maybe when the sun comes up tomorrow, you'll see everything's rosy. You sure you don't want to tell me what happened? Maybe I can help. Whatever it is, I've been there."

The claim was so preposterous, I almost laughed. "There's

nothing you can do, except get the money from Heinz as fast as possible."

"And I already told you, I'll do that."

I grabbed my bath towel and my muddy shoes. "I'm done talking."

He'd been rubbing his eyes with his fist, but now he looked at me again. "Whose shirt are you wearing, anyhow? Is it—*lilac?*"

"It's light blue. Never mind that. I'm not keeping it. Shut off the light and go to sleep. I promise I won't wake Del."

I stepped into the hall and pulled the bedroom door closed behind me.

In the bathroom, I opened the linen cupboard. I took a hand towel and folded the cash from Mr. Kenrick inside. This was enough to cover the bills at home for months. Now the cash from Heinz could truly fund my future. It would give me real options. I should have been dancing on Cloud Nine. For the moment, however, I felt short-changed of any joy in it.

I stored the hand towel in a spot at the very back of the cupboard, behind some hot water bottles, the rubber skins coated in dust.

I washed up. When I returned to the dark room, I found Bernie sawing logs in bed. I moved carefully this time, avoiding the tin ashtray, relieved I didn't have to discuss matters any further.

TWENTY-THREE

BERNIE WAS WRONG ABOUT ONE THING: I felt no better when I woke up. I needed fresh air to clear my muddled head. I was awake, dressed, and down on the sidewalk before my cousin opened his eyes.

I went for a long walk, heading in the opposite direction of Raymond's house.

The carpet was a ticking time bomb. Somebody would pull it from the river, and quick. Once the body was ID'd, the cops would be over at the Kenricks' house, asking questions. I needed to get lost before that bomb went off.

At Division Street, I stopped at a corner diner. The joint's green-and-red floor tiles reminded me of Christmas. By December, I told myself, the whole grisly episode would be ancient history. I only had to put it behind me.

I didn't have an appetite, but the apple-cheeked waitress's pleasant demeanor calmed my nerves, and I ordered coffee and eggs. When the food arrived, I pushed the plate away and stared out the window. I had that odd feeling again of watching a movie screen: that's how far I felt from ordinary people on the street.

The check came, and I reached into the pocket of my trousers. Along with the coins, I pulled out a piece of paper folded into a triangle. I unfolded it and smoothed it against the tabletop. One of Madame Monk's dittos from French class. When I flipped it over, I saw the list of names and addresses I'd copied sloppily from the attendance sheet. I recalled writing out the information quickly, the paper pressed against the rough wall in the church toilet. I'd forgotten I had it.

Finding it now seemed like a sign. A tiny chance to redeem myself. I needed to complete one more task before I skipped town. The sooner, the better.

I asked the pleasant waitress to hold the seat for me. She pleasantly asked me to pay for the grub first. I dropped some change, then went around the corner to a drugstore, where I purchased four picture postcards and four two-cent stamps. The cards all featured the same image: a colorized photograph of Buckingham Fountain, with its billowy plumes of water.

I took the cards and the stamps back to the diner and asked the waitress for a pencil. On each card, using standard Palmer Method lettering that would have made my grammar-school teachers proud, I wrote identical messages:

DEAR FRIEND,

FAR TOO OFTEN, BURGLARS PREY UPON THE HOMES OF UNSUSPECTING TRAVELERS, SO TAKE EVERY SENSIBLE PRECAUTION TO PROTECT ALL VALUABLES. LEAVE THEM WITH TRUSTED FRIENDS OR USE A SAFE DEPOSIT BOX. WISHING YOU A WONDERFUL TRIP! SEE YOU UPON YOUR RETURN.

-S

I felt especially proud of "see you upon your return" and the mysterious sign-off: S. I didn't have a reason for choosing the letter, other than it wasn't the first letter of my real or fictional names. More than anything, I hoped the recipients of the cards would simply heed the warning and lock up their treasures. Maybe that would be enough.

Since the Kenricks had already left for Canada, I did not send them a card. I addressed the cards to the Palmers, the Feeneys, the Shaws, and even to sour Mrs. Moore. Based on what I'd learned from class, none of these families knew one another. No one would pick up the telephone and make calls upon receiving a postcard.

While the cards were a tiny act of penance and didn't make up for my role in Heinz's crooked scheme, the moment I dropped them into the mailbox, I felt a little better.

That feeling lasted two minutes, replaced by a cold sweat on my hands and neck.

What if, I considered, the recipients took the cards to the local police station to ask for extra security? What if a sharp detective at one of these various police stations made a brilliant connection? I could picture Madame Monk saying, "Oui, I remember now, there was the young man who came alone, so friendly with everyone, asking for the travel dates . . ."

I told myself to relax. There was no way anyone would connect me to the postcards. I hadn't used my own initial. Anyone involved would assume I had received a postcard, too. Nobody in the class knew my real name or address, anyway. Besides, in another few days, I'd be sitting on a passenger train heading out of town.

Hotel kitchens serve hundreds and hundreds of identical plates every night. Some nights, the monotony can drive a person batty. That Monday night, the repetition kept me sane. Compared to

Raymond's house and the car and the bridge, the kitchen at the Lago Vista might have been on Pluto. I felt grateful for the distance.

Jackson and I took the elevator to the ballroom, where a large gathering of ladies sat listening to a bearded, bespectacled professor lecturing on Shakespeare. In the back, tables had been set up with rows of dessert plates covering the white banquet tablecloths. Once again, I held the trays of sheet cake as Jackson plated each piece. He used a ladle to drizzle the raspberry sauce, taking time to make sure each plate looked perfect. The sight of the dark red sauce made me feel queasy.

"Feeling fine," he said, "about the games this week. By the time you leave town at the end of the month, one of us is bound to have his pockets filled."

I didn't have the heart to tell him I'd be gone long before the end of the month. Or that I had two hundred in cash stowed back at the apartment. After griping for weeks about my financial troubles, how could I explain a windfall like that?

"Tell me what you're planning," I said, to stave off the nausea.

"Planning?"

"The honeymoon."

He smiled. "Gertrude wants to take a long drive east, up to see Buffalo and Niagara. That's her dream, to get a look at those falls."

"Nice. You got a car?"

"We can borrow a car."

"Whose?"

"My brother's."

"How long will it take to get all the way up there?"

"Three days, I expect."

The whole time we plated those cakes, I kept asking for more details. Attractions, motels, numbered highways—I didn't care about which part. I only liked listening to the sound of his voice, steady and patient, describing a future where things might turn out swell for everybody.

✱✱✱

Hours later, Bernie and I punched out and headed back to Del's. Over the traffic roar, Bernie whistled "Tip Toe Through the Tulips" like he had all the vim and vigor in the world.

Kitchen work and talking to Jackson had distracted and calmed me, but now the anxiety coursed through my veins again. I wanted nothing more than to jump on a train out of Chicago, but I couldn't split without the rest of the cash. I wished I could tell Bernie everything, but I couldn't think how. If I left out the queer element, none of it would hold water.

We were only at Grand Avenue when my cousin clapped his hand on my shoulder. "See you back at Del's," he said. "Don't wait up."

"Bern, wait—you'll talk to Heinz? About getting us that payout?"

"Didn't I say I would? I'll see him tonight, in fact. I'll remind him we're ready just as soon as he is. You look like hell, kid. Go get some beauty sleep."

He started down the block. His figure grew smaller as he threaded the sidewalk traffic.

Bernie knew how much I needed that money. Only trouble was, he didn't know how fast the clock was ticking now.

His warnings had been clear as glass. He'd told me what kind of fellow Heinz was. He'd urged me to do my part without angering Heinz or attracting his attention. I knew I should go back to Del's and wait.

Instead, I followed him down Grand Avenue.

TWENTY-FOUR

I N A BIG CITY, it's a piece of cake to trail somebody without being
seen. Even at that hour, there were enough people around that
I never worried about Bernie spotting me. I stuck to him like glue
for five long blocks, hanging back at every corner to be safe.

I wasn't sure what I might do when we got to where we were
going. All I knew was that if Bernie was going to see Heinz, I
wanted to get my cash.

After Franklin Street, Bernie walked a little farther, crossed
Grand Avenue in the middle of the block, and approached a shop
with a pink-and-green neon sign that read SAN TROPEZ TROPICAL
FISH. The sign was illuminated, even though the windows were
dark. Bernie pushed open the door and went inside.

I headed to the intersection before crossing over and doubling
back. When I tried the door, it was locked. I wanted to peer through
the window, but scummy tanks blocked the view.

I knocked hard. Twice.

Bernie's scowling face appeared behind the glass. When he
pulled open the door, the shop bell jingled above our heads. "What
the hell, Joe? Did you follow me?"

"I lost my key."

"Lost it? Aw, no—"

"I'm sure it's back in the room. Probably left it there like a dope. You know how my brain has been today."

A voice I didn't recognize came from the depths of the shop. It sounded low and reedy, almost froglike: "*Who's out there?*"

"No one important!" Bernie called. "Hold tight!" He fished a key out of his pocket and spoke quietly: "Now take this and beat it. Slide a newspaper or something in the doorjamb so I can get in later."

Taking the key, I sniffed the malodorous air wafting out of the shop. It all felt too close to give up now. "Is Heinz in there? Can I speak with him?"

"Not a smart idea," he said. "You better move along."

"Come on, I know the score, don't I? Let me shake the man's hand, at least."

The frog-voice croaked again in the distance: "*Who's out there?*"

"Hello! Heinz?" I called over my cousin's shoulder.

Bernie muttered a colorful, double-hyphenated profanity I'd never heard from him before. But he stepped out of the way, letting me pass.

The shop was dark, only one ceiling fixture turned on in the back near the cash register. Even in dim light, I could see silvery fish darting in the murky tanks. The tanks closer to the register held turtles and snails, shadowy and still. The linoleum floor hadn't seen a mop in a while.

For weeks, I'd been picturing Heinz as being the same age as Bernie, but the man resting on a metal folding chair behind the counter was in his midthirties, at least. Thin brown hair, the yellowish skin on his face and neck marked with scars, almost like potato skin.

He gazed up from a ledger spread out on his lap and gave a blank stare. "Who's shopping for guppies at this hour?"

Bernie cleared his throat. "Yeah, Heinz, this is Joe, my cousin. I told you about him. He's the one that's been helping us." He gestured toward me with an uncomfortable laugh. "Dope lost his key and followed me here after work."

Heinz looked me up and down. "Joe, right. You took the French class for us? The little church over on Dearborn."

"That's correct, sir. I did everything you asked. I got all the names and the addresses and the travel dates."

"Goody for you, kid. We're certainly obliged."

The counter was littered with empty tins of sardines. Now I recognized part of the stench, at least. Heinz still had the key for the sardine tin on his finger, wearing it like a ring or something.

Bernie placed his hand on my shoulder. "Okay, then, Joe—"

"Thing is," I interrupted, "I need my share now."

Heinz only nodded. "You'll get it soon. We honor our promises."

Bernie cleared his throat again. All that water in the room, and he sounded dry as a desert. "The kid here is eager to head home, Heinz. Back to the farm, I mean."

Heinz looked surprised. "What the hell for?"

"My mother needs me. We need the money back home."

"Mother isn't going anywhere, junior. You'll get your full payment soon enough."

"But my part's done."

Heinz's open hands gestured in the air. "And we appreciate the time you've put in. We gotta wait for the families to start traveling. That's next month. It wouldn't be smart for us to pay up before we know for sure what a good job you did. Didn't Bernie explain it to you? You get paid after we work the first house. That's the standard."

"What did I tell you?" Bernie said. "After the first house. That's the standard, like I told you."

"The Kenricks," I blurted. "They've already left for Canada. Start with them."

Bernie folded his arms, staring at Heinz. "Townhouse on State Parkway."

"With the housekeeper?" Heinz asked.

"The housekeeper's a drunk," I said. "She's out like a light by eleven."

Heinz nodded. "We're on it, kid."

"They've already gone," I said. "They won't be back until the weekend. Sunday at the soonest."

Heinz closed the ledger and stood up. On his feet, he was almost as tall as Hannigan. "We are aware of everything." He set the book next to the register, then yanked open a drawer and grabbed another tin of the sardines. With an economy of movement, he used the key to roll the lid, then lifted his chin to drop a few silvery fish into his mouth. He swallowed and gave me a shrug.

"Okay, then, Joe, since you're in such a rush to go home and see Mama, maybe you can help move things along. Can you get this tomato off the premises for us?"

I turned to Bernie. "You said all I needed to do was take the class and get the information. That's all I agreed to."

Heinz answered for him: "And that's what we'll pay you for. But now you're asking for the money early. So work with us. Find a way to meet her. We only need—what? An hour, maybe less. When we've got the time, we can work real quick."

Bernie punched my shoulder playfully. "What's the problem? Ask her out for a Coca-Cola."

"Maybe you should ask her out," I suggested.

"No way, I can't go knocking on her door. She doesn't know me from Mickey Mouse. Hasn't she seen you with Raymond?"

Heinz leaned forward. "She's *seen* you already? How come?"

"Because that's what it took to get the travel information, that's all."

Heinz winced.

The thought of being anywhere near State Parkway again made me feel sick. I wanted nothing to do with that house or that family. But I needed the rest of the cash. I looked again at Heinz. "If I help with the housekeeper, you'd give us the total payout right away?"

He took a deep breath, nodded. "After we work that house, then, yeah, you'll get all the money you earned. Every cent. That's the standard."

"What if I take her out, and you get caught?"

"Caught?" Bernie made a goofy face. "By who? You said the family's out of town."

"I mean by the cops."

Heinz swallowed another sardine. "Nothing to worry about, kid."

"Why not?"

"Because it's not!" Heinz pounded his fists on the counter so hard, I heard the coins rattle in the register. "I got family on the force. I got people everywhere. There won't be any trouble." He grabbed the sardine tin and rooted in the corners for the last fragments. The oily key, still on his finger, danced in the light.

His steam was only building. With a beet-red face, he slammed the sardine tin against the floor at my feet. Threw it with such force, the oil splashed up and hit my bare arm. He pointed, his greasy finger nearly touching my face.

"Listen, you prissy clown, maybe you're a complete moron and your cousin never clued me in. But there's one thing I need you to be very clear on, which is that *I'm* the brains here. You got that? I make the decisions, I say how it goes, and you do exactly what I tell you to do, without wasting my time with questions."

A droplet of oil from the sardine can snaked down my forearm, but I couldn't swipe it away. I'd never been hollered at like this.

"If we can't get into these houses," Heinz continued, "then the information you gave us is worthless. So don't get any more ideas into your stupid head. You don't *make* suggestions. You don't worry about the cops. Want to worry about something? Worry about keeping your mouth shut in every room you find me in. You got that?"

I nodded, even though I felt tricked. This wasn't what we had agreed to at all. But they were telling me, clear as day, how I could get the money sooner. The whole racket had been a game of pretend, and this would be the last round.

I braced myself for whatever came next, but Heinz only waved his hands at Bernie in a furious, dismissive gesture. "Now get this moron outta my sight!"

I followed Bernie to the exit. My cousin looked as steamed and scared as I'd ever seen him. I went out to the sidewalk. Bernie tried to close the door, but I stopped him.

"Bern, wait." I held up his house key. "Take this. Turns out I've got mine."

With a glare that rivaled the neon sign hanging above us, he took the key and then slammed the door in my face.

TWENTY-FIVE

EVEN AT BREAKFAST, Bernie looked like he wanted to murder his fried eggs.

He was sore, but I no longer had use for his lectures. All I'd come to Chicago to do was bail out the farm and look out for my own future. I never planned to fence people's travel information. I never planned to help dispose of a body. I never planned to assist in a residential burglary. But I'd agreed to every one of those plans, and by the end of the week I'd have all the money I needed.

I couldn't wait to escape that trouble for a few hours by spending the afternoon with Eddie. Eddie, who never encouraged me to jaywalk, much less anything worse. He'd promised to pick me up at noon. The thought of seeing him again kept me from cracking up.

At the kitchen counter, Del read from the paper. "Now here's a grim item. 'Body Fished Out of the River Wearing Wool Overcoat.'"

I didn't even blink, that's how big a sap I was. I only said, "Must have been in the water a long time. Nobody wears an overcoat this time of year."

Del gave a pitying smile. "Not really an overcoat, child. That's a thing newspaper men say."

"What does it mean?"

Bernie sneered at my stupidity. "A corpse inside a carpet, Joe. Rolled up like that. Happens all the time."

As soon as he spoke, my whole vision went wacky. I set down my fork, as the eggs appeared to spin around the plate like tops. So that was that: The carpet hadn't sunk to the bottom of the river like we hoped. It was discovered right away. The cops would identify him, like I predicted. They'd have our number in no time.

Del kept reading, "It says here that a hobo sleeping on the riverbank found the carpet in the water just north of Goose Island. Well, that's an unpleasant surprise. You start out thinking you found this swell carpet, and then you unroll it and see something like that!"

Bernie nodded. "Oldest story in the book."

My hands were quaking on the table, so I moved them to my lap.

Del squinted at the story. "It doesn't say how long the carpet had been in the water. How long do you suppose a body would *keep*, in those circumstances?"

"Does it say—how the person died?" I sputtered. "He or she?"

"They haven't identified the poor soul yet." She set down the newspaper. "Sorry, Joe. I shouldn't read the paper before you've finished your breakfast. Put it out of your mind now, and eat your eggs."

Maybe Bernie was right. What was I blowing my wig for? The story said they'd pulled a corpse from the river. Could have been anyone's. Male or female. Happens all the time, Bernie said.

Sure it did.

I couldn't regulate my breathing, and I couldn't let them see I'd lost my cool. I got up from the table and went down the hall to the bathroom. I shut the door and stood at the linen cupboard. The cash from Mr. Kenrick was still there. Now that the carpet was out of the river, we needed to finish the Kenrick job quick.

I had two hours before Eddie picked me up. The whole time, all I could picture was an army of energetic cops fanning out across the city, knocking on doors and asking too many questions. I felt lousy about everything.

Eddie's family had a contract at Comiskey Park, so he took me to a ballgame. He claimed the vendors there had the best root beer *and* the best pretzels in town. He bought us cheap seats, but then slipped a few coins to an usher so we could sit closer to the field. "We're not second class to nobody," he told me.

It felt batty as hell to be sitting at the sunny ballpark, surrounded by families enjoying the game. Eddie treated us to root beers, pretzels, and a sack of peanuts, but my nerves felt so jangly I couldn't even finish the pretzel. Food wasn't what I wanted or needed. I needed distraction, and baseball wasn't it.

"I've been thinking," Eddie whispered. "Maybe I'll take you to one of the pansy joints some night soon. You said you liked to go, right?"

The last thing I wanted was to get near another queer place, but I couldn't explain it with people around. "You told me you don't like them."

"Naw, they're okay. I only meant you gotta be smart about who you talk to. We'd stick close and have a swell time. You won't have the chance once—"

"I'd rather have a swell time by ourselves."

He nodded with a grin.

We'd been at the game three innings. When he lifted a hand to signal the hot dog vendor, I stopped him.

"I'm not a baseball fan," I admitted.

"So what? Me neither."

"And I've had enough to eat."

Eddie stood up. "Let's beat it."

We left the ballpark. He drove us to a vast gravel lot next to an abandoned warehouse, a brown-brick building with iron cages protecting the windows. White-and-gray pigeons passed easily through the broken glass. *Like ghosts*, I thought. I said so to Eddie. "Ghosts of the people who used to work inside. A little sad, right?"

"No excuse for not working," he said. "But let's not think about work."

The lot wasn't ideal for fooling around, but it was quiet; if anyone approached, we'd hear footsteps on the gravel.

I felt safe in Eddie's truck. Plus, this particular method of distraction couldn't be beat. Being alone with Eddie made me feel loose again, almost drunk. I wanted to record the encounter in my head, every part of him, every touch and taste, so there was no room in my mind for any other thoughts.

"We gotta cut this short," Eddie finally said, buttoning his trousers.

"Why?"

"Deliveries later. West side."

"Think you'll work for your dad a long time?" I asked.

"Oh, yeah. I'd be a chump to walk away from what my pop

is building. There'll be plenty to go around someday. Me and my brothers, we'll all pick up different corners of it."

"That makes sense," I said.

He reached down to his feet and picked up the sack of peanuts from the ballpark. He grabbed a handful and unrolled the window.

"Except, the way I see it," he said, "I gotta learn how a business runs. I won't drive a delivery truck forever. Once I've learned how to balance a ledger, then maybe I can expand the business in some other city. Like St. Louis or Indianapolis. Somewhere I can make my own life. I can't stick around here, doing what my family expects." He tossed some shells out the window.

"Really?"

"They'll want me to get married, set up house with a girl, all that. Aw, you know what I mean. I'll make it on my own."

I was so surprised to hear him speak like this, I almost slid across the seat to kiss him again. It was so unlike the way Raymond had spoken. Eddie would be free to build a life somewhere else, like me.

"I'll be eager to see where life takes you," I told him. "See, this is why I want us to write. Not often. Just every now and then to send news. Wouldn't that be swell?"

He only smiled, dusting off his hands, before starting the engine. "We better get you back now."

There it was again, the wall that went up whenever I spoke about the future. I couldn't figure it out. Eddie always came on so warm and eager. He acted like he was crazy about me.

193

Not everybody, it turned out, was crazy about me. On Wednesday, an envelope arrived with a postmark from home. Inside, the note-card showed a blue jay sitting on the branch of an oak tree.

Mary Toomey's message was short and to the point: "Drop dead, Gentleman Joe."

I stared at the card for a long minute. I wanted to cover it with kisses.

TWENTY-SIX

"**W**E GOT *OPTIONS*," Heinz explained through a haze of cigarette smoke. It was Thursday, nearly noon. We were sitting
in his black Model A Ford, parked on North Boulevard around the
corner from the Kenrick residence. Heinz and Bernie sat in the
front seat, and I was in back. The back seat had three ugly tears
in the upholstery, like it had been the site of a very unpleasant
conversation. "If she's not there now, we try again tonight. If she's
not there tonight, we try tomorrow."

He spoke easily, like he was planning a picnic. He seemed in
better spirits than he'd been Monday in the fish store, when he'd
hollered at me to keep my trap shut.

It opened anyway. "I gotta be at the hotel," I said. "Three thirty,
at the latest."

Heinz turned his greasy potato head to stare at my nerve. "Call
in sick."

"Tell 'em diarrhea," Bern suggested. "Nobody argues with
diarrhea. Now remember, Joe, you keep Dollface at that diner on
Division Street until you see me come in. At that point, go ahead
and shake her loose any way you can. You got that?"

"How much time will you need?"

"I don't know," Heinz snarled. "How much time will you need to take a dump tomorrow? Now shake a leg!"

I stepped out of the Ford on shaky feet. I hadn't been so nervous to approach the Kenricks' townhouse since the day I first met Raymond to practice French. I kept my head down. What were the chances an insomniac neighbor had spotted us that night with the carpet?

The first thing I noticed was that the window to the side of the front door had been repaired. Sparkling new glass, white trim painted fresh. Like nothing had ever happened.

I rang the bell and waited.

No answer.

I prayed Agnes would open the door. The faster the job was done, the sooner we'd get the money from Heinz. I needed to be on a train already.

No answer.

Moreover, if Agnes appeared, it would be proof, at least, that the body in the carpet had not been her. It would lend credence to Raymond's account of the blackmailer's assault.

Just when I was about to give up hope, the door swung open.

For once, Agnes wasn't in her housekeeper's uniform. Instead, she wore a pink gingham sundress, with a lacy collar that plunged farther down on the chest than I was used to seeing on any girl, except in pictures.

"Is Raymond home?"

She looked me up and down with the usual indifference. "Nope."

"Think he'll be back soon?"

Her penciled eyebrows drew closer together as she seemed to

think about it. "The whole family is away. Didn't nobody tell you that?"

I shook my head.

"Family event, up there in Canada."

"Will they be back soon?"

"Too soon, in my opinion, but keep it to yourself. Late Sunday."

"That's disappointing. I was in the neighborhood and hoped Raymond would have lunch with me."

She only stared over my shoulder, watching traffic.

"I wanted to take him out," I explained, "because I'm leaving town. I was going to treat him to lunch at a diner we like over on Division Street." I paused, the way Bernie had coached me. "Say, would you like to have lunch with me instead?"

Finally, her eyes woke up: "Me? Have lunch with you?"

"You need to eat, don't you?"

"Plenty of chow in this place. As you know perfectly well."

"Yes, but if you come with me, I'll treat, and you won't have to do any dishes. Please join me, Agnes. I don't want to eat by myself."

"I mean . . ." She looked over my shoulder again and then warily at me. "I haven't got all day. I'm meeting a girlfriend later."

"I got an appointment later, too. Come on, say yes."

My invitation didn't seem to flatter or offend her. She only bounced her narrow shoulders. "Hold your horses."

The door closed again.

I reminded myself: It was nothing but lunch. I only had to entertain her until Bernie showed up at the diner. It was the last crooked task I needed to do before I left town. And it wouldn't harm Agnes; she'd get a free sandwich out of the deal.

Several minutes passed. I almost rang the bell again.

When the door opened, she was holding her pocketbook. She'd put on eye makeup and lipstick. Her white-blond hair was pulled back and fastened with a gadget I couldn't see. There was no question she turned heads whenever she went out.

She locked the door, and we made our way south on State Parkway.

"Listen," she said, dropping the keys into her pocketbook. "I know the diner you're talking about over on Division. Coffee there tastes like gasoline. I know a better place."

"But I like that diner. I'm craving their pancakes."

"Trust me, my place is better."

I didn't want to argue, but we needed to go to that specific diner, or else I wouldn't be sure when Bernie and Heinz were through with the job.

We turned west on Division. Agnes slowed her step when we passed a shop with a green-and-brown awning. Gold-painted lettering on the window read E. BRADLEY & SONS, BOOKSELLERS.

Agnes gave me another once-over. "You said you're paying for lunch?"

"That's right."

"Let's make a quick stop, then. I've got a dollar in my pocket, and I know exactly how to spend it."

I agreed eagerly, thinking that the longer it took to get to the diner, the less time I'd spend waiting for Bernie to show up.

The shop was surprisingly deep, with shelves that climbed all the way to the ceiling. Persian carpets covered the floor. At the center of the store, two circular tables held piles of new hardcovers. *Tender Is the Night. Anthony Adverse. Five Silver Daughters.* One called *Lamb in His Bosom* showed a couple sitting on a wagon pulled by a horse. Nothing to look at, but since I was standing there with Agnes, the word *bosom* in the title embarrassed me.

"What sort of novels do you like?" I asked her.

"It's not for me. It's for my folks. Where I'm from, there's nowhere to buy books, so every now and then I send one home."

I recalled Raymond telling me that Agnes had fled her tiny hometown in the middle of the night. Something about a scandal.

"So what sort of books do they like?"

"No clue. We're not close like that. Tell you the truth, I don't even enclose a letter with the book. But I slide a few dollars between pages one and two."

"Gee, I bet they appreciate it."

She lifted a novel to stare at the cover. "Probably they do. They never write back."

"Why not?"

Her shoulders lifted again in response. "I even put the Kenricks' street address right there on the package. It don't bother me, not really. As long as I send a book every once in a blue moon, the family knows I'm breathing. That's how I see it."

She returned the book to its place, then headed toward a wall in the back of the shop. "Look here." She pointed. "This place has autographed copies of popular books. I like to send those sometimes, so maybe folks will think I'm rubbing shoulders with hotshots." The idea made her smile.

A framed, hand-lettered sign read AUTOGRAPHED FIRST EDITIONS— THIS SHELF ONLY. Roughly two dozen volumes filled the space. My heart sank a little when I realized what I was seeing.

Agnes reached for a book, carefully opening the cover to examine the title page. I glanced over her shoulder. Sure enough, it was one of Bernie's autographed copies. *The Good Earth* by Pearl S. Buck.

"This one's famous, right?" she asked.

"Don't buy that one," I said.

"Why not?"

"Because—I've read it." This part was true.

She gave me the side eye. "Nobody's buying it for you."

"I don't recommend it. It's about . . . farmers."

"Bite your devil tongue!" she laughed. "My own family are farmers. And the book is famous. Honestly it don't matter. They won't even read it. Like I said, I only like the impression the signature gives." Book in hand, she brushed past me and headed toward the register up front.

"Hold on, Agnes. Tell you what. I'll buy your lunch *and* this book for you. But only if we go to my diner."

She smiled. "You must really like them pancakes."

"Deal?"

"Okay, then, Mr. Rockefeller, here you go. And much obliged."

I paid for the book and we kept moving. When we got to the diner, we took a booth at the sunny window. This was the same place I'd come to on Monday morning, the one with the Christmas-candy floor tiles. The same pleasant waitress dropped menus and cold water at the table. "Bring your appetite this time, fella?" she asked.

I ordered coffee.

Agnes took her time with the menu, as if considering every option. When the waitress returned, I ordered pancakes. Agnes ordered a lettuce, tomato, and Swiss cheese sandwich and a Dr Pepper.

"That's all you want?" I said. "Order a side, too, if you want."

She only studied me. "You're not *Charles*, not really."

"What do you mean? Who else would I be?"

"It's only that name. Charles. It don't suit you. Don't nobody ever call you Charlie?"

"Not even once," I answered honestly. "Did anyone ever call you . . ." I was stuck, unsure of what the nickname might be for Agnes. "Aggie?"

"*Nessie.* Sure, they did. Back home, everyone called me Nessie. But when I came here, I got to be someone different. Agnes sounds more grown up. That's what I needed, a chance to be someone different. If you ever get the chance, I recommend it."

When the food came, Agnes gave me a grin and ordered a side of cottage cheese. She moved her gum to the rim of her water glass. The pancakes were fine, but the coffee did taste lousy.

She told me about the crowd she ran with, mostly other housekeepers and shop girls, who made regular trips to a place called the Limehouse in Rogers Park. "Up on Howard Street. Barney Richards and his band are there every week, and they don't charge a cover. We eat and then dance all night. You might like it. Hey, this sandwich isn't half bad."

"I'll be gone by the weekend," I said.

She had a fellow who took her out sometimes. "Walt's only a med student, but he acts like a high roller. He's nuts about Chez Paree over on Fairbanks. You heard about Mike Fritzel's big show there? I can take it or leave it, but the supper there is something else."

Raymond never mentioned how friendly Agnes could be when she warmed up. Sitting in the booth, I said a silent prayer that she wouldn't personally end up in trouble for anything that went missing from the Kenricks' house. I'd never be able to vouch for her if she did.

We finished with the food, still no sign of Bernie.

"Save room for dessert?"

She laughed. "After pancakes? Now who do you think you're fooling, Charlie? You're still a kiddo, after all. Nothing for me, thanks much."

I wasn't hungry, but I ordered a slice of apple pie. Heated and à la mode, hoping both elements would add more time.

A bell rang when the door opened, and Bernie walked in. He sat at the counter and performed the role of Indecisive Man Seeing Lackluster Menu.

I signaled the waitress to cancel the pie. "And bring the check."

Agnes stared at me.

"My eyes are bigger than my stomach," I explained. "You were right. Sorry."

"Anyway, thanks again for lunch. And for the book."

"I'm sure your family will enjoy it."

I left eighty cents on the table, and we got to the sidewalk. Agnes said she was heading south to meet her girlfriend at Carson's. "Much obliged, Charlie," she said. "I'll be seein' ya."

She headed down LaSalle without looking back.

Bernie came outside. His gaze trailed her legs, and he muttered, "Jeez, I can't believe you made a stink about spending time with a juicy dish like her."

We walked back to Del's. I almost asked, "How'd it go?" But I stopped myself. I didn't need details. I never wanted to think of Bernie breaking into someone's house.

Back in the room, he took off his shoes and began cleaning them.

I sat on the cot. "So did Heinz give you the payment? Our part's over now."

"Give him time, Joe. It's not like Heinz carries bags of money everywhere he goes. He's got people he needs to work with now."

"Which people?"

He frowned at the shoes. "Nobody we know, trust me. Listen, I ought to give you hell. Your landscaping efforts didn't make things easy for us. Every basement window was exposed to the heavens, thanks to you."

"I wish you hadn't gone in there yourself, Bern. In broad daylight, too. You could have been caught."

"Haven't we told you not to worry about that? We were careful. And Heinz has pals on the force. But forget about that. You told me you quit your friendship with that Kenrick kid. Didn't you tell me that?"

"You bet I did. I regret it all now, because he got me involved in something real bad. I told you the other night."

"What did he get you involved with, exactly?"

I wouldn't tell him. I never could tell him about the night on the bridge.

"Never mind the details," I said. "The important part is, it's all over now. I washed my hands of it. But I feel lousy about this break-in. I went over there half a dozen times. My fingerprints are all over that stupid house."

"Relax. Home burglaries happen all the time in the big city. Cops don't have time to work most of these cases. Especially not if Heinz is involved." He lifted the shoes again and inspected them from another angle. "Tell you something, buddy, the experience was a kick. I never did nothing big like that before."

"Don't ever do it again. Promise me now."

"I'll promise you squat."

"You don't understand. I *warned* them. I warned all the others in the French class."

"What the hell does that mean?"

I hesitated, but he needed to know. "I sent them all postcards. Everyone but the Kenricks. I kept the notes short and didn't sign my name."

"What did you write?"

"Nothing, just warned them about burglaries and suggested they get someone to keep an eye on their houses when they traveled."

Bernie's mouth opened and closed like one of Heinz's fish, but he didn't speak.

"You can't go into any more of those houses, Bern. It's not safe."

"Goddammit, what'd you go and gum the works like that for? If Heinz finds out, we'll never get the payout. And that's the *nicest* thing that will happen to you. What the hell were you thinking?"

"I was in a panic, and my conscience got the better of me. But that's a good thing, isn't it? I'm listening to my conscience again—"

"Says the fellow who turned rat on his own people?" He set down the shoes and stared at the floor for a long minute. When he lifted his head again, he looked lousy. "That's gotta be one hell of a thing to learn about yourself. Listen, as long as we're giving each other the business, we need to talk about something."

"I need to wash up and get changed."

Before I could stand, he reached for my arm. "Park it and

listen. It's like this. When we were inside the house, I visited your pal Raymond's bedroom."

"Yeah? What'd you take from him?"

"Not a thing. Trust me, I hightailed it outta there. That room gave me the creeps."

"How come?"

"The whole thing! The furniture, the art prints, and all those recordings of crooning dames. The clippings of John Dillinger tucked in the mirror frame, like the guy's some film star to admire. If I didn't know for certain that a *boy* slept there, I never would have guessed. I may be a drop-out, but I still can put two and two together."

"What are you saying?"

"The kid's a fruit, Joe."

"Oh, give it a rest."

"I'm telling you something here, so listen. He's queer as a cockatoo. Couldn't you see that?"

I felt my face burn, hearing the accusation out loud. "What, because he's got a fancy bedroom?"

"You'd have to be blind not to notice it. Didn't you see all the expensive threads in his closet? Anyone can see he enjoys *shopping with the girls*."

"Says you, who spends more time polishing shoes than anyone I ever met."

"Think what you like. I'm only saying I'm glad you put some distance between you. Trust me, you don't want an element like him in your life. I warned you the very first day you got here, didn't I? Told you to stay away from Bughouse Square and all the nelly places. It's too easy for a kid from out of town to get tricked."

"You speaking from experience?"

205

"Don't bet on it. Any fellow who gives me a grin isn't grinning very long. Listen now, you gotta be careful. It's true what they say about a man's reputation. You lose your reputation, you lose everything."

The hypocrisy was too much. I didn't want to say something I couldn't take back, so I got up and took my work shirt to the bathroom. I scrubbed a gravy stain with soap, and rinsed it, squeezing it out over the tub. I had an hour, at least, before I needed to leave for work. The shirt would dry anyway on the walk to the hotel.

When I got back to the room, Bernie was gone. I looked out the window and saw him getting into a taxi.

His harsh words about Raymond made me feel rotten. My cousin and I had once been close as brothers, but it was clear we didn't know each other at all anymore. Were we even still family?

Just then, a terrible notion came to me.

I went to the closet and pulled out my old suitcase, with its frayed leather straps. Farther back, the space was crammed with Bernie's own suitcase, a can of Flit bug spray, and the two shoeboxes where we kept our down payments from the French class. Holding my breath, I brought both shoeboxes to the cot. My heart was pounding so hard, any fellow standing in the room would have heard it.

I counted out the money on the floor. Except for what we'd already sent home, it was all still there, both portions. Satisfied, I returned the cash and put both shoeboxes back where they belonged. I shut the closet door and lay on the cot, staring at the cracks in the ceiling. I should have felt relieved to see the money still there, but instead I only felt lousy for doubting my own cousin's loyalty.

TWENTY-SEVEN

THE LAWMEN STALKED MY THOUGHTS. I pictured cherry tops prowling the streets, every turn leading them closer to us. And all I could do was keep to my schedule and wait for Heinz's payout.

Deliveries kept Eddie busy most mornings, leaving us only an hour or two before my hotel shifts. "Pop couldn't manage without me," he bragged. "I practically run the deliveries myself." The responsibilities he took on added to my admiration for him.

Turned out, I wasn't the only one enjoying a cuddle. After a long shift on Saturday, I returned to the apartment and found Bernie in bed with a complete stranger. A poodle with tight white curls and shiny black eyes.

Of all breeds, I thought miserably, Bernie had to bring home a dead ringer for the porcelain figurine that once resided in the Kenricks' front window.

"What the hell?" I exclaimed. "Whose pooch is this?"

"Cute, right? Sweet as a peach, too. I'm holding her for a friend."

The dog came over to greet me. She licked my hands like they were still covered in kitchen grease.

"Which friend? Heinz?"

He stretched out on the bed, arms crossed behind his head. "Not Heinz."

"It's been two days."

"The timing's not up to us. Jeez, we've been over that. Anyhow, the dog's from over on Burton Place."

Burton Place was one of the swankiest streets in the Gold Coast; parts of it were even fancier than Raymond's street. Ray and I had walked down Burton together plenty of times, passing one ornate townhouse after the next.

The dog smelled clean, not like a farm mutt. Her shiny eyes looked a little desperate.

"If we're sharing the room with a pooch, even for one night, you owe me the true story. There's no way you've got friends over there on Burton Place."

He shrugged. "Future friends, I guess. They sure better be friendly when I return this dog to them."

"Aw, Bern, you stole someone's dog?"

He laughed. "Nah, nothing like that. Honest to god, I was walking over there earlier, minding my business, and this bitch came bouncing over to greet me. All by herself, too. Came up like we were old pals. Didn't yap or nothing. I couldn't let her run out into the street, could I? So I brought her straight back here, where she'll be safe and sound."

"Good Samaritan. That's you all the way."

The dog had returned to Bernie and put her head down on the bed, as if she'd made peace with this reversal of fortune.

Bernie sighed. "I'll head back over there tomorrow, hang some signs. That's the only way to find the owner."

"Might even be a reward, if you're lucky."

"Yeah, that's what I'm thinking, too. People always feel grateful to get their pets back." He scratched her belly like he was already growing fond of her. "Fortunately, I've got a leash, thanks to the previous occasions when I found myself in this extremely unusual situation."

The dog spent half the night jumping between the beds, moving from one to the other, her little paws click-clacking on the wooden floor like some form of torture. It didn't matter. Thanks to the cops patrolling in my dreams, I wasn't getting forty winks anyhow.

$$* * *$$

Sunday afternoon at work, Jackson pulled me aside and told me our numbers hadn't paid out. "Policy's never a sure thing, Joe," he said. "But it's got to pay out sooner or later. Gertrude showed me the ring she wants. Our luck has got to change."

"It will," I said, trying to sound as confident as he did. Now that I had the cash from Kenrick and nearly the payout from Heinz, I wanted to believe luck could change for any fellow.

Later, I punched out and hoofed it north on Michigan Avenue on dead feet. The sweltering air felt extra heavy, due to the humidity. Past the old water tower, my eyes scanned every sidewalk, looking for familiar faces. The Kenricks were due back from Canada by now. I pictured Raymond and his father explaining the new living room carpet and the missing porcelain dog. Would Mrs. Kenrick even notice that the front window had been replaced?

At Del's, Bernie was waiting for me, dog on the leash already. "Let's take a stroll. I want a milkshake, and I need you to hold the pooch when I go inside."

"Go on without me. Tie her to a lamppost, if you have to."

"Nuts to that. Some jerk might take her."

"I feel pretty licked, Bern."

"I've hardly seen you all weekend. What's the point in having you here for the summer if we never have some grins together?"

I didn't have the energy to argue. It was almost eleven and the heat was even worse inside the room. I washed up and followed my cousin and the dog downstairs.

On Clark Street, the sidewalks were mobbed, since it was too hot for anyone to sit indoors. The dog stopped to take a leak at every lamppost and fire hydrant. I couldn't figure where she kept all the piss.

Bernie slipped me the leash and went inside a corner store. I expected him to come back with his milkshake, but he appeared holding a frozen treat. He tore off the paper wrapper, revealing a shocking red gelatinous core. He broke it apart and handed me one half on a stick.

"What is it? Some kind of ice cream?"

"Nah, it's something different. It's a cherry Popsicle."

"That's a funny name," I said. "Two parts, like bicycle?"

"No, you numbskull, like icicle. Just try it, you'll like it."

The Popsicle was tart and sweet. I did like it, although it didn't taste like cherries. More than anything, it tasted cold. It made my whole mouth feel like an icebox.

We cut west and continued north on Lincoln. It was still hot as blazes, but better than being inside four walls, so we kept on walking. At one point, Bernie slipped me the leash again and got another cherry Popsicle. He broke it apart and gave me half.

My own summer, I reflected, was broken in two halves like a Popsicle. Different flavors completely. I wanted to kick myself for wasting so much time building a house of lies with Raymond when I should have been laying a stronger foundation with Eddie.

I'd taken a dumb risk by helping Heinz with Agnes. But that was the last time I'd go anywhere near the Kenrick residence. Raymond didn't know my real name, or where I was staying. He knew I worked in a hotel downtown, but he didn't know which one. There were dozens of big hotels, maybe a hundred.

While I missed Ray's company, the experience had led to a night that would haunt me forever. I couldn't believe a word from him or his family. I didn't need that kind of trouble in my life. The problems of rich people never interested me, anyway.

On the flip side, Eddie was the genuine article. No games and no trouble. My friendship with him was the one thing I would take with me after the summer without any mixed feelings at all. He was exactly the kind of fellow I needed to begin my syndicate.

When Bernie flicked his Popsicle stick into the street, the dog jumped, stretching the leash, trying to fetch it. "Chin up, Joe, we're gonna get the payout from Heinz soon. I don't see why you're moping around all the time. If you ask me, you ought to be skipping up the street."

"No one's asking you."

"What you should do," he added, "you should take some girl out and have a good time. Before you go, I could introduce you to some real friendly lookers, if you want. You'll have the cash. Enough to save and enough to spend, if you ask me."

"No one's asking you," I repeated.

If Bernie's newest "little plan" was to hook me up with a girl, then it was only one more reason to get lost as soon as possible.

At Fullerton, we reached a three-way intersection. We were about to turn south on Halsted when we saw a hubbub north of us on Lincoln. My instinct was to walk the other way, but Bernie wandered closer.

Near a picture house called the Biograph, the block was jammed with patrol cars and ambulances, lights flashing, plus a mob of onlookers. We couldn't get any closer. The crowd was so noisy, they nearly drowned out the sirens.

"What's the story?" Bernie asked a kid standing in front of us.

"They've shot people!" he squealed.

"Who shot people?" Bernie craned his neck to see right over him. "Whose gang?"

"No, the police," he said. "They carried away two ladies and a gentleman."

A lady next to Bernie said, "That wasn't a gentleman. It was Dillinger, the outlaw."

I finally spoke up: "John Dillinger, you said?"

"And not by cops, neither," the woman said. "Federal agents. Kid oughta get his facts straight."

Bernie jostled my shoulder. "This we got to see."

Because of the pooch, he couldn't go farther, so I pushed ahead on my own to see better. The people had already formed a line that snaked around the alley. Blood covered the bricks, shiny as motor oil.

That's when I spotted him, standing in the middle of the crowd. Raymond Kenrick. He was in line, his hands stuffed in the pockets of his twill trousers. Had I conjured him with my thoughts? I searched the crowd for his parents, but Raymond seemed to be alone. The outlaw's number one fan. In the thick of this swelling mob, Raymond somehow had managed to nab a view from the very front row. Maybe he'd been inside the theater, watching Clark Gable in *Manhattan Melodrama,* when it all went down.

The rowdy crowd treated the scene like a carnival, laughing and posing for pictures. Reporters held up flares for the photographers, pointing to where Dillinger had fallen. Raymond moved slowly around the circle, not speaking to anybody. He looked almost sad. When he came to the exact spot where Dillinger fell, he did what so many of the others were doing: crouched down and dipped a handkerchief in the blood pooled on the pavement.

I turned around and shouldered my way back to Bernie. "Let's head back," I said, pulling on his elbow. "Now."

He looked surprised. "What? Joe, this is historic."

"Since when are you interested in history?"

"Go spit in yer hat, I love history!"

"Raymond Kenrick's over there," I whispered. "I don't want to see him."

Bernie's face snapped back, searching the crowd. "Which one? Point him out."

I didn't answer, just stepped around him and moved away. Sure enough, Bernie and the dog followed. My cousin called me to wait, but I ignored him. We retraced our steps back to Clark Street. It seemed to take forever to get back, since the dog kept stopping to piss. My whole body felt sore.

At Del's, I trudged up the stairs on heavy feet.

"What the hell was that about?" Bernie asked in the hallway. "You scared of someone like Kenrick now?"

"For Pete's sake," I said, "would you get the money from Heinz, so I can beat it?"

"I'm working on it!"

TWENTY-EIGHT

ANOTHER NIGHT OF THE POOCH DRIVING US BATTY, barking out the window at every passing car. When I did sleep, I dreamed about the dog's stupid head rolling off, leaving a row of jagged teeth around the neck. "Nuts to you," I muttered groggily, pulling the pillow over my ears.

Del made flapjacks to celebrate the Dillinger ink spilled through the papers. She even rewarded the dog with a bone it didn't deserve. Still, when Del smiled at Bernie, I could see the fatigue in her eyes. "This . . . energetic creature won't be in your room after today, will she, Bernard?"

"Absolutely not. Don't give it another thought."

"If the landlord hears about a dog—"

"I heard you, Del. Hand me the classifieds, somebody. Maybe the family put a notice in there." He scanned the paper, reading out loud: "Let's see . . . Lost purses, lost teeth even. Right, look here. Lost dogs, a bunch of them. Irish Setter. Scotch Terrier. Pomeranian. Huh. In this whole section, not a single poodle."

"Maybe you should hang up those flyers you had in mind," I said. "You could do it today."

"Yeah, I'll take care of it."

Del's attention returned to the paper. "Why, here's an update for us," she said brightly. "Remember the corpse they fished out of the river last week? The one rolled in a wool carpet?"

I lowered my head, pretending to watch the dog gnawing her bone under the table.

"According to the medical examiner, the man was called George Drummond, thirty-one years of age. It says he was a film-projector operator at the Terminal Theater up on Lawrence Avenue. A member of the union. What a nasty piece of luck for him."

The name Drummond meant squat to me. And a film-projector operator didn't fit into either of the scenarios the Kenricks had given me. Maybe it wasn't the same wool carpet after all.

I lifted my head. "How do they know his name?"

"Says here they took X-rays of the fellow's teeth. They sent them to dental offices all over town, until they found the man's dentist. Well, I don't welcome the idea of strangers poking equipment around my mouth after I'm dead. Makes me sick to my stomach to think of it."

Bernie drowned his flapjacks in syrup. "Does it say who put him in the river?"

She shook her head no. "But there's a sergeant quoted here, who claims that *five* members of that union have been killed so far this year. All unsolved murders. The coroner estimates the man's death occurred last weekend. Stabbed right in the neck. According to the coroner, the body hadn't been in the water more than a day before the hobo wandered along the riverbank and pulled it out."

I reminded myself to breathe, as memories came flooding back: the weight of that carpet as Raymond and I dragged it through the house, the rotten stench of blood as I steered the unfamiliar Packard along Armitage Avenue. I felt sick, but I couldn't share my fear with anyone. My own cousin had spent time in that house, and I couldn't even tell him.

When Del took her plate to the sink, I reached for the newspaper. The story included a photo of George Drummond, a man with a small forehead and dark hair that parted in the middle; his wide-set eyes stared off to the side, as if startled or distracted. Could this be the person we'd dropped into the river? The thought made my skin crawl. I had to get out of the apartment.

"I'll take the dog over to Burton Place," I told Bernie.

He drained his coffee cup. "How come?"

"I can't lose another night of sleep, Bern. I'll parade her around, see if anybody knows her. I'll hang the signs myself, if I have to."

"You think you can handle it?"

Bernie's tone was so condescending, I refused to answer.

"I've got rubber cement somewhere," Del said, pulling open kitchen drawers.

"I'll take the dog," I told Bernie, "but only if you go see Heinz about the money he owes us. Go see him this morning. Deal?"

"Way ahead of you, pally. I agree, it's time."

If Del was curious about this line of talk, she knew better than to ask questions. She located her tub of rubber cement and placed it on the table.

"You sure it was Burton Place?" I asked Bernie.

"Hand to God, it was Burton. I can't recall if it was east or west of Astor. I found her shivering on the sidewalk and came to the rescue."

"Shivering. In July."

Bernie nodded. "That's right. Shaking, like she was scared out of her wits."

The dog looked too stupid to have wits, with its pink tongue hanging out all the time.

"Finish your food first," Del said, looking at me. "I won't have a bite of that go to waste."

I finished my flapjacks, and Del made three flyers with her fountain pen: *Sweet Snowball Poodle Dearly Misses Her Ma & Pa! Inquire at Klein Drug Cosmetics Counter, Division St.*

When nobody was looking, I removed the page with the news item about Drummond, folded it up, and stuffed it into my pocket.

Grabbing my hat, the flyers, the rubber cement, the leash, and the poodle, I set out uneasily toward the lake. We crossed Clark Street, Dearborn, and State Parkway, stopping every half block so the dog could do her business. Her freak bladder belonged in a circus tent. Finally, we made it to the fancy block where Bernie claimed she belonged. It wasn't even ten thirty, and the heat was unbearable. No breeze from the lake.

I led the dog back and forth on Burton Place, between State Parkway and Lake Shore Drive. I searched every lamppost and telephone pole for signs advertising a lost dog. Nothing. I tried to hang all three signs, but every surface was too hot for the rubber cement to adhere to. The soggy flyers dropped to the pavement like wet dishrags, and I got left with fingers coated in rubber.

I'd strayed too close to where the Kenricks lived now. In spite of my better judgment, I sat on a bus bench, where I could observe their house from a safe distance. Raymond was home from his trip, and I was tired of keeping secrets I couldn't tell. Fears I couldn't share. I half prayed the front door would open and Raymond would simply walk out—a foolish wish, given he was never out of bed this early. Much more likely, Agnes would appear or Mr. Kenrick, and those possibilities made me tug for the dog, conscious of my recklessness, ready to return to Del's.

"Charles," said a soft voice behind me. "Is that you?"

My head spun around. I almost dropped the leash.

Raymond was wearing clothes I'd seen before, but he sported a new straw hat. Sunglasses, too, made of yellow celluloid. He looked as if he was just as surprised to see me.

I stood. "Are you wearing a disguise?"

He pointed, as if he was seeing a ghost. "Is that your dog?"

"No. I'm looking for the owner. What are you doing awake this early? I hardly know you."

"I haven't been sleeping well, but—never mind that. I hardly know you, either. What's your real name?"

"Joe."

He tilted his head, as if he was struggling to view me through the sunglasses. "I must say, I prefer Charles."

"Call me whatever you like, Ray. I don't really care."

"I forgive you for giving me a false name. After all, many people in Chicago know me as Ricardo. It's a safety issue in some places. But why use a false name at a French class?"

When the dog pulled at the leash, I sat on the bench again so she would come sit by me. "That's a story for another time. Let's start with you telling me who George Drummond was to your family."

"George Drummond?" Raymond sat next to me. "Where did *you* hear that name?"

I removed the newspaper clipping from my pocket, but he only gave it a quick look. His expression confirmed what I suspected. The same carpet. The same body.

"I'm telling you, Ray, this is bad. Not only did they find the carpet, the police have identified the body."

He didn't speak. He only leaned back with a despondent sigh.

I wanted to slap him or shake him into action. "Say something, will you? When the police detectives talk to his people and retrace his last steps, we could find ourselves in big trouble."

"I don't know how much more trouble I can take."

"Raymond, tell me what really happened."

"Happened?" he said. "It's still happening. First thing this morning, another goon came knocking on our door. I'm back now from my father's office to get more cash. And there's nothing we can do about it. We never got the wallet back, and they're still holding it over my head. And now they're asking questions about their *friend*, George Drummond. I only learned his name this morning, when the fink threatened us."

"And?"

"And, the difference is, this time Mother answered the door. She didn't hesitate for a minute. She grabbed a century note and paid the man. But he promised to pay another visit before long, the nasty rat. It's all out in the open now, all my secrets. Even Mother can hardly stand to look at me."

I didn't know what to say. He was facing my own worst nightmare, piled upon the existing trouble we were already in. All along, I'd been wrong about Raymond: He wasn't a fellow who could lose a wallet without consequences.

"Ray, I'm sorry. I didn't believe you. Until today, I wasn't sure what to believe."

"Nobody would blame you for that."

"But I deserve some blame. If we hadn't gone to Vi's that

220

night—if I hadn't insisted—then your wallet wouldn't have been stolen, and you wouldn't be in this jam."

"It's normal to be curious, and I could see what being there meant to you. Besides, I knew the risks. What Father and I pulled you into was much worse. Unforgivable, really."

"What will you do now?"

He took off the sunglasses and stared out at the street. "I'll leave town, just as soon as I can. But not for school—I'm leaving for good this time. I'll start over, someplace else. The way you suggested, the last time we had lunch together. You were right all along. Fellows like us, we need to start fresh, far away from home. I can never be married. Maybe I'll join the priesthood."

One thing about Raymond Kenrick: He always surprised me. "The priesthood?"

"I hardly ever miss Mass on Sundays. I'd say that qualifies me as much as anyone. I won't cut ties with my family completely. I'll tell them where I am, so they won't worry. But I'll never be happy until I can live in a place where nobody has anything on me. I won't have brutes like this shaking down my family."

"I'm very, very sorry," I said again.

"I only need to work out a way to get out of town. The basics. If I told my parents I wanted to go, they wouldn't let me. But I can't stay."

"There are too many cons in this town," I said.

"But there are swell people, too. Like you, Charles. Excuse me, Joe. You were aces to me. You helped us out that night with Drummond. I'll always be grateful. I owe you so much."

"But, Ray, what happened that night has only led to worse trouble for you. You owe me nothing."

I hoped he believed me, because I really meant it. If anything, of course, I owed him. For his affection and amusing company. For showing me the ropes. For trusting me. And how had I repaid him? Not only had I participated in the French-class scheme, but I'd sold him out to Heinz when I thought it might get me the payout sooner. I'd treated Raymond no better than the brutes who kept coming to his door and demanding money.

There didn't seem to be anything left for us to say, except good-bye.

"Ray, I wish you nothing but—"

"Daisy!" Out of the clear blue, a child came running down the street. The girl was about eleven years old, with a polka-dot ribbon in her hair. "You found our dog!" she shouted. "You found Daisy!"

I stood, handing the leash right over. "Take her, please. Good riddance."

"Oh, Daisy, Daisy, *Daisy* . . ." she bawled, pressing her face against the dog's snowy curls.

She was only a child, but I couldn't help scolding her. "We haven't slept all weekend. Why didn't your parents put up a sign? Or place an ad in the classifieds?"

The girl seemed too overjoyed to answer. The dog pressed its paws against her pinafore and licked her face. No question, the two were acquainted.

"Gee, thanks!" She tugged on the leash with some confidence, and the dog followed her, the two of them skipping down the street like old pals.

Raymond had remained on the bench. He reached for my sleeve, pulling me back down. His other hand covered his mouth.

"It's especially complicated right now, because . . ." He stopped, and I realized he was crying.

"Ray, tell me."

"On top of everything else, our house was *burgled* while we were away. Can you imagine? The very same punks, I expect. Agnes says it happened on Thursday, when she was out. She must have been gone for a long while. The prowler went all through the place, taking silver, jewelry, any little thing he could pocket. My mother called the police last night to report it. Father tried to stop her, of course. The very last thing we need is police in our house, after what happened with Drummond. My parents are furious with Agnes. How did she not notice a broken window? I never trusted her for a—"

I stopped him. "I was with Agnes on Thursday."

"Yes, she told us."

"We had lunch together, before she met a friend for shopping. I'll vouch for her if it comes to that. I'm sure Agnes had nothing to do with the burglary."

"Goody for her, but what about you?"

"Me?"

"From anyone's point of view, you taking Agnes out for lunch looks very . . . I suppose it looks very *strange*. You barely know her. What was that about?"

I folded my hands on my lap, trying to think how to explain. "It wasn't about anything. We visited a bookshop and had a bite to eat. When we said good-bye, she left for downtown and I went to work."

"But it's not like you ran into her on the street. She said you came to the door looking for me. You knew we were out of town."

I took a deep breath. "After that horrible night on the bridge, I was hoping you'd changed your plans and stayed home. So I took a chance. I was *upset*, Ray. Haven't you been feeling afraid? When you weren't there, I asked Agnes to join me for lunch."

He nodded, as if satisfied by the explanation. "The police came last night. They looked everywhere. I fled the house, terrified they'd see something in my eyes. If the police only knew what happened in that house last week."

"Did they find anything?"

"The prowler entered through a basement window. The detectives found some odd tracks in the mud in the garden, where we'd been working. Tracks in the basement, too. The police said they might be useful."

So much for Bernie, I thought. His reckless confidence would be the end of him.

"They found about a million fingerprints, too," he added.

"Drummond's?"

"Not likely. Father and I wiped everything down that night. But I'm sorry to tell you, some of the fingerprints may be yours."

"So what? I went to your house a few times, at your invitation."

"Yes, but the detective asked for the names of everyone who visited this summer. Mother gave them your name with the others. The police may want to interview you. And since the name you gave us is false, how's it going to look? As it is, it must have seemed very strange when I couldn't provide an address or a phone number for you. Tell the truth now, why *had* you called yourself Charles Powell for a ridiculous French class?"

I could never tell him about the work I did for Heinz. "It's . . . it's a long story, and I don't have enough time to tell it—"

Raymond interrupted, "It doesn't matter now, anyway. You must leave town right away. If the police somehow connect us to Drummond's death, I won't let it involve you."

"I am leaving, soon as possible. I'm only waiting for . . . my final paycheck."

"A paycheck?" He looked confused again. "Your weekly wages aren't worth your safety. Just pack up and get lost."

"You don't understand. My family isn't wealthy like yours. I need every penny I can earn this summer."

Even as I spoke, I doubted the words registered with him. Raymond never knew what it meant for me to pay for our meals and taxis and cinema tickets. He never could have understood how dear that money was to me. At the same time, considering our friendship had led to so many troubles for him, maybe the two of us were even after all.

He only said, "This town isn't safe for either of us now. Go back to St. Louis the first moment you can. I'll leave, too, as soon as I have some money. I can sell my records and my tennis gear. A priest doesn't even need a tuxedo, I suppose."

When I rose to my feet, he did the same.

"Again," I said. "I'm truly sorry. About all of it."

"Stop apologizing, please. I'm the one who's sorry."

I began to step away. "Tell your mother I said good-bye."

"She adores you, too. That's the truth."

"She adores Charles Powell, not me."

"You're only splitting hairs now. Listen, I've said this before, but I want us to stay in touch. You want that, too, don't you? I'll write to you in a few weeks, after I'm settled somewhere. Nothing that will shock your family, I promise. To them, I'll only be the friend you made at a French class. Give me your home address, will you?"

I pretended to pat down my pockets, just as I'd done the first time we met, when he asked for my card. "I haven't got anything to write on."

"In that case, write to me when you get home. You have our address. But don't wait too long, because I won't be anywhere near Chicago by the end of the month."

Could I ever write? I supposed I could write a long letter and explain everything: how difficult things were for us on the farm, and how it led me to lie and betray his family for money. And how, despite that invisible barrier that had always existed between us, I'd genuinely appreciated his kindness and affection. I could tell him how much his example had meant to me.

No. I would only apologize. I owed him that, at least. I wouldn't include my return address. Just the one letter.

"Of course I'll write. I won't forget."

"So long," he called, "but only for now!"

When he lifted his hand to wave, I stepped close enough to squeeze it for a long moment, not wanting to let go. "Thank you, Ray. For everything. Good-bye."

With that, I released him, and we went our separate ways.

TWENTY-NINE

DEL STARED AT MY FEET. "Well? Where's the dog?"

I couldn't speak. My head was in a fog after saying good-bye to Raymond. Sweat made my skin feel sticky. At the kitchen sink, I filled a tall glass with cold water. I drank it like I'd returned from the Sahara, then filled up the glass again.

"You *found* the *owner!*" Del guessed brightly. "What's the family like? Did they seem awful relieved?"

"Over on Burton Place," I said, between gulps. "Just like Bernie told us. A little girl recognized her. Named Daisy."

"The girl?"

"No, the dog."

"How sweet. Daisy. Oh, I'm so pleased, Joe."

Bernie's voice came from the hallway: "Attaboy, Joe!"

I set the glass on the counter. When I turned around, Bernie stood in the doorframe with his hands raised in the air, celebratory, like a circus showman. His cheeks could hardly contain his wide smile. "Did you get a reward?"

"Did you see Heinz?"

"Nah, not yet. Haven't been out of the apartment yet. Forget about that now and tell us what happened."

"Bernie, you *promised*. We made a deal. I'd take your pooch to find the owner, and you'd go see Heinz."

Bernie only stared at me with that goofy grin, as if waiting to hear the biggest story of the year. "So come on, let's have it. What'd they give you?"

"I never met the parents," I said. "The funny part was—I mean, it happened so fast. I didn't think to ask for a reward."

The kitchen fell dead silent, and I realized it wasn't the funny part after all. The mantel clock ticked loudly in the front room.

"At least we got the dog back where she belongs," I added, "so we can all get some sleep tonight."

Bernie's face turned pink. He began shouting: "You didn't *think* to ask for a reward? After all that *crap* with the *dog*, and us losing *sleep* all weekend, and the goddamn *food* we gave it, you didn't take two seconds to ask for some *compensation* for the trouble?"

I couldn't think what to say. I'd been so distracted by my conversation with Raymond, it never crossed my mind to ask the girl for a reward. I couldn't have asked for money, not with Ray sitting right there.

Even Del lifted her eyebrows at my foolishness. "You should have spoken with the girl's parents, Joe. To make sure she was telling the truth. A family like that, over on Burton Place, they gladly would have paid a reward."

"The two of them belonged together, anyone could see that," I said. "The dog danced around the girl's legs like a young pup."

Bernie's enraged face had gone from pink to green, as if he might be sick just from looking at me. His eyes became shiny, the first time in years I'd seen him even close to crying. He shouted, "Who the hell *cares* about *the stupid dog*, Joe? You—you *moron!*"

Turning, he stormed down the hall. I knew better than to follow him. He was too angry to listen. I only heard him swearing a blue streak and his bedroom drawers squealing until finally the apartment door slammed behind him.

I sank into a chair at the table, hoping Del might have some comforting words. But she only stared like she agreed with my cousin's assessment. We sat in silence for a minute or so, before she turned to face the kitchen window.

"It's a nasty piece of luck, and that's all there is to it."

* * *

After the dustup with Bernie, I needed some time to calm down. I wasn't sure who I was angrier with: my cousin, for not making it crystal clear the reward was so important; or myself, for forgetting it.

I splashed water on my face and neck, changed into my work clothes, and went downstairs. At the end of the block, Eddie was waiting in the delivery truck. When I climbed onto the seat, he gave my knee a friendly squeeze. He always made everything seem better. He knew he could lift my spirits. Today I was especially grateful for it.

"Wanna go visit your favorite warehouse pigeons?" he asked.

"I'm due at the hotel early. Let's go cool off near the water."

He drove us to the lake, and I treated him to a cherry Popsicle. We sat on a bench near the beach and watched the cruise liners sailing north from Navy Pier. Every now and then, Eddie knocked his foot against mine, or his knee against mine, or his massive shoulder against mine. I had never felt the need for my own personal bodyguard, but I always felt secure when I sat next to him.

I told him the story about taking the lost dog over to Burton Place. I tried to make it sound comical: walking back and forth along the empty street, the endless piss, and my struggle with the flyers and the rubber cement. How the little girl, when she found us, bawled into the dog's curly coat.

"Nice work!" Eddie said. "How much you get?"

I hoped my disappointment didn't show. "I forgot to ask for a reward. Does that mean I'm a chump?"

He laughed. "Listen, it's no crime to make a buck when opportunities come your way. Stick with me, I'll show you how to live in the big city."

I wanted to kiss him, but the park was too crowded. This was always the trouble for us. Finding private spots to be alone. Eddie shared a bedroom with three brothers, and at Del's, there was always the risk Bernie might burst in.

Eddie must have seen the desire in my eyes. "Listen, Peaches, I'm working on it."

"I'm leaving soon."

"Naw, you can't. Not 'til we figure this out. And like I said, I want us to visit some of the pansy parlors together. I'll make everything worth your while. Can't you be patient?"

I couldn't tell him why I had to beat it. I wanted Eddie always to think the best of me.

"It's lousy to think I won't see you after this summer," I said.

"Sure as hell lousy."

"You've told me you won't be married. But do you think you'll have someone? Someday?"

He turned toward the water, eyes scanning the horizon. "Hard to predict the future, Joe. But we'll take things day by day. Year by year. We'll meet fellows now and then—like this, what you and I have. We can have something really good. And then we'll move on."

I didn't agree with this bleak vision of the future, any more than I agreed with Raymond's.

"Eddie, like I've said before, I believe we *can* stay in touch after I go home."

"It's a swell thought but . . ."

"But what? Why can't we exchange letters as friends? I've promised to be discreet."

He sighed with a funny shake of his head.

"What? Tell me."

"Peaches, we both know the score. Don't we? Given the situation we're in, something temporary is the best we can have."

He spelled things out so plainly. On some level, I felt relieved to know his reluctance wasn't about me.

"But that's not what I want for my life," I said. "I want friendships that last. Affection that lasts. When I picture my future and think about myself coming home from work every day, I want to have somebody there waiting for me."

"What can I say, Joe?" he said with another laugh. "Maybe you should've held on to that poodle."

He rocked his shoulder against me playfully, but I didn't see the humor in what he said.

$$***$$

Inside the hotel kitchen, I was prepared to meet Bernie's fury again, but he wasn't there.

I stopped by Mertz's office. He lifted his shiny red nose from the books when I knocked. He looked peeved, even before I opened my trap.

"My cousin working tonight?"

"Nope."

Good, I thought. Give him time to cool down. And time to speak to Heinz.

Bernie wasn't at Del's when I got home from work and still no sign of him in the morning. If the point of his disappearing act was to get under my skin, it was working. Was Bernie ever going to get that money? If he did, would I ever see it?

Before she left for the drugstore, Del stood in her uniform washing breakfast dishes at the sink. "It's nothing for us to fret about."

"He's only got a girl, I bet," I said.

She rinsed the dishpan and hung it on a hook in the cupboard to dry. "He's a grown man, and I'm too young to be his mother," she concluded, although neither claim seemed entirely credible.

✳✳✳

On the way to the Lago Vista, I stopped by San Tropez Tropical Fish. The shop was locked and dark, with a sign in the window that read SEA YA REAL SOON. I knocked and waited, but nobody came. I stood far back on the sidewalk to look upstairs. No lights there either.

When I spun around to cross the street, a taxi nearly killed me. That's when I realized I'd stopped hearing all the traffic noise. I'd gotten used to it, the way Bernie had predicted.

I visited Mertz's office again, and he gave me another glare.

"My cousin working tonight?"

"Didn't he tell you?" he snapped. "Called up earlier. Quit on me, out of the blue."

"Quit? What for?"

"Hell if I know, kid. He's your family. Ask him yourself."

Family loyalty stopped me from telling Mertz I *couldn't* ask Bernie. I wouldn't let Mertz think my cousin was some stray cat.

"What, you didn't know?" Hannigan called from the meat counter.

"Why? You think I know every bit of his business just because he's my cousin?"

"No, because you can read minds, Nostradamus."

"Oh, right. Sure."

I grabbed my apron, facing a mountain of spuds to peel.

The fact that Bernie had called Mertz meant he was breathing, at least.

I went to find Jackson, stacking butter in the cooler.

"When are you playing policy again?" I asked him.

"Tomorrow night."

I gave him two more dollars. "Same three numbers. Three, fifteen and sixteen."

He smiled. "You sure? We've talked about this, Joe."

I'd never felt less sure of anything in my life.

"Positive," I said.

✱✱✱

My cousin didn't show his face at Del's that night or in the morning. Now my blood was running colder than ever. Returning to

Del's after work on Wednesday, I pulled the shoeboxes out of the closet again so I could check the money. I counted it out on the cot. Both down payments, still there. Bernie had hardly touched his.

This time, I didn't feel the least bit guilty about checking. If Bernie was willing to quit the hotel job without breathing a word to me, what made me think he'd ever come back with the money from Heinz?

I took the share from my shoebox and crept down the hallway to the bathroom. Opening the linen cupboard, I grabbed the towel containing the two hundred from Mr. Kenrick. I added my down payments for safekeeping and put the towel back.

Without the payout from Heinz, I'd be returning home with just enough money to save the farm and not one cent to fund my own future.

Nobody ever said life was fair. My cousin had warned me on the very first day.

THIRTY

"**W**HAT DO YOU KNOW?" Bernie said. "Rip Van Winkle awakes."

My eyes opened to the sight of my cousin on the bed, still in his skivvies. I'd never been happier to see those dumb hairy legs.

On the floor were more hardcovers, now with yellow-and-black covers. Dashiell Hammett. Bernie was back at it with the fountain pen. He finished blowing on a new signature to dry the ink.

"What time is it?" I asked.

"What do you care?"

"I got in pretty late. You must have crept in later . . ." *Like a thief,* I didn't add.

He slapped the book closed and reached for a cigarette. "I feel perfectly rested."

I pushed myself up and stood to face him. I braced myself to hear the hard truth.

"Level with me, Bern. I can take it, whatever you say. Are we ever gonna get that money from Heinz? We've been patient as hell, but once and for all—"

He reached to his side, near the window, and tossed a brown paper sack over to my cot. I scooped it up and looked inside. Nothing but stacks of green.

"Golly."

"Go ahead, count it. It's all there. I told you, Heinz is a man you can rely on."

I made piles of cash on the cot. Heinz had already paid me forty-eight dollars, so I counted out the balance of three hundred fifty-two. That sum, plus the two hundred from Mr. Kenrick, plus my hotel wages, was everything I needed. I hardly dared acknowledge what it meant for me. Now home would only be a pit stop on my way to something bigger.

I put the rest back in the sack. "Thanks, Bern," I said sincerely. Despite everything the scheme had put me through, I was grateful to be holding that cash at last. "Haven't seen much of you this week. You had us worried."

"You, maybe. Del knows better than to worry. I've been peachy."

"Good for you."

He reached for another book. "Then again, something nutty happened yesterday, when I was walking over in the Gold Coast. Over there on Dearborn."

"Looking for another poodle to pinch?" I teased.

He wrote a signature and gave it some air before slapping the cover closed. "In fact, I was over there to check out the bulletin board at St. Chrysostom's. Seeing when the next language class might start."

"Count me out, thanks."

"No argument there. But listen to this. Instead of a sign for a new language course, guess what I saw?"

"What?"

"A drawing of your stupid mug."

"Hold on, really? There's a sign up?"

"Honest to god. Like a police sketch or something."

"It looked like me?"

"Big poster, too. 'Charles Powell,' it says, and that's you, last time I checked. 'Charles Powell—Wanted for Questioning.' A poster up like that, and in a lousy church. Your postcards really gummed things up for us."

"I guess the foolproof plan you cooked up with Heinz wasn't so foolproof."

"That's one way to put it. I'd say it's the last time we work with a fool. Any flunky could have done that job, and you know it."

"Listen, Bern. The Kenricks are back from their trip. Raymond told me they've got cops there at their house, taking fingerprints and asking questions. Sounds like you left some unusual-looking footprints in the basement over there."

He sat up. "Wait a minute, you got together with Kenrick—after what we talked about? Nah, that's no good. You gotta stay away from there."

"It wasn't planned," I said. "We ran into each other on the street when I took the dog over there. I'm not a jerk. If it were my choice, I wouldn't go anywhere near that house. But here's the problem. When Raymond told me about the robbery, he said it's possible people think it's *me* that broke in."

"Does he think so?"

"Ray knows I'd never do something like that. But now that you tell me about my face on a poster, it seems like I should pack up and get lost."

He nodded. "You got your money now. At this point, making tracks is not the worst idea. Especially if it means saying sayonara to Raymond Kenrick. Yeesh."

"You never even met him."

"Be a man for once, Joe! You and I both know what I saw in that bedroom. People will judge you based on the crowd you hang around."

"Yeah? And what about you? Mertz says you quit the Lago Vista. You working with Heinz full-time now?"

"We help each other out, sure."

"Listen to yourself. You say people will judge me for spending time with Raymond. But aren't those same people going to judge you for working with Heinz?"

"It takes real nerve for you to say that, sitting there with that cash."

"I'm only saying I don't like the garbage he pulled us into."

"Joe, the whole point of us coming here was to make some dough for our families. You don't make any dough by standing around watching. You make it by using your brain and taking risks."

"But we've been taking risks *without* using our brains."

"What, you expected me to keep working in that lousy hotel kitchen for the rest of my miserable life? You want me to end up like Hannigan or Jackson?"

"They're honest men, hard workers."

"You think that would make the family proud?"

"You could get training and find better jobs over time. That's the way people should do it."

"Nah, that's how chumps do it. Waiting for their luck to change. Waiting by the mailbox for their kids to send money home. That's a loser strategy, Joe."

"You think working with someone like Heinz is a better plan?"

"I take the opportunities I see. That's my only plan. And you can judge me for that, but keep it to yourself. Especially after all the ways I've helped you out this summer. Got you a job. Found you a place to sleep, helped you earn some easy cash. Now you have the nerve to judge me for my choices? Come on."

He was right. I owned my choices, like he owned his.

"I thanked you already. Something wrong with your ears, Bern?"

He didn't answer. He got out of bed with the bag of cash. He put it in the shoebox in the closet with his down payments. If he noticed my box felt empty, he didn't mention it.

I pulled on some trousers and stuffed my share of the payout in my pocket. When the coast was clear, I'd add it to my stash in the bathroom cupboard.

"The sooner you pack up and get lost, the better," he said. "That's my advice."

"I will. Having lunch with a friend first."

"Who? Not Kenrick."

"Someone else. I told you, I won't see Raymond again."

"You better not. The family wouldn't like you going down the wrong street, not like that. You understand what I'm saying?"

I wouldn't acknowledge the accusation. But he studied me so intently, I finally turned toward the sink to brush my teeth.

After a moment, he lit up a smoke, leaning against the headboard.

"The saddest part is," he said, "I genuinely looked forward to having you here this summer. I figured we'd come in handy for each other whenever we needed something. The way family does."

I had to admit, one thing Bernie had always done for family

was come in handy. He'd sent that money, envelope after envelope, never missing a month.

"We've done that. We always will."

"Okay, then, Joe, see you in church."

I went into the hallway and closed the door. After I deposited the money in the bathroom, I went to the kitchen and had a bowl of Wheaties. When I came back to the room, my cousin was gone.

THIRTY-ONE

I WOULDN'T HAVE STUCK AROUND AT ALL, except for one last chance to see Eddie. I needed to make our last date a real humdinger.

I sat on the cot and wrote my address on a scrap of paper. I'd force it on him, if I had to. I felt certain we could write to each other safely. Nothing romantic or queer, nothing risky. We just needed to stay connected. I even had the money to come visit now and again, after things had cooled down.

The thought made me smile, and I drew a heart around the address. My name wasn't anywhere on it. If Eddie's mother found it in his pocket when she was doing laundry, he could claim he'd gotten it from a girl on his delivery route.

I pulled on the new twill trousers, along with a clean Oxford shirt. Even though I wouldn't have occasions to wear these things back home, I treated the clothes gently. They'd serve a purpose, now that I could see the future. A future beyond college, even. It didn't take any special powers either. Someday I would move freely, as needed, wherever my degree might take me. I'd make a good life in a big city, a life without secrets in a place built for exploring. My salary would be enough to pay my bills and my mother's, and I'd still have plenty left over to spend on pictures and restaurants, shopping, maybe even on ocean liners. I'd build my queer syndicate, one by one, starting with Eddie. We'd form lasting friendships, not temporary ones, and over time we'd find a whole community of people who truly understood, and they'd become family. Now that I had the money in hand, none of it felt like a daydream anymore. It felt like a plan.

✳✳✳

At noon, I found Eddie on the sidewalk outside Del's building, grinning like a lunatic. I was up for anything, as long as we were nowhere near the Gold Coast and that stupid sign hanging at the church. I pulled down the brim of my hat to hide my face.

I didn't spot the delivery truck anywhere. "Did you walk?"

"No truck today. Today is special."

"Yeah?"

"Didn't I promise I'd figure it out?" He pointed to a nice car parked at the curb. A gleaming, apple-red Buick. "Jump in. Thirty minutes ago, I dropped the whole family off at the big fair downtown. They'll be occupied all day."

I got in and ran my fingers across the seat, which was upholstered in ivory fabric. "Gee, Eddie, it's real nice."

"Sure is. Pop uses this car when he's hobnobbing with clients. Looks swell, right? It's my genuine style, to be honest."

Eddie looked swell, too. He was wearing a striped blue shirt with a bright white collar, the fabric tight against his chest. Gray trousers. He always looked sharp when he dressed up even a little.

"Say, Eddie, let's take a drive somewhere. Show me something new."

"I'm taking you back to my house," he said. "You wanted to see it, right? We'll have the whole place to ourselves. I'm not collecting the family until after supper."

I couldn't think of a better way to say good-bye. But I didn't have all day. I wanted to get the bad news out of the way first. "Mind if we grab a bite on the way?"

"I'd swear you *can* read my mind sometimes. I could eat a horse!"

He drove south for a while, then turned onto Taylor Street. He parked in front of an Italian restaurant, a walk-down place, with windows high up on the brick wall and a view of shoes passing on the sidewalk. We could hear a lively violin playing at a nicer joint across the street. All I cared about was that we were plenty far from the church on Dearborn.

At the table, Eddie put aside the menus like we didn't need them. "You gotta try the pizza pie here," he said.

"Shouldn't we have lunch first?"

"Before what?"

"Before we have pie?"

"No, Joe, it's not a dessert. Pizza pie is the main dish, you'll see."

When the pizza pie came, it wasn't like any pie I'd ever seen. Salami and mushrooms on top, rather than fruit. Plus, it was a wreck; it looked unfinished. But once Eddie demonstrated how to go about eating it, I decided it was the most delicious thing I ever tasted.

The second I'd wolfed down the last slice, Eddie's face turned serious. "Listen, I want to talk to you about something."

"Me, too. Let me go first."

He laughed. "Aw, c'mon—"

"Eddie, listen, I'm not joking." I glanced over my shoulder. "I'm leaving."

"I know you are. I hate even to consider it. But we'll make the most of it before you go. It's what I want us to talk about."

"No, I mean I'm leaving tonight. I only need to collect my paycheck and make a train."

His head cocked back in surprise. "What happened to you staying another week?"

I stared into his handsome brown eyes. I could never tell him the truth—not about the poster up at the church or the burglary. "There aren't enough bookings at the hotel. Mertz can't give me the hours anymore."

"He canned you? When?"

"Last night. He sounded awful sorry."

Eddie blinked twice, like he needed to process the news. Then he lifted his hands jovially. "I mean, so what? That only means you got more free time. I can treat when we go out, if money's the problem. Hell, I'll drive you all the way home myself, when the time comes."

"Eddie, that's swell, but you don't—"

"I want to! I just need to convince my folks to lend me the car. I'd need help with the gasoline, but it's cheaper than the cost of a train ticket."

He was trying so hard, but I couldn't stay in town another week. "Tomorrow's my mother's birthday. I want to surprise her." The lies kept pouring out, like water from a garden hose.

I reached into my pocket and took out the scrap of paper I'd brought for him. "Anyhow, take this. That's my home address right there. We talked about this. I want us to stay in touch. Can't we try, at least?"

He examined the address, looking almost sad. "Aw, you drew a little heart on it."

"Throw it away once you write it down somewhere permanent." I glanced around again, making sure no one could overhear. "I'd never write something queer in a letter. Never. I'd only write about school, or college, or I'd send you a joke now and then. You could tell me about work or your family, whatever you want. What I'm saying is, I want what we have to be more than temporary."

"I want that, too. Let's start with you not leaving town so quick. You really can't stay? Not even for one more week?"

"I've got to get some money back to the farm, or we'll be in even sorrier shape than we are right now."

His face brightened. "But that's what I want to talk about, Joe. I know a way to earn more money, right here in the city." Now he was the one checking for snoops. "C'mon, let's beat it."

He paid for the pizza pie, and we returned to the Buick. We sat facing each other in the front seat. It was scorching inside the car. We lowered the windows, but he didn't start the motor.

"Joe, don't you ever wonder how I have cash to pay for things when we go out? Like that pizza pie you enjoyed so much?"

I hadn't wondered about it at all. "I see you working hard. Figured your dad gives you spending money when you need it."

"Believe me, I've tried. I get squat from him."

"So what then?"

"It's easy." He took a deep breath. "You asked me once to go to the pansy bars, and I told you I don't care for them. Remember? That's the truth. I only go when I need to."

"What does that mean?"

"You can make money in those places. Ten bucks a night without even trying. I'd make more if I worked with a buddy. We could work it together."

Uncomfortably, I recalled my first night in town, and the geezer who offered me two dollars in the park.

"Doing what?" I asked, even though I wasn't sure I wanted the answer.

Eddie's cheeks had turned pink. He looked almost shy. "Plucking feathers, Joe." He laughed. "It's the silly name they give it. Plucking feathers. It's just lifting wallets. I get five bucks each. More, if there's something juicy in the wallet. That gets me ten."

"From who? Who calls it plucking feathers?"

He shrugged. "Some fellows I met last year."

I sat back against the car door. "No, no . . . Eddie, that happened to my pal. He's in terrible trouble now."

"There's a risk to going to them places. Everybody knows that."

"But—ever since my pal's wallet was stolen, these goons have been showing up at his house. Threatening him and his folks. Demanding payment."

"And what happened?"

I hesitated. "The father took care of him."

"Paid him the money?"

I nodded.

"Yeah, well, that's what you do, when you deal with those

people. It's a dangerous city if a person isn't careful. Sounds like your pal learned a valuable lesson."

"But it's wrong. You shouldn't be part of it." Even then, I recognized the hypocrisy in my own words. I hated to ask, but I needed to know: "Did you ever try to take *my* wallet?"

He looked injured by the question. "What? Naw, Peaches, never gave it a thought."

"How come?"

"The fellows you meet out there, they're all full of it. Nobody ever tells the truth. Not about who they are, or where they're going, or what they want. It's like a game with them. When a fellow does tell the truth, turns out it's only half the story, at best."

"But don't you feel sorry for them? Telling the truth can make a person vulnerable."

"Joe, you showed me your library card without me even asking. I admired that about you. From the first second when I saw you in that stinkin' alley, I never once thought about messing with you."

"But those people you know, they harassed my pal. Exposed him to his parents. How many men's lives have been ruined?"

"I never did *nothing* like that. All I did was sell the feathers I plucked for five dollars each. They all can survive the loss of a feather."

"That's not all they're losing, and you know it."

He sighed. "The way I see it, times have been hard. Our options are limited. I'm offering you a way to earn some easy cash before you leave. I'll show you exactly how to do it. There's no risk, not when you're with me."

He sounded like my cousin now, and I didn't want to listen. The sweat running down my face made my eyes sting.

"It's not for me, thanks," I said. "Say, do you mind if we cut things short? Heat's getting to me, and I've got a train to catch."

He didn't start the engine. He only leaned closer, squeezing my knee. For once, I tried to move my leg out of reach.

"You act like such a saint sometimes," he whispered.

"I'm no saint. Never claimed to be."

"Haven't we all done things we're not proud of? Say, very late at night? Like dumping some old carpet off a bridge?"

There was a long moment when we only stared at each other. A bomb might have exploded on the sidewalk and we wouldn't have noticed.

"What did you say?"

"You heard me."

"Hold the phone. You know about that? How?"

His smile looked almost guilty. "I was there, Peaches."

I dimly recalled a car crossing the steel bridge just after Raymond and I dropped the carpet. We'd kept our backs to the street. I hadn't thought twice about it.

"It didn't sound like your truck."

"I wasn't in the truck. I was right where I'm sitting now, behind the wheel of this Buick."

"And what? You just happened to drive by and see us at that particular moment? What are the chances?"

"Chance had nothing to do with it. C'mon, Joe, I'd been following you."

"Following me?" It took a moment before my mouth could form the obvious word: "Why?"

"I knew you weren't being straight with me. From the very beginning, I liked you a hell of a lot. You worked hard. You told me your name. But you kept giving me the runaround. You never had time for me, even when you weren't at the hotel. I could tell you were leaving something out."

"So you tailed me?"

"Only a few times. I followed you to that church on Dearborn where you took your French classes. Even followed you to the pictures once." He gave an unhappy laugh. "*Fog Over Frisco*, now that one had a nutty story. I didn't stay long."

I felt a hole form in my stomach, the size of a pizza pie.

"Twice, when I asked directly if you were seeing anybody else, you said no. That's when I knew I couldn't trust you. Not completely. I never could figure out your angle, spending time with your rich pal. You'll have to explain it sometime—"

"If you didn't trust me, why give me any time at all?"

"Because I like you a lot, Peaches. Always have. And then the idea struck me that we might make some cash real easy, working it together."

I looked out the window. I couldn't face him. Part of me wanted to run, but I needed to know the full story. "My pal, the one you saw me with. Blond—"

"Believe me, I'm familiar."

"Did you see us that night at Vi's Little Grapevine and take his wallet?"

Just like that, the light in his eyes went out. I never saw those dimples again.

"Was it because you were jealous?" I asked.

"Don't ask questions you don't want answers to," he said. "After all, I'm not giving *you* the third degree. I haven't even asked what you were doing on that bridge that night. Not even after the newspapers reported they pulled a carpet from the river—"

"That was different."

"A corpse rolled up in a carpet. What do you say about that? I don't want to know them answers, do I?"

I didn't respond. No reason to. "Take me back to where I'm staying. Please."

"The thing is, I actually knew the piece of garbage you dropped in the water. Nobody's crying any tears for George Drummond, that's for sure. Dirtiest devil rat there ever was. Tell you the truth, Joe, he's the one who got me into this racket. I didn't volunteer for it, not at first. That fink found me when I was only—"

"I'm sorry, Eddie, I need to go."

He groaned angrily. "I'm still not asking you questions, am I? But I could."

"I was helping my friend."

"You and I can help each other, too! My whole point here was to offer you some extra cash. Pluck a few feathers at five dollars each. That's all."

"But it's more than that. It's ruining the lives of people."

He struck the steering wheel with his fists. "I'm telling you, they never told me what they do with the wallets!"

He was lying. I knew it because of his childish anger, his desperation to justify his actions. I recognized it in myself.

Clouds passed over the sun, and everything around us went gray, nothing but the blur of automobile traffic.

"Let's settle down a second," Eddie said. "I can put that night on the bridge out of my mind. Can't you forget what I told you about plucking feathers?"

The request made me feel like the biggest fool in the world. I needed to stop ignoring the wrong side of things. Stop separating actions from their consequences.

"The scrap of paper," I said. "The one I gave you at the restaurant with my address. You still have it?"

"Sure, I do."

"Prove it."

He reached into his trousers and pulled out the paper to show me.

"Give it back."

His eyes narrowed in confusion.

I didn't wait—I tore the scrap out of his hand. I couldn't believe I got it so easily. The paper was soaking wet from sweat, the ink cloudy. "Thanks," I said, turning forward in the seat. "Now let's go."

"Sure," Eddie said. "We can even make a stop first. It's well over a week since Drummond was killed. I expect the cops would welcome leads from anybody. Even someone like me. There might be a reward."

Finally, there it was: a threat.

"You won't go to the cops," I said. "You'd only be ratting on yourself. You admitted already, you don't know the first thing about what happened."

"Forgive me, I'm such a dumb onion, I thought maybe I knew *the first thing*. Tell me something. Did you kill George Drummond? Was it because he was threatening your friend?"

"No, Eddie. You really don't know. It was an accident. Drummond forced himself into the house and attacked the family. He got injured in the fight. It wasn't planned."

Eddie leaned forward against the steering wheel, wiping his mouth with his thick forearm. "That's one version of the story.

We can come up with some others. I'll wager Raymond Kenrick is capable of more than you even think."

I froze. I'd been careful not to mention Raymond's name. First name or last. Not even once. Eddie knew both. Maybe he knew all about him. I needed two seconds to absorb it all.

"It's a shame, Joe. We could've been friends. We might've written pretty letters back and forth, like you wanted. But for whatever reason, you can't admit that you and I are exactly the same. Out of the same can."

I didn't want to believe it, but maybe he was right. Either way, the person he thought he knew wasn't the person I wanted to be.

In a flash, I got out of the car, leaving the door open behind me. I stopped a taxi passing on Taylor Street and jumped in, giving the driver Del's address.

Through the grimy window, I saw Eddie standing in the street next to the Buick. He hollered for me to wait, but I told the driver to step on it.

THIRTY-TWO

EDDIE'S THREAT WAS THE LAST STRAW. I needed to disappear. If I chanced another night at Del's, I might wake up to find either Heinz or the cops standing above me. No telling which would be worse.

The taxi dropped me at the corner drugstore so I could use the telephone. Mertz seemed neither surprised nor disappointed to hear I was quitting. I hadn't lied to Eddie about that part; the August bookings were as dead as George Drummond.

"It's only Thursday, kid," Mertz said. "Won't have your paycheck until tomorrow."

"But—I need to leave tonight. Couldn't I pick it up today? I'll come by as soon as I can."

Nothing but static on the line for three or four seconds. "I'll see what I can do." Mertz hung up before I could thank him.

Leaving the drugstore, I scanned the street, wondering if Eddie had followed me, but saw no sign of him or the red Buick.

Inside the apartment, Del sat on the davenport in the front room, her feet soaking in a pan of Epsom salts. I went to the bathroom to make a withdrawal.

When I returned, I announced, "Del, I'm packing up and leaving today."

Her face lit up. "What for? Has something *terrible* happened at home?"

"Nothing like that. The hotel cut my position, and I'm eager to catch a train as soon as possible."

She nodded, but didn't say anything. It wasn't the kind of story she liked.

"Anyhow, I want to settle up for the room."

I placed two fives and four ones on the seat cushion next to her.

Her expression softened. "Why, that's too much, Joe."

"It's for the next two weeks," I explained. "I'm leaving sooner than we agreed upon."

"But the room is only three per week."

"Three total?"

"Same as it's always been. Same as the day Bernard moved in last year."

"I thought—" I started. But of course, I'd already suspected it. Rather than splitting the rent with me, Bernie had charged me the total cost and slept in the better bed for free. And increased the rent.

"I shouldn't even charge you," she added. "I feel safer having you boys in the apartment. You can't imagine what happens to single girls who live alone. The other day, I read the most shocking story in *True Detective* about a gal in Reno who—"

"Keep it all, please," I interrupted. "Put it toward my cousin's charges."

"That's generous, Joe. By the way, this came for you." She lifted an envelope from the side table and handed it to me.

I went to the bedroom to read it. The letter was the shortest my mother had sent. No clippings either, like she no longer worried about squandering postage.

First she reported that she'd seen Mary Toomey's mother. "I do wish you'd told me about it yourself, Joe. I must have looked awfully embarrassed."

Then the letter took an unpleasant turn. "A mother cannot be blind to her child's true nature, especially when that child is her only son. Please don't think I don't know what's going on. I have lived on this planet for a long time, and I understand some things. I know all men are not the same. Men are as various as flowers in a garden, and some of them need tending to. I won't let your bashfulness be your doom, Joe. Every woman wants to find a husband, and when everything comes to pass, I promise you won't be one of the poor souls left standing alone."

In the final lines, she reminded me that I would be home soon: "All the people who know you are still here. Nothing has changed. And isn't that a comfort?"

The letter fell from my hand to the cot, as a familiar dread washed over me.

Home would never change, and college was still a year away. Or longer. And the danger of staying in Chicago loomed larger every hour.

I grabbed my suitcase from the closet and pulled out my things. I was struck by the shabbiness of my farm clothes: faded fabrics, buttons loose, cuffs on the trousers frayed beyond repair. There had been times that summer when I dreamed I would never wear these old threads again. Now that I was heading home, I felt glad I'd saved them. This was the real Joe Garbe, the one I'd almost lost by pretending to be someone else.

It was like Bernie had said: I needed to grow up, be a man. And face whatever hell came of it.

I didn't want to believe Eddie and I were out of the same can. Maybe I could prove that we weren't, once and for all.

Suitcase packed, I went to the kitchen and sat with the newspaper. I studied the travel advertisements.

When I found what I needed, I visited the bathroom and withdrew the rest of my cash. I took it back to the room and set the money on the cot.

Next, I found Bernie's share, waiting in the shoebox in the closet, right next to the Flit roach spray. I added this money to the pile on the cot.

Life wasn't fair; it had never been fair.

The combined payout from Heinz was six hundred. Except for what we'd sent home already and what I'd spent with Raymond, most of it was there. Plus the two hundred from Mr. Kenrick. Plus my wages from work.

The envelopes from my mother were stacked on the bureau. I'd saved them all. I took three of them and dumped the news clippings into the wastebasket.

I took the two hundred from Mr. Kenrick and stuffed it into one envelope.

Into a second envelope went one hundred and twenty dollars.

On the back of the third, I printed a quick note to my cousin: *For the clothes and the class. Thanks for coming in handy.* I inserted one hundred and forty dollars, dropped it into the shoebox, and returned it to the closet. Bernie would be sore as hell, maybe forever, but he wouldn't rat on me. We knew too much about each other now.

I slid the other two envelopes and the rest of the cash into my pocket. With a final look around the room, I grabbed my suitcase and found Del standing on bare wet feet near the door.

"Good luck to you, Joe," she said. As if she knew I truly needed it.

✳ ✳ ✳

I walked east along Elm Street until I got to State Parkway. With my hat pulled low and my nose to the ground, I wondered how long it would take to shake the paranoid feeling of being followed.

The sky had grown overcast. My suitcase was heavy, and I alternated hands at each new block. Everything felt the same as it did the first time I walked over to see Raymond. Same drop in air temperature, same cool breeze from the lake. Same nerves running through my veins.

I knocked on the door, praying that Agnes wouldn't answer.

She answered anyway. The friendliness we'd forged was gone. "Look what the cat dragged in," she said with a scowl.

"Is Raymond here?"

"You're not supposed to see him. Not unless his parents are here."

"Agnes, please—"

To my relief, Ray appeared behind her. He wore cream-colored linen pants and a thin cotton undershirt. He always looked even more slender, almost vulnerable, without a proper shirt. Like Agnes, he didn't seem overjoyed to see me.

When she backed off, Ray stepped outside and pulled the door closed behind him. "What are you doing here? I thought you cleared out of town."

"I'm leaving today. It's not safe to stick around any longer."

The panic rose in his voice. "That's exactly what I told you. You can't be seen here."

"It's not safe for you either, Ray. Do you remember that night on the bridge—a car driving by? The driver of the car knows who you are. Your name and where you live. He knows all about Drummond. He could tip off the police."

His mouth fell open, but he didn't speak.

"I needed to warn you. And to give you this." I handed him the first envelope, containing two hundred cash.

He looked inside the envelope. When he saw the stack of bills, his blue eyes widened. "Holy cats, have you robbed a bank?"

"No, your father gave me that money after that awful trip to the river with Drummond. There's enough there for a train ride to anywhere you want to go. Enough to live on, too, until you're settled."

He was thumbing the bills, as if making sure they were real. "Look, my hands are trembling. Don't you need this cash?"

"Not that money, no. I have enough to pay down some bills at home. That's all I came here to do, anyway."

"How can I thank you?" he asked.

"Well—for starters, please don't go hiding in the priesthood."

"Why not?"

"Do you even believe in God?"

"Listen, we haven't got time for a religious debate right now. You must leave, *please*. Agnes will telephone my parents. Worse, she'll call the police!"

"Take that cash and start somewhere new, just like you said. Someplace where nobody knows you or your family. You can get a job and finish school."

His eyes were watery now. "I'm speechless for once."

A siren wailed in the distance, but I didn't see anything.

"Real quick," I said, "here's how you can thank me. My true name is Joe Garbe, and I live on a bankrupt farm with my mother in a town you've never heard of called Kickapoo. My address is there, see? The return address on the envelope. Write to me when you find a permanent place. Will you do that?"

He bit his lip, glancing at the envelope. "After all this, I don't know why you'd ever want to hear from me again."

"Where I'm from, Ray, I don't know anyone like you. Anyone like us, I mean. I want to be part of your syndicate. And when I'm back home, it will cheer me to know you're out there. Out in the world."

He smiled, at last. "I'll write, I promise."

The siren got louder, and I grabbed my suitcase. "I better beat it."

He held up a hand as if he wanted to say more, but there wasn't time. "*Adieu,*" he said in our secret language.

"*Au revoir!*" I called, bounding down the steps to the sidewalk.

I raced down the block and jumped into the first taxi I saw heading downtown. In the rearview mirror, I could see a cherry top turning onto Raymond's street.

✻✻✻

I gave the driver the address of the Lago Vista, my heart pumping fast. It was the first time all summer I splurged on a taxi between the Gold Coast and the hotel. Bernie always said it was a point of pride to use our feet.

This time I felt proud again, but in a different way. For the first time in weeks, I felt more like myself. The conversation with Eddie had helped me see everything. Just because I was queer didn't mean I had to be crooked. And now Raymond knew my real name. First and last. It felt swell to be introduced.

When the taxi moved to Wabash, I watched the crowded sidewalks and buildings. I tried to read the thousand advertising signs rushing by, recording them to memory.

LIFEBUOY SOAP – NO "B.O." NOW!

PRICES NEVER TO BE REPEATED

KENMORE IMPERIAL – THE SAFEST WRINGER WE KNOW!

3 HOUR SERVICE – SAME DAY SERVICE

SKY RIDE TAP – PACKAGE GOODS – SANDWICHES

The sight made me feel teary again, because I couldn't stay.

My mother would be glad to see me, at least. That's what I told myself. I'd surprise her with more cash than she'd seen in years. We'd pay down some bills and figure things out. Home was the one place Bernie couldn't tell the whole story. The only place I could afford to go was home.

THIRTY-THREE

I PUSHED INTO THE KITCHEN AT THE LAGO VISTA, savoring the aroma of meat grilling in fry pans and Jackson's cakes browning in the oven. I sure would miss the good smells. I'd miss the cold gelatin molds pressing against my forearms, and the elegant silence of the carpeted, air-cooled hallways upstairs, and the remarkable sound of waitresses cussing.

When I went to Mertz's office, he plucked the paycheck from his ledger and handed it to me. "Any time you need work, kid, you stop by."

"I'm obliged, and grateful for the opportunity."

He mopped his sweaty nose with a handkerchief. "Don't take any wooden nickels," he said, before returning to his ledger.

Looking unhappy, Hannigan called from the freezer. "Mertz says you're leaving?"

When I nodded, he reached out his huge, clammy mitt and we shook for the first and last time. "You know what'll work out best, Nostradamus."

"No," I said. "I never claimed I could see the future."

Funny thing was, for once, I knew exactly what my future held. A journey home to the world I knew. Same comforts and same discomforts. If I wasn't careful, there'd be Sunday dinners with Mary Toomey and her folks. But I'd be more careful this time.

I found Jackson standing at the pastry counter, slicing apples for tarts. When he saw me, he set down the paring knife. He placed his fists on his hips, as if ready to scold me. "Planning to leave without saying good-bye?"

"I'm saying it now. But hold on, have you ever heard of *pizza pie*?"

With a helpless shrug, he said, "I'd make it for you, if you weren't going. I don't miss your cousin one bit, but I'll miss you."

"I'm grateful to you, Jackson. For everything. I'm heading to the station now, but wanted to give you something first." I handed him the second envelope. "A seven-day Great Lakes Cruise to Niagara Falls costs sixty dollars per person. There's enough here for two tickets."

His smile looked uncertain.

"Fed came through with the farm aid," I lied. I couldn't tell him the real story. Jackson only liked stories with happy endings. "We're all set back home, and so I want you to have that."

"That's awful kind of you. But the thing is . . . To be perfectly honest, I don't know if Gertrude and I would feel comfortable on one of those cruises."

"What do you mean?"

"I'm sure they're wonderful, but they're not, you know, for everyone. No, what we'd like to do is drive to Niagara. We'd lodge in places we've heard about. Establishments that are more welcoming . . . Maybe that sounds strange to you."

I recalled the places Raymond had taken me to. The places Mayor Kelly planned to shut down. "I think I understand. But say, you can get a decent used car for a hundred dollars. Use this money to buy the car, then. Go on, take it, please."

Jackson pressed the envelope into his apron belt. "I appreciate it, Joe, I really do. But before you go, we need to talk." He removed his toque, setting it on the counter. "Not here. Come along now, and not a word to anyone."

I followed him out to the alley. The sky had grown dark with clouds. The humidity only strengthened the stench of food rotting in the bins. I would miss Jackson and his baking, but I wouldn't miss this stinkhole alley.

He motioned us into a corner. Making sure no one was watching, he pulled a thick stack of bills out of his pocket. Hundreds of bills.

I didn't trust my eyes. All I could think was that maybe our numbers had been lucky, at last. "You won?" I said. "Or I did?"

He pushed the cash back into his trousers, looking over his shoulder again. "Neither. I never win at that stupid game. Or, hardly ever. Told you that a few times."

"So where'd you get it?"

He grinned. "Close your mouth and I'll tell you. Near where Gertrude and me stay, there's this nice house on Oak Park Avenue. Solid brick, built before the Great War, the kind of house you can't *help* but notice, see? We admire it every time we pass by. Except the grass in front has looked like trash all summer. Weeks go by and the lawn is looking sorrier and sorrier."

"Did you knock on the door?"

He shook his head no. "I figured it was abandoned. You see that sometimes, even in those neighborhoods. Those folks who lost real coin in the crash. I figured, why knock on the door of an abandoned house?"

"So what happened?"

"Be patient now." He was enjoying the story too much to rush it. "First thing this morning, when I was passing by, I saw a man in front. White fellow, dressed to impress. A businessman or a banker, I figured, standing with his hands in his pockets. He was frowning at the grass like he'd seen a snake. But I never saw any snakes up here, not like the cottonmouths or copperheads we got back home."

"What was he staring at?"

"At the sorry-looking grass! Well, I told him I'd cut the lawn for him if he had a mower. I thought I might make up for what I'd lost playing policy last night."

"He gave you *all that* to cut his grass?"

"Two dollars, that's what he offered. And I agreed. He asked me to come back next week. Cut the lawn until he sells the house. Said he's going back to his wife and family in South Carolina. That's his plan. He said if I do that, then I can keep the mower for myself to use. He gave it to me, Joe."

I still didn't understand. "So where'd the rest of the money come from? You went out cutting grass all day?"

"Keep listening now. When I pulled the mower from the garage, I noticed an automobile in there, all covered in blankets. The man told me it belonged to his dead brother. *The whole place* belongs to his dead brother. See, that was the thing all along. The man is selling his brother's house. He's got to empty it out fast. The man told me the car hadn't been driven in two years. Said the motor probably didn't even run. He told me, 'If you can drive it, it's yours.'"

"So you took it?"

"He signed over the registration to me. I spread the blankets on the back seat and put the mower on the blankets. Turns out, the car ran pretty good, just needed some fresh oil and air in the tires. Cadillac two-door coupe, only a few years old."

"That's unbelievable, Jackson."

"Best part is, this afternoon I drove it to a dealer on Randolph who offered me *nine hundred dollars* for it. Probably worth more, but I took it."

"Hold on, you sold it already?"

He burst out a big laugh. "I wasn't gonna pay a garage to keep it for me, was I?"

"What a story! I've never heard anything like it."

"Now we've got the money to buy a sensible car *and* a wedding ring. And extra, for lodging and meals, the works. We'll do it next month, when I can get away from here. It's all happening."

"Gee, I'm happy for you," I said. And I was. Until that moment, I hadn't realized how badly I needed to hear some good news.

"So, you see," he said, "I don't need this gift from you." He took the envelope from his apron belt and tried to give it back.

"No, keep it—"

"Listen now, take it back and put it safe in your own pocket. You're a good kid, Joe. Everyone who meets you sees that. But you're acting like a fool right now. You may not need that money today, but you'll need it someday."

"But I didn't tell you how I got it—"

"Did you steal it?"

"My cousin and I earned it . . . but not honestly."

"It's yours now, isn't it? We both got lucky for once. That's something to celebrate."

I didn't feel lucky. He wouldn't be celebrating if he knew how we earned it. "At least write your home address on the back of that thing, will you?" I said. "Can we stay in touch?"

Nodding, he removed a pencil from his apron and wrote down his address. He handed me the envelope, and we shook mitts.

"So long, Jackson."

He hesitated. "You know something? My name isn't Jackson."

"It isn't?"

"Jackson is where I came from. Jackson, Mississippi. Starting on my first day at the hotel, Mertz and Hannigan called me that. My real name is William. Family calls me Billy, or Baker, on account of my work. I put it there with my address. When you write, call me Billy. And be sure to say hello to Gertrude. She knows who you are. Good luck, Joe."

He gave me a playful knock on the arm, before turning around and going back through the screen door to the kitchen.

I picked up my suitcase and began making tracks toward LaSalle Street Station.

A drop of rain struck the brim of my hat, followed by another, then a steady drizzle. The suitcase felt almost too heavy to carry. Zigzagging through the blocks of the South Loop, I turned onto Congress, within sight of the station. The rain was steady now, and I was sweating something fierce. But I kept walking. I wasn't going to spend another dime on taxis.

Maybe Jackson was right and I should be celebrating. I still had over four hundred dollars in my pocket. Enough for us to survive at home, month by month, until our luck changed. Until the weather improved. Until the government aid came through.

That was the worst part, I realized. I'd be stuck waiting by the mailbox, too, hoping to hear from Raymond, just as my mother waited to hear from the Fed.

It was nearly six o'clock, and a hard rain pelted the sidewalks.

THIRTY-FOUR

B Y THE TIME I PULLED OPEN THE HEAVY DOOR AT THE STATION, my clothes were soaked and my socks itched.

Inside the waiting area, I recalled how lost I'd felt when I arrived. The mob of people, the countless terminals and baggage stands. The flower stalls and vaulted ceiling still dazzled me, but this was the end of an adventure rather than the beginning. The wet shoes of travelers following me into the station sounded squeaky, almost sad.

I followed the crowd to the main concourse. There were ticket windows on either side, with long lines forming at each counter. I walked up and back, searching to see which of them served the Rock Island Railroad.

Passing the rows of long benches, I recalled how they'd reminded me of church pews. Hundreds of passengers, sitting and waiting, reciting their silent prayers. Not everyone's prayers got answered, it turned out.

Just then, in the very last bench, a slender figure sat upright. He raised his hand to signal my attention, fingers wiggling.

Raymond.

I walked straight up to him and dropped my suitcase at his

feet. "Gee whiz, Ray, here you are. Out in the world, just like I hoped you'd be."

He had two suitcases at his feet and a film magazine unopened on his lap. "I've been sitting here for twenty minutes, watching all the people coming and going. In a way, it comforts me to see them all. It makes it feel almost *ordinary* to be leaving."

I sat next to him. "You didn't waste any time."

"There wasn't a reason to stay a minute longer. Not with the warning you gave me and the cash. I'll go directly to a new city and get settled so I can enroll in school. Classes will be starting in a few weeks."

"Didn't your father try to stop you?"

"I didn't tell him. Didn't breathe a word to anyone. I packed some clothes and raced out the door."

"Ray, your parents will panic."

"I wrote them a note and tucked it in the pocket of Mother's dressing robe. She'll find it tonight, before she even starts to worry."

"They'll worry a lot if they don't hear from you."

"Once I find a place to settle, I'll write."

"I expect they'll send a detective after you to bring you home."

For a moment, he only stared at the travelers passing by. "No. I think they'll be relieved. Among other things, they won't have to deal with thugs knocking on the door and threatening to expose their pansy son. They're free of that worry now, at least. I explained it all in the note."

"But how will they explain it to everyone else? To their friends and your neighbors? Their golden boy, gone . . ."

Raymond shrugged. "That's for them to decide. Maybe they'll

tell them I've popped off and joined a monastery." The notion seemed to amuse him.

"Don't even joke about that."

"Look here," he insisted, "the two of us meeting up like this, so we could see each other one last time. Wouldn't you say God has intervened in our case?"

"It is nice to think so," I admitted. "But where are you going?"

"First to Kansas City. When I get there, I'll poke my head out the door of the train. If I don't like what I see, I'll spend a few more dollars and keep on going to Texas. Maybe to California. You can tell a lot about things from your very first look, don't you think?"

I didn't agree with this theory at all, especially after the past few weeks. "Why west?"

"I'd like to see the wide-open landscapes, and the cowboys. I'd hoped to get a train from Union Station called the Zephyr. A zephyr! Carried west by a gentle breeze. Doesn't that sound marvelous?"

I nodded. It did sound wonderful.

"Unfortunately, it doesn't have any service today," he explained, "so I came to this station instead and purchased a ticket on the Golden State Limited. It doesn't leave for another two hours. When does your train take you downstate?"

"I don't have a ticket yet. I was looking for the Rock Island counter when I saw you."

There was one subject I needed to discuss with him before we parted, but I wasn't sure how to broach it. I dreaded thinking about it at all, but meeting him again seemed like a sign.

"Ray, about what happened that night, the carpet and the bridge—"

He pretended to cover his ears. "No, let's not talk about it."

"But we have to talk about it. I still can't believe it happened. I can't go through something like that ever, *ever* again."

He looked suddenly defiant. "We may have to! Who knows what life will throw at us? We must be tougher than anyone. Even now, after everything, don't you see how it is?"

I knew he was right. I would need to be prepared for anything.

I reached for my suitcase.

"Say," he began.

"What?"

He only sat back, biting his lip. "Never mind."

I wasn't ready to leave yet. "Wait, how was Canada?"

"Oh my word, abundantly *awkward* between my father and me. Tense beyond belief. That won't surprise you. But we stayed at the most incredible lodge, built out of white birch timber, with views of the St. Lawrence River. In the lobby, I chatted with a group of rugged Canadian *Mounties*, all wearing their scarlet waistcoats and those thrilling leather belts and sashes. They were on a visit from New Brunswick. Seeing them lifted my spirits somewhat. And the family kept me busy. And the food—I wish I had time to tell you everything."

"Me, too."

We both held our tongues, listening to the loudspeakers calling out platform numbers and destinations.

I took the deepest breath of my life. "The thing is, Ray, I wouldn't mind going west, too. How would it be if I bought a ticket for your train? With you?"

He reached for my shoulder. "I was about to suggest the same thing."

"As friends, I mean."

"Of course as friends. *Dearest* friends. What else would we be, Charles?"

"Joe," I corrected gently.

"Joe, yes, of course. That part may take some getting used to."

"The trouble is," I explained, "I can't go home again, either. I thought I could. I thought I needed to. But if I go back, everything will be the same as it was before. It would be awful, pretending all the time. It didn't used to feel that way, but now it would feel like a lie. Every day would be a lie."

He understood. Of course he did. "Won't your mother worry when you don't come home tonight?"

"No, she's not expecting me. The plan was for me to keep working here for another week. Anyway, I'll do the same as you. I'll send a card, so she knows I'm safe. And I'll keep working and send her money as often as possible."

He nodded, as if to encourage me.

"Besides," I reasoned, "I have work experience now. I can find something steady."

"Nothing stopping you."

"And it would be easier, if we did it together. If we're not starting out somewhere alone. If one of us gets into trouble—"

I didn't finish the sentence. I couldn't let him think I only wanted to travel with him for safety reasons. "I don't mean it would only be useful. It's just—I can't think of a better fellow to start my syndicate with."

He was beaming now. "I feel the exact same way."

For most of my life, I realized, I'd felt safe at home. I'd felt safe with my cousin, too. I'd felt safe with Eddie for a while. It was never like that with Raymond. But whenever I was with him, I felt something different than safe. Something more important. I felt joy.

He showed me where to buy the ticket and stood with me in line. "Oh, I'll miss my piano," he said, lighting a cigarette. "I'll miss 'Stardust.'"

"I hope you won't smoke too much. Not at all, really."

"Don't give it another thought. I'll tuck them away, so you'll never see them. We can keep *some* secrets from each other, I think."

"Let's make that the only one for now."

The full ticket fare would be ten dollars and twenty cents. I reached into my pocket and pulled out my cash.

Raymond drew nearer, in order to block any stranger's view. He whispered into my ear, "The moment we sit down on the train, I demand you tell me about all this money. Are you secretly rich, after all?"

"It's a long story, and I'm not proud of it. But I will tell you the full, true story. The most important thing to know is, I'm not rich. In fact, I need to wire this money home. A quarter of it, at least."

"Is that right?"

"More like three quarters," I clarified. "As soon as possible."

"Western Union office is right over there," he said, pointing.

"I won't have much left. That's the situation. I'll need a job just as soon as we find a place. Maybe I'll work in a hotel kitchen."

If Raymond minded, he didn't show it. "And I'll work in a clothing shop or a department store. I don't have a lick of experience, but I could get a job as a sales clerk somewhere, don't you think?"

"Look at you, with your remarkable face. You'll be hired on the spot anywhere you apply. And we'll finish school, of course. We'll enroll together. But how will we find an apartment?"

"I've already thought of that. We'll find a place near some university. A neglected attic that we can spruce up with cans of paint. We'll add some cheerful ferns and bookshelves . . . Landlords these days are in no position to turn away any applicant who can cover the rent."

I nodded. "All we'll tell the landlord is that we're taking courses to complete our degrees."

"Exactly! Anyone would believe us. Best of all, a cover story like that has the benefit of being *true*, technically speaking." He smiled, the same lighthearted spirit I first encountered in the church gym. "I'll only work retail until I finish college," he added. "I really would like to become a doctor. That wasn't just talk, you know. You'd never guess, but I'm a very hard worker and quite studious when I need to be."

"Ray, you can be whoever you want to be."

"Yes, you'd better believe it."

We'd reached the very front of the line. There was so much more I wanted to discuss with him, but now it was my turn to approach the counter and buy a ticket to somewhere totally new.

AUTHOR'S NOTE

More than twenty years ago, at a barn sale near Sturgeon Bay, Wisconsin, I found an old hardcover book. According to the penciled notation inside the cover, the price was $28.00, pretty steep for a used book in a dusty barn. But I opened my wallet anyway, in part because the copyright page declares—in all caps—"THE MATERIAL IN THIS BOOK HAS BEEN PREPARED FOR THE USE OF THE MEDICAL AND ALLIED PROFESSIONS ONLY." As everyone knows, there's nothing better than getting your hands on a book you are not allowed to read.

First published in 1941, the book contains clinical profiles of eighty men and women, all given pseudonyms, who are classified as either "bisexual," "homosexual," or "narcissistic." Most were young adults when interviewed; many were teenagers in the late 1920s and early 1930s. The profiles are remarkably intimate: family histories, childhood memories, anatomical measurements, explicit romantic encounters, plenty of fun and outrageous trouble. It's difficult to stomach the author's outdated theories about sexuality (and his purpose: "prevention" and "treatment of sexual maladjustment"). I will not include his name here. But the time capsule he left behind was worth every penny.

I'll Take Everything You Have does not contain any of those individual stories, but I thought about those eighty "patients" often when I was imagining Joe's story. In the decades before Stonewall, a lot of high drama took place right under the nose of mainstream society. Invisibility had its advantages: Most parents wouldn't think twice if two boys or two girls disappeared behind closed doors for hours, or even spent the night together. But secrecy made queer people vulnerable, too. Violence and harassment were common experiences. Fifty years later, at the height of the AIDS crisis, the buttons and bumper stickers warned, "Silence = Death." It always does.

Teens who want to learn more about Chicago's queer history should find a copy of Tracy Baim's *Out and Proud in Chicago: An Overview of the City's Gay Community* (Surrey Books, 2008). Visually stunning, it's jam-packed with fascinating true stories and colorful biographies. In 2011, the Chicago History Museum presented an exhibit called *Out in Chicago: LGBT History at the Crossroads*. As part of the show, the museum published an excellent collection of essays with the same title, edited by Jill Austin and Jennifer Brier (Chicago History Museum, 2011). I also enjoyed Jim Elledge's wonderful *The Boys of Fairy Town: Sodomites, Female Impersonators, Third-Sexers, Pansies, Queers, and Sex Morons in Chicago's First Century* (Chicago Review Press, 2018).

For younger readers, I'm a big fan of Jerome Pohlen's *Gay & Lesbian History for Kids: The Century-Long Struggle for LGBT Rights* (Chicago Review Press, 2015). We use passages for Gay-Straight Alliance meetings all the time.

To learn more about American life during the early 1930s, check out *Hard Times: An Oral History of the Great Depression* (The New Press, 1986). Studs Terkel's collection of 150+ interviews represents a wide range of experiences and captures what those difficult years were like. I like its Midwestern focus, too.

When I began work on this novel, I explored every issue of the *Chicago Tribune* from the summer of 1934. There's nothing like daily newspapers to summon the mindset, preoccupations, and temperature (literal temperature) of a community. I'm grateful, always, for the essential work of journalists, and also for the Chicago Public Library, without which I wouldn't have had such easy access to the newspaper archive.

If readers are curious to know what it might have been like for Jackson and his fiancé to take a cross-country road trip in 1934, I'd steer you to Candacy Taylor's well-researched, entertaining book, *Overground Railroad: The Green Book and the Roots of Black Travel in America* (Amulet Books, 2022).

***

Finally, some quick thanks:

To the welcoming queer spaces of my youth, especially Tracks in Washington, DC, and Big Chicks and Sidetrack in Chicago: You granted every wish and tolerated so much foolishness. I'm getting sentimental over you.

To my family and friends: I get a kick out of you. You're my thrill.

To two local communities that have enlightened me, entertained me, and employed me: CICS Northtown Academy and StoryStudio Chicago. Nice work if you can get it.

Come rain or come shine, I've benefited from the wisdom and good humor of my agent, Jennifer Laughran.

Kate Klise, beloved by generations of young readers and by her brother, saw early drafts of the manuscript and offered smart feedback, as did my patient and generous editor, Elise Howard, along with Adah Li, Ashley Mason, Jody Corbett, Krestyna Lypen, and others, all of whose contributions made the book stronger. The whole team at Algonquin Young Readers, now led by Stacy Lellos and Cheryl Klein, is second to none. I've been a fan of Patrick Leger's work for years; what a kick to have his evocative illustration grace the cover, designed by the brilliant Laura Williams.

John Henricks, lifelong Chicagoan and passionate "train-iac," generously answered my questions about local train travel in the 1930s.

Six-plus decades ago, my pal Russ Langford devoured a massive meal at an Italian restaurant, then ordered a funny-sounding dish called "pizza pie" for dessert. That was his mistake, just as any factual or logical errors in this book belong to me and me alone.

The time-capsule medical book was dedicated to the author's wife, and I dedicate this one to my husband. Night and day, Mike, all I do is dream of you. For everything, thanks.